HOKAS ON DECK

Alex saw a line-of-battle ship, the admiral's pennant at its masthead and the name *Victory* on its bows. As he walked up the gangplank, Hokas on deck broke into a hornpipe. A Hoka in blue coat and cocked hat, telescope tucked beneath his left arm, hurried across the tarry-smelling planks.

"Welcome, Your Excellency, welcome," he said. "Bligh's the name, Captain William Bligh, sir, at your service."

"I must see His Lordship," Alex said. "I have an important message for him."

Bligh looked embarrassed. He shuffled his feet. "His Lordship is resting in his stateroom, sir. Indisposed."

Alex knew full well. Horatio Lord Nelson's public appearances were few and short. The nuisance of having to wear an eyepatch and keep his right arm inside his coat was too much.

"But we shall have the honor of dining with His Lordship this evening," Bligh said. "Meanwhile, we've time for a tot of rum in my cabin, Commodore, to welcome you into our company."

"Commodore? Huh?" Alex asked.

Bligh winked and took the man's elbow. "Ah, yes, I know full well. Ashore the walls have ears. Mustn't let the Frenchies learn Commodore Hornblower is on a secret mission in disguise. . . ."

Other Books in This Series:

Hoka! Hoka! Hoka!

Baen Books by Poul Anderson

Fire Time
Three Hearts and Three Lions

Baen Books by Gordon R. Dickson

The Magnificent Wilf
Mindspan

HOKAS POKAS!

Poul Anderson
&
Gordon R. Dickson

Hokas Pokas

A Baen Book

Baen Publishing Enterprises
P.O. Box 1403
Riverdale, NY 10471

ISBN: 0-671-57858-8

Cover art by Michael Whelan, designed by Patrick Turner

First printing, February 2000

Distributed by Simon & Schuster
1230 Avenue of the Americas
New York, NY 10020

Typeset by Windhaven Press: Auburn, NH
Printed in the United States of America

CONTENTS

Part I:

I.
FULL PACK (HOKAS WILD)

Prologue

From the *Encyclopaedia Galactica*, 11th edition:

TOKA: Brackney's Star III. The sun (NSC 7-190853426) is of type G2, located in Region Deneb, approximately 503 light-years from Sol. . . . The third planet appears Earthlike, to a sufficiently superficial observer . . . There are three small moons, their League names being Uha, Buha, and Huha. As is customary in the case of inhabited planets, these derive from a major autochthonous language (see NOMENCLATURE: Astronomical). It was discovered too late that they mean, respectively, "Fat," "Drunk," and "Sluggish." . . .

At least "Toka" means "Earth." However, indigenous tongues have become little more than historical curiosities, displaced by whatever Terrestrial speech suits the role of the moment. . . .

Two intelligent species evolved, known today as the Hokas and the Slissii. The former are quasi-mammalian, the latter reptiloid. . . . Conflict was

3

ineluctable. . . . It terminated after human explorers had come upon the system and the Interbeing League took charge. . . . In effect, the Slissii were bought out. Abandoning their home world *en masse*, they became free wanderers throughout civilization, much to its detriment. (See SLISSII. See also COMPUTER CRIME; CONFIDENCE GAMES; EMBEZZLE- MENT; GAMBLING: Crooked; MISREPRESENTA- TION; POLITICS.)

The ursinoid Hokas generally stayed in place. No nation of theirs refused to accept League tutelage, which of course has had the objective of raising their level of civilization to a point where autonomy and full membership can be granted. Rather, they all agreed with an eagerness which should have warned the Commissioners. . . .

The fact is that the Hokas are the most imagi- native race of beings in known space, and doubtless in unknown space too. Any role that strikes their fancy they will play, individually or as a group, to the limits of the preposterous and beyond. This does not imply deficiency of intellect, for they are remark- ably quick to learn. It does not even imply that they lose touch with reality; indeed, they have been heard to complain that reality often loses touch with them. It does demonstrate a completely protean person- ality. Added to that are a physical strength and energy astonishing in such comparatively small bodies. Thus, in the course of a few short years, the "demon teddy bears," to use a popular phrase for them, have covered their planet with an implausible kaleidoscope of harlequin societies describable only by some such metaphor as the foregoing. . . .

Full Pack

When one is a regular ambassador to a civilized planet with full membership in the Interbeing League, it is quite sufficient to marry a girl who is only blond and beautiful. However, a plenipotentiary, guiding a backward world along the tortuous path to modern culture and full status, needs a wife who is also competent to handle the unexpected.

Alexander Jones had no reason to doubt that his Tanni met all the requirements of blondness, beauty, and competence. Neither did she. After a dozen years of Toka, he did not hesitate to leave her in charge while he took a native delegation to Earth and arranged for the planet's advancement in grade. And for a while things went smoothly—as smoothly, at least, as they can go on a world of eager, energetic teddy bears with imaginations active to the point of autohypnosis.

Picture her, then, on a sunny day shortly after lunch, walking through her official residence in the

city Mixumaxu. Bright sunshine streamed through the
glassite wall, revealing a pleasant view of cobbled
streets, peaked roofs, and the grim towers of the
Bastille. (This was annually erected by a self-appointed
Roi Soleil, and torn down again by happy sans-culottes
every July 14.) Tanni Jones' brief tunic and long
golden hair were in the latest Bangkok fashion, even
on this remote outpost, and her slim tanned figure
would never be outmoded and she was comfortably
aware of the fact. She had just checked the nursery,
finding her two younger children safe at play. A newly
arrived letter from her husband was tucked into her
bosom. It announced in one sentence that his mission had been successful; thereafter several pages
were devoted to more important matters, such as his
imminent return with a new fur coat and he wished
he could have been in the envelope and meanwhile
he loved her madly, passionately, etc. She was mur-
muring to herself. Let us listen.

"Damn and blast it to hell, anyway! Where *is* that
little monster?"

As she passed the utility room, a small, round-
bellied, yellow-furred ursinoid popped out. This was
Carruthers. His official title was Secretary-in-Chief-
to-the-Plenipotentiary, which meant whatever Carruthers decided it should mean. Tanni felt relieved
that today he was dressed merely in anachronistic
trousers, spats, coat, and bowler hat, umbrella furled
beneath one arm, and spoke proper Oxford English.
Last week it had been a toga, and he had brought
her messages written in Latin with Greek characters; he had also buttonholed every passerby with
the information that she, Tanni, was above suspicion.

"The newsfax sheet, madam," he bowed. "Just
came off the jolly old printer, don't y'know."

"Oh. Thanks." She took the bulletin and swept her

eyes down it. Sensational tidings from Earth Headquarters: the delegates from Worben and Porkelans
accused of conspiracy; Goldfarb's Planet awarded to
Bagdadburgh; a League-wide alert for a Starflash
space yacht which had been seen carrying the Tertiary Receptacle of Wisdom of Sanussi and the as-
yet-unidentified dastards who had kidnaped him from
his planet's Terrestrial embassy; commercial agree-
ment governing the xisfthikl traffic signed between
Jruthn and Ptrfsk—Tanni handed it back. There were
too many worlds for anyone to remember; none of
the names meant a thing to her.

"Have you seen young Alex?" she inquired.

Carruthers screwed a monocle into one beady
black eye and tapped his short muzzle with the
umbrella handle. "Why, yes, I do believe so, eh, what,
what, what?"

"Well, where is he?"

"He asked me not to tell, madam." Carruthers eyed
her reproachfully. "Couldn't peach on him, now could
I? Old School Tie and all that sort of bally old . . ."

Tanni stalked off with the secretary still bleating
behind her. True, she thought, her children did
attend the same school which educated the adult
Hokas, but . . . Hah! In way, it was too bad Alex
was returning so soon. She had long felt that he
didn't take a firm enough line with his mercurial
charges. He was too easily reduced to gibbering
bewilderment. Now she was made of sterner stuff,
and—in a Boadicean mood, she swept through a
glassite passageway to the flitter garage.

Yes, there was her oldest son, Alexander Braith-
waite Jones, Jr., curled up on the front seat with his
nose buried in an ancient but well-preserved folio
volume. She much regretted giving it to him. Her idea
had been that he could carry it under one arm and

enjoy it between bouts of healthful outdoor play, rather than having to sit hunched over a microset; but all he did was read it, sneaking off to places like—

"Alexander!"

The boy, a nine-year-old, tanglehaired pocket edition of his father, started guiltily. "Oh, hello, Mom," he smiled. It quite melted her resolve.

"Now, Alex," said Tanni in a reasonable tone, "you know you ought to be out getting some exercise. You've already read those *Jungle Books* a dozen times."

"Aw, golly, Mom," protested the younger generation. "You give me a book and then you won't let me read it!"

"*Alexander!*" Boadicea had returned in full armor. "You know perfectly well what I mean. Now I told you to—"

"Madam," squeaked a voice, "the devil's to pay!"

Tanni yipped and jumped. Remembering herself, she turned in a suitably dignified manner to see Carruthers, hastily clad in pith helmet and fake walrus mustache.

"Message on the transtype just came," said the Hoka. "From Injah, don't y' know. Seems a bit urgent."

Tanni snatched the paper he extended and read:

FROM: *Captain O'Neil of the Black Tyrone*
TO: *Rt. Hon. Plen. A. Jones*
SUBJECT: *UFO (Unidentified Flying Object) identified. Your Excellency:*

While burying dead and bolting beef north of the Kathun road, received word from native scout of UFO crashed in jungle nearby, containing three beasts of unknown origin. Interesting, what?

> Yr. Humble & Obt. Svt., etc.,
> "Crook" O'Neil

For a moment Tanni had a dreamlike sense of unreality. Then, slowly, she translated the Hokaese. Yes . . . there were some Hokas from this northern hemisphere who had moved down to the subcontinent due south which the natives had gleefully rechristened India, and set themselves up as Imperialists. The Indians were quite happy to cooperate, since it meant that they could wear turbans and mysterious expressions. Vaguely she recalled Kipling's Ballad of Boh Da Thone. It dealt with Burma, to be sure, but if consistency is the virtue of little minds, then the Hokas were very large-minded indeed. India was mostly Kipling country, with portions here and there belonging to Clive, the Grand Mogul, and lesser lights.

The UFO must be a spaceship and the "beasts," of course, its crew, from some other planet. God alone knew what they would think if the Indians located them first and assumed they were—*what* would Hokas convinced they were Hindus, Pathans, and Britishers imagine alien space travelers to be?

"Carruthers!" said Tanni sharply. "Has there been any distress call on the radio?"

"No, madam, there has not. And damme, I don't like it. Don't like it at all. When I was with Her Majesty's Very Own Royal, Loyal, and Excessively Brave Fifth Fusiliers, I—"

Tanni's mind worked swiftly. This was just the sort of situation in which Alex, Sr., was always getting involved and coming off second best. It was her chance to show him how these matters ought to be handled.

"Carruthers," she snapped, "you and I will take the flitter and go to the rescue of these aliens. And I want it clearly understood that—"

"*Mom!* Can I go? Can I go, huh, Mom, can I?"

It was Alex, Jr., hopping up and down with excitement, his eyes shining.

"No," began Tanni. "You stay here and read your book and—" She checked herself, aware of the pitfall. Countermanding her own orders! Here was a heaven-sent opportunity to get the boy out of the house and interested in something new—like, for example, these castaways. They were clearly beings of authority or means, important beings, or they could not afford a private spaceship. There was no danger involved; Toka's India was a land of congenial climate, without any life-forms harmful to man.

"You can go," she told Alex severely, "if you'll do exactly as I say at all times. Now that means exactly."

"Yes, yes, yes. Sure, Mom, sure."

"All right, then," said Tanni. She ran back into the house, making hasty arrangements with the servants, while Carruthers set the flitter's autopilot to locating the British bivouac. In minutes, two humans and one Hoka were skyborne.

The camp proved to be a collection of tents set among fronded trees and tangled vines, drowsy under the late afternoon sun. A radio and a transtype were the only modern equipment, a reluctant concession to the plenipotentiary's program of technological education. They stood at the edge of the clearing, covered with jungle mold, while the Black Tyrone, a hundred strong, drilled with musket, fife, and drum.

Captain O'Neil was a grizzled, hard-bitten Hoka in shorts, tunic, and bandolier. He. limped across the clearing, pith helmet in hand, as Tanni emerged from the flitter with Alex and Carruthers.

"Honored, ma'am," he bowed. "Pardon my one-sided gait, ma'am. Caught a slug in the ulnar bone recently." (Tanni knew very well he had not; there was no war on Toka, and anyway the ulnar bone is in the arm.) "Now a slug that is hammered from telegraph wire—ah, a book?"

His eyes lit up with characteristic enthusiasm, and Tanni, looking around, discovered the reason in her son's arms.

"Alex!" she said. "Did you bring that *Jungle Books* thing along?" His downcast face told her that he had. "I'm not going to bother with it any longer. You hand that right over to Captain O'Neil and let him keep it for you till we leave for home again."

"Awwwww, Mom!"

"Right now!"

"—is a thorn in the flesh and a rankling fire," murmured Captain O'Neil. "Ah, thank you, m'boy. Well, well, what have we here? The *Jungle Books*, by Rudyard Kipling himself! Never seen 'em before." Humming a little tune, he opened the volume.

"Now, where is that UFO?" demanded Tanni. "Have you rescued its crew yet?"

"No, ma'am," said the Captain, with his nose between the pages. "Going to go look for 'em this morning, but we were hanging Danny Deever and—" His voice trailed off into a mumble.

Tanni compressed her lips. "Well, we shall have to find them," she clipped. "Is it far? Should we go overland or take the flitter?"

"Er . . . yes, ma'am? Ha, hum," said O'Neil, closing the book reluctantly but marking the place with a furry forefinger. "Not far. Overland, I would recommend. You'd find landing difficult in our jungles here in the Seeonee Hills—"

"The what?"

"Er . . . I mean north of the Kathun road. A wolf . . . I mean, a native scout brought us the word. Perhaps you'd care to talk to him, ma'am?"

"I would," said Tanni. "Right away."

O'Neil shouted for Gunga Din and sent him off to look, then dove back into the volume. Presently another Hoka slouched from behind a tent. He was of the local race, which had fur of midnight black, but was otherwise indistinguishable from the portly northern variety. Unless, of course, you specified his costume: turban, baggy trousers, loose shirt, assorted cutlery thrust into a sash, and a flaming red false beard. He salaamed.

"What's your name?" asked Tanni.

"Mahbub Ali, memsahib," replied the newcomer. "Horse trader."

"You saw the ship land?"

"Yes, memsahib. I had stopped to patch my bridles and count my gear—whee, a book!"

"It's mine!" said O'Neil, pulling it away from him.

"Oh. Well, ah—" Mahbub Ali edged around so that he could read over the Captain's shoulder. "I, er, saw the thing flash through the air and went to see. I, um, glimpsed three beasts of a new sort coming out, but, um, they were back inside before I could . . . By that time the moon was shining into the cave where I lived and I said to myself, 'Augrh!' I said, 'it is time to hunt again—'"

"*Gentlebeings!*" cried Tanni. The book snapped shut and two fuzzy faces looked dreamily up at her. "I shall want the regiment to escort me to that ship tomorrow."

"Why, er, to be sure, ma'am," said O'Neil vaguely. "I'll tell the pack and we'll move out at dawn."

A couple of extra tents were set up in the clearing, and there was a supper at which the humans shared top honors with Danny Deaver. (A Hoka's muscles are so strong that hanging does not injure him.) When night fell, with subtropical swiftness, Alex

crawled into one tent and Tanni into the other. She
lay for a while, thinking cheerfully that her theories
of management were bearing fruit. True, there had
been some small waverings on the part of the auto-
chthones, but she had kept things rolling firmly in
the proper direction. Why in the Galaxy did her
husband insist it was so difficult to . . .

The last thing she remembered as she drifted into
sleep was the murmur of a voice from the camp-
fire. "Crook" O'Neil had assembled his command and
was reading to them. . . .

She blinked her eyes open to dazzling sunlight.
Dawn was hours past, and a great stillness brooded
over the clearing. More indignant than alarmed, she
scrambled out of her sleeping bag, threw on tunic
and shoes, and went into the open.

The camp was deserted. Uniforms and equipment
were piled by the cold ashes of the fire, and a
flying snake was opening a can of bully beef with
its saw-edged beak. For a moment the world
wavered before her.

"Alex!" she screamed.

Running from tent to tent, she found them all
empty. She remembered wildly that she did not even
have a raythrower along. Sobbing, she dashed toward
the flitter—get an aerial view—

Bush crackled, and a round black-nosed head
thrust cautiously forth. Tanni whirled, blinked, and
recognized the gray-shot pelt of O'Neil.

"Captain!" she gasped. "What's happened? Come
out this minute!"

The brush parted, and the Hoka trotted out on
all fours, attired in nothing but his own fur.

"Captain O'Neil!" wailed Tanni. "What's the
meaning of this?"

The native reached up, got the hem of her tunic between his jaws, and tugged. Then he let go and moved toward the canebrake, looking back at her.

"Captain," said Tanni helplessly. She followed him for a moment, but stopped. Her voice grew shrill. "I'm not moving another centimeter till you explain this—this outrageous—" The Hoka waddled back to her. "Well, speak up! Don't whine at me! Stand up and talk like a . . . like a . . . a Captain. *And stop licking my hand!*"

O'Neil headed into the jungle. Tanni gave up. Throttling her fears, she went after him. Colorful birds whistled overhead, and flowers drooped on long vines and snagged in her hair. Presently she found herself on a trail. It ran for some two kilometers, an uneventful trip except for the pounding of her heart and the Captain's tendency to dash off after small game.

At the end, they reached a meadow surrounding a large flat-topped rock. The Black Tyrone were there. Like their commander, they had stripped off their uniforms and now frisked about in the grass, tumbling like puppies and snarling between their teeth. She caught fragments of continuous conversation:

"—Sambhur belled, once, twice, and again . . . wash daily from nose-tip to tail-tip . . . the meat is very near the bone—" and other interesting though possibly irrelevant information.

Rolling about, Tanni's eyes found her son. He was seated on top of the rock, wearing only a wreath of flowers and a kitchen knife on a string about his neck. At his feet, equally nude and happy, sprawled Carruthers and the black-furred Mahbub Ali.

"Alex!" cried Tanni. She sped to the rock and stared up at her offspring, uncertain whether to kiss and cry over him or turn him across her knee. "What are you doing here?"

Captain O'Neil spoke for the first time. "Thy mother was doubtful about coming, Little Frog."

"Oh, so you *can* talk!" said Tanni, glaring at him.

"He can't talk to you, Mom," said Alex.

"What do you mean, he can't?"

"But that's wolf talk, Mom. You can't understand it. I'll have to translate for you."

"*Wolf?*"

"The Seeonee Pack," said Alex proudly. He nodded at O'Neil. "Thou hast done well, Akela."

"*Argh!*" said Mahbub Ali. "*I* run with no pack, Little Frog."

"By the Bull that brought me!" exclaimed Alex, contrite. "I forgot, Bagheera." He stroked the black head. "This is Bagheera, Mom, the Black Panther, you know." Pointing to the erstwhile Carruthers: "And this is Baloo the Bear. And I'm Mowgli. Isn't it terrific, Mom?"

"No, it isn't!" snapped Tanni. Now, if ever, was the time to take the strong line she believed in. "Captain O'Neil, will you stop being Akela this minute? I'm here to rescue some very important people, and—"

"What says thy mother Messua?" asked the Captain—or, rather, Akela—lolling out his tongue and looking at Mowgli-Alex.

The boy started gravely to translate.

"Alex, stop that!" Tanni found her voice wobbling. "Don't encourage him in this . . . this game!"

"But it isn't a game, Mom," protested her son. "It's real. Honest!"

"You know it isn't," scolded Tanni. "He's not really Akela at all. He should be sensible and go back to being himself."

"Himself?" murmured Baloo-Carruthers, forgetting in his surprise that he wasn't supposed to understand English.

"Captain O'Neil," explained Tanni, holding on to her patience with both hands. "Captain—"

"But he wasn't really Captain O'Neil either," pointed out Baloo.

On many occasions Tanni had listened sympathetically, but with a hidden sense of superiority, to her husband's description of his latest encounter with Hoka logic. She had never really believed in all the dizzy sensations he spoke of. Now she felt them. She gasped feebly and sat down in the grass.

"I wanted to let you know, Mom," chattered Alex. "The Pack's got Shere Khan treed a little ways from here. I wanted to know if it was all right for me to go call him a Lame Thief of the Waingunga. Can I, Mom, huh, can I?"

Tanni drew a long, shuddering breath. She remembered Alex, Sr.'s advice: 'Roll with the punches. Play along and watch for a chance to use their own logic on them.' There didn't seem to be anything else to do at the moment. "All right," she whispered.

Akela took the lead, yapping; Baloo and Bagheera closed in on either side of Alex; and the Pack followed. Brush crackled. It was not easy for a naturally bipedal species to go on all fours, and Tanni saw Akela walking erect when he thought she wasn't looking. He caught her eye, blushed under his fur, and crouched down again.

She decided that this new lunacy would prove rather unstable. It just wasn't practical to run around on your hands and try to bring down game with your teeth. But it would probably take days for the Hokas to weary of the sport and return to being the Black Tyrone, and meanwhile what was she to do?

"By the Broken Lock that freed me!" exclaimed Bagheera, coming to a halt. "One approaches—I mean approacheth."

"Two approach," corrected Baloo, sitting up on his haunches bear-fashion. Being an ursinoid, he did this rather well.

Tanni looked ahead. Through a clump of bamboo-like plants emerged a black-haired form with a blunt snout under heavy brow ridges, the size of a man but stooped over, long arms dangling past bent knees. He wore a sadly stained and ragged suit. She recognized him as a native of the full-status planet Chakba. Behind him lifted the serpentine head of a being from some world unknown to her.

Akela bristled. "The Bandar-log!" he snarled.

"But see," pointed Baloo, "Kaa the Python follows him, and yet the shameless Bandar is not afraid." He scratched his head. "This is not supposed to be," he said plaintively.

The Chakban spotted Tanni and hurried toward her. "Ah, dear lady," he cried. His voice was high-pitched, but he spoke fluent English. "At last, a civilized face!" He bowed. "Permit me to introduce myself. I am Echpo of Doralik-Li, and my poor friend is named Seesis."

Tanni, glancing at the friend in question, was moved to agree that he was, indeed, poor. Seesis had come into full view now, revealing ten meters of snake body, limbless except for two delicate arms just under the big bald head. A pair of gold-rimmed pince-nez wobbled on his nose. He hissed dolefully and undulated toward the woman, wringing his small hands.

Tanni gave her name and asked: "Are you the beings who crashlanded here?"

"Yes, dear lady," said Echpo. "A most—"

Seesis tugged at the woman's tunic and began to scratch on the ground with his forefinger.

"What?" Tanni bent over to look.

"Poor chap, poor chap," said Echpo, shaking his head. "He doesn't speak English, you know. Moreover, the crash . . ." He revolved a finger near his own right temple and gave her a meaningful look.

"Oh, how terrible!" Tanni got to her feet in spite of Seesis' desperate efforts to hold her down and make her look at his dirt scratchings. "We'll have to get him to a doctor—Dr. Arrowsmith in Mixumaxu is really very good if I can drag him away from discovering bacteriophage—"

"That is not necessary, madam," said Echpo. "Seesis will recover naturally. I know his race. But if I may presume upon your kindness, we do need transportation."

The Hokas crowded around Seesis, addressing him as Kaa and asking him if he was casting his skin and obliterating his marks on the ground. The herpetoid seemed ready to burst into tears.

"But weren't there three of you?" asked Tanni.

"Yes, indeed," said Echpo. "But—well—I am afraid, dear lady, that your little friends do not seem to approve of our companion Heragli. They have, er, chased him up a tree."

"Why, how could they?" Gently, Tanni detached the fingers of Seesis from her skirt, patted him on his scaly head, and turned an accusing eye on Alex. "Young man, what do you know about this?"

The boy squirmed. "That must be Shere Khan." Defiantly: "He does look like a tiger too." He glared at Echpo. "Believe thou not the Bandar-log."

"These gentlebeings are no such thing!" snapped Tanni.

"Surely thy mother has been bitten by Tabaqui,

the Jackal," said Baloo to Alex. "All the Jungle knows Shere Khan."

"This is *dewanee*, the madness," agreed Bagheera. "Heed thy old tutor who taught thee the Law, Little Frog."

"But—" began Alex. "But the hairy one dares say that—"

"Surely, Little Brother," interrupted Baloo, "thou hast learned by this time to take no notice of the Bandar-log. They have no Law. They are very many, evil, dirty, shameless, and they desire, if they have any fixed desire, to be noticed by the Jungle-People. But we do *not* notice them even when they throw nuts and filth on our heads."

"Oh!" groaned Echpo. "That I, an ex-cabinet minister of the Chakban Federation, B.A., M.S., Ph.D., LL.D., graduate of Hasolbath, Trmp, and the Sorbonne, should be accused of throwing nuts and filth on people's heads to attract attention!"

"I'm so sorry!" apologized Tanni. "It's the imagination these Hokas have. Please, please forgive them, sir!"

"Your slightest whim, dear lady, is my most solemn command and highest joy," bowed Echpo.

Tanni returned gallantly to the subject: "But how did you happen to be marooned here?"

"Ah . . . we were outward bound, madam, on a mission from Earth to the Rim Stars." Echpo produced a box of lozenges and politely offered them around. "A cultural mission, headed by our poor friend Seesis—is he bothering you, dear lady? Just slap his hands down. The shock, you know . . . Ah . . . A most important and urgent mission, I may say with all due modesty, undertaken to—pardon me, I cannot say more. Our converter began giving trouble as we passed near this sun, so we approached your planet—

Toka, is that the name?—to get help. We knew from the pilot's manual that it had civilization, though we scarcely expected such delightful company as yours. At any rate, the converter failed us completely as we were entering the atmosphere, and though we glided down, the landing was still hard enough to wreck our communications equipment. That was yesterday, and today we were setting out in quest of help—we had seen from the air that there is a city some fifty kilometers hence—when, ah, your Hokas appeared and our poor friend Heragli—"

"Oh, dear!" said Tanni. "We'd better go get him right away. Can you guide me?"

"I should be honored," said Echpo. "I know the very tree."

"Does thy mother hunt with the Bandar-log, O Mowgli?" inquired Akela.

"Certainly not!" snapped Tanni, whirling on him. "You ought to be ashamed of yourself, Captain."

"What says she?" asked Akela agreeably.

Alex repeated it for him.

"Oh!" said Tanni, stamping off.

"Ah . . . poor dear Seesis," murmured Echpo. "He should not be left unguarded. He could hurt himself. Would your, ah, Hokas watch him while we rescue Heragli?"

"Of course," said Tanni. "Alex, you stay here and see to it."

The boy protested, was *Alexander*'d down, and gave in and announced importantly that he, the Man-Cub, wished the Pack to remain with him and not let Kaa depart. Tanni and Echpo started into the woods. Baloo and Bagheera followed.

"Hey, there!" said the woman. "Didn't Mowgli tell you to—"

"By the Broken Lock that freed me," squeaked

Bagheera, slapping his paunch with indignation, "dost thou take *us* for wolves?"

Tanni sighed and traded a glance with Echpo. As they went among the trees, she calmed down enough to say: "I can fly you to Mixumaxu, of course, and put you up; but it may take weeks before you can get off the planet. Not many deep-space ships stop here."

"Oh, dear." The Chakban wrung hairy hands. "Our mission is so vital. Could we not even get transportation to Gelkar?"

"Well . . ." Tanni considered. "Why, yes, it's only a few lightyears off. I can take you myself in our courier boat, and you can charter a ship there."

"Blessed damosel, my gratitude knows no limits," said Echpo.

Tanni preened herself. She was no snob, but certainly a favor done for beings as important as these would hurt no one's career.

Through the ruffling leaves, she heard a hoarse, angry bellow. "That must be your friend," she remarked brightly, or as brightly as possible when battling through a humid jungle with hair uncombed and no breakfast. "What did you say his name was?"

"Heragli. A Rowra of Drus. A most gentlemanly felino-centauroid, dear lady. I can't conceive why your Hokas insist on chasing him up trees."

A minute later the girl saw him, perched in the branches seven meters above ground. She had to admit that he was not unlike a tiger. The long, black-striped orange body was there, and the short yellow-eyed head, though a stumpy torso with two muscular arms was between. His whiskers were magnificent, and a couple of saber teeth did the resemblance no harm. Like Echpo, he wore the thorn-ripped tatters of a civilized business suit.

"Heragli, dear friend," called the Chakban, "I have

found a most agreeable lady who has graciously promised to help us."

"Are those unprintables around?" floated down a bass rumble. "Every blanked time I set foot to earth, the thus-and-so's have gone for me."

"It's all right!" snapped Tanni. She was not, she told herself, a prude; but Heragli's language was scarcely what she had been led to expect from the Bandar's—oops!—from Echpo's description of him as a most gentlemanly felino-centauroid.

"Why, sputter dash censored!" rasped the alien. "I see two of 'em just behind you!"

"Oh, them?" said Tanni. "Never mind them. They're only a bear and a black panther."

"They're *what*?"

"They're . . . well . . . oh, never mind! Come on down."

Heragli descended, two meters of rippling muscle hot in the leaf-filtered sunlight. "Very well, very well," he grumbled. "But I don't trust 'em. Lick my weight in flaming wildcats, but these asterisk unmentionables wreck my nerves. Where's the snake?"

Echpo winced. "My dear fellow!" he protested delicately.

"All right, all right!" bawled the Rowra. "The herpetoid, then. Don't hold with these dashed euphemisms. Call an encarnadined spade a cursed spade is my way. Where is he?"

"We left him back at—"

"Should've knocked'm on the mucking head. Said so all along. Save all this deleted trouble."

Echpo flinched again. "The, ah, the Rowra is an old military felino-centauroid," he explained hastily. "Believes in curing shock with counter-shock. Isn't that right, Heragli?"

"What? What're you babbling about now? Oh . . .

oh, yes. Your servant, ma'am," thundered the other. "Which bleeding way out, eh?"

"A rough exterior, dear lady," whispered Echpo in Tanni's ear, "but a heart of gold."

"That may be," answered the woman sharply, "but I'm going to have to ask him to moderate his voice and expurgate his language. What if the Hokas should hear him?"

"Blunderbore and killecrantz!" swore Heragli. "Let'm hear. I've had enough of this deifically anathematized tree climbing. Let'm show up once more and I'll gut 'em, I'll skin 'em, I'll—"

A chorus of falsetto wolfish howls interrupted him, and a second later the space around the tree was filled with leaping, yelling Hokas and the Rowra was up in the branches again.

"Come down, Striped Killer!" bawled Akela, bounding a good two meters up the trunk. "Come down ere I forget wolves cannot climb! I myself will tear thy heart out!"

"Sput! Meowr!" snarled Heragli, swiping a taloned paw at him. "Meeourl spss rowul rhnrrrr!"

"What's he saying?" demanded Tanni.

"Dear lady," replied Echpo with a shudder, "don't ask. General! General!—His old rank may snap him out of it—General, remember your duty!"

"LAME THIEF OF THE WAINGUNGA!" shouted Alex, bombarding him with fallen fruits.

Heragli closed his eyes and panted. "Oh, m'nerves!" he gasped above the roar of the Hokas. "All your fault, Echpo, you insisting on no sidearms. Of all the la-di-da conspir—"

"*General!*" cried the Chakban.

Tanni struggled around the Hokas and collared her son. "Alex," she said ominously, "I told you to keep them away."

"But they outvoted me, Mom," he answered. "They're the Free People, you know, and it's the full Pack—"

"FOR THE PACK, FOR THE FULL PACK, IT IS MET!" chorused the Hokas, leaping up and snapping at Heragli's tail.

Tanni put her hands over her ears and tried to think. It hurt her pride, but she sought desperately to imagine what Alex, Sr., would have done. Play along with them . . . use their own fantasy . . . yes and she had read the *Jungle Books* herself—Ah!

She snatched a nut from her boy just before he launched it and said sweetly: "Alex, dear, shouldn't the Pack be in bed now?"

"Huh, Mom?"

"Doesn't the Law of the Jungle say so? Ask Baloo."

"Indeed, Man-Cub," replied Baloo pontifically when Alex had repeated it, "the Law of the Jungle specifically states: 'And remember the night is for hunting, and forget not the day is for sleep.' Now that you remind me—thou remindest me, it is broad daylight and all the wolves ought to be in their lairs."

It took a little while to calm down the Hokas, but then they trotted obediently off into the forest. Tanni was a bit disconcerted to note that Baloo and Bagheera were still present. She racked her brains for something in the *Jungle Books* specifically dealing with the obligation of bears and black panthers also to go off and sleep in the daytime. Nothing, however, came to mind. And Heragli refused to climb down while—

Inspiration came. She turned to the last Hokas. "Aren't you thirsty?" she asked.

"What says thy mother, Little Frog?" demanded Bagheera, washing his nose with his hand and trying to purr.

"She asked if thou and Baloo were not thirsty," said Alex.

"Thirsty?" The two Hokas looked at each other. The extreme suggestibility of their race came into play. Two tongues reached out and licked two muzzles.

"Indeed, the Rains have been scant this year," agreed Bagheera.

"Perhaps I had better go shake the *mohwa* tree and check the petals that fall down," said Baloo.

"I hear," said the girl slyly, "that Hathi proclaimed the Water Truce last night."

"Oh . . . *ah*?" said Bagheera.

"And you know that according to the Law of the Jungle, that means all the animals must drink peaceably together," went on Tanni. "Tell them, Alex."

"Quite true," nodded Baloo sagely when the boy had translated. "Macmillan edition, 1933, page 68."

"So," said Tanni, springing her trap, "you'll have to take Shere Khan off and let him drink with you."

"*Wuh!*" said Baloo, sitting down on his haunches to consider the situation. "It is the Law," he decided at length.

"You can come down now," called Tanni to Heragli. "They won't hurt you."

"Blood and bones!" grumbled the Rowra, but descended and looked at the Hokas with a noticeable lack of enthusiasm. "Har d'ja do."

"Hello, Lame Thief," said Bagheera amiably.

"*Lame Thief?* Why—" Heragli began to roar, and Bagheera tried manfully to arch his back, which is not easy for a barrel-shaped Hoka.

"General! General!" interrupted Echpo. "It's the only way. Go off and have a drink with them, and as soon as you can, meet us here again."

"Oh, very well. Blank dash flaming etcetera."

Heragli trotted off into the brush, accompanied by his foes. Their voices trailed back:

"Hast hunted recently, Striped Killer?"

"Eh? What? Hunted? Well, as a matter of fact, in England on Earth last month—the Quorn—Master of the Hunt told me—went to earth at—"

The jungle swallowed them up.

"And now, dear lady," said Echpo nervously, "I must presume still further upon your patience. Poor Seesis has been left unguarded all this time—"

"Oh, yes!" The woman's long slim legs broke into a trot, back toward the place where she had first met the herpetoid. Echpo lumbered beside her and Alex followed.

"Ah . . . it is a difficult situation," declared the Chakban. "I fear the concussion has made my valued friend Seesis, ah, distrust the General and myself. His closest comrades! Can you imagine? He has, I think, some strange delusion that we mean to harm him."

Tanni slowed down. She felt no great eagerness to confront a paranoid python.

"He won't get violent," reassured Echpo. "I just wanted to warn you to discount anything he may do. He might, for example, try to write messages . . . Ah, here we are!"

They looked around the trampled vegetation. "He must have slipped away," said Tanni. "But he can't have gone far."

"Oh, he can move rapidly when he chooses, gracious madam," said Echpo, rubbing his hands in an agitated fashion. "Normally, of course, he does not so choose. You see, his race places an almost fanatical emphasis on self-restraint. Dignity, honor, and the like . . . those are the important things. A code, dear lady, which"—Echpo's deep-set eyes took on an odd gleam—"renders them vulnerable to, er, manipulation by those alert enough to press the proper semantic keys. But one which also renders them quite unpredictable. We had better find him at once."

It was not a large area in which they stood, and it soon became apparent that they had not simply overlooked the presence of ten meters of snake-like alien. A shout from Alex brought them to a trail crushed into the soft green herbage, as if someone had dragged a barrel through it. "This," said the boy, "must be the road of Kaa."

"Excellent spotting, young man," said Echpo. "Let us follow it."

They went rapidly along the track for several minutes. Tanni brushed the tangled golden hair from her eyes and wished for a comb, breakfast, a hot bath and—She noticed that the trail suddenly bent northward and continued in a straight line, as if Kaa—Seesis, blast it!—had realized where he was and set off toward some definite goal.

Echpo stopped, frowning, his flat nostrils a-twitch. "Dear me," he murmured, "this is *most* distressing."

"Why—he's headed toward your ship, hasn't he?" asked Tanni. "He should be easy to find. Let's go!"

"Oh, no, no, no!" The Chakban shook his bat-eared head. "I wouldn't dream of letting you and your son—delightful boy, madam!—go any further. It is much too dangerous."

"Nonsense! There's nothing harmful here, and you said yourself he isn't violent."

"Please! Not another word!" The long hands waved her back. "No, dear lady, just return to the meeting place, if you will, and when Heragli gets there send him on to the ship. Meanwhile I will follow poor Seesis and, ah, do what I can."

Before Tanni could reply, Echpo had bounded off and the tall grasses hid him.

She stood for a moment, frowning. The Chakban was a curious and contradictory personality. Though his manners were impeccable, she had not felt herself warming to him. There was something, something almost . . . well, *Bandar-loggish* about him. *Ridiculous*! she told herself. *But why did he suddenly change his mind about having me along? Just because Seesis headed back toward the wrecked ship?*

"Shucks, Mom," pouted Alex, "everybody's gone. All the wolves are in bed—in their lairs, I mean, and Bagheera and Baloo gone off with Shere Khan, and the Bandar's gone to the Cold Lairs and we can't even watch Kaa fight him. Nobody lets me have any fun."

Decision came to Tanni. The demented Seesis might, after all, turn on Echpo. If she had any chance of preventing such a catastrophe, her duty was clear. In plain language, she felt an infernal curiosity. "Come along, Alex," she said.

They had not far to go. Breaking through a tall screen of pseudo-bamboo, they looked out on a meadow.

And in the center of that meadow rested a small, luxurious Starflash space rambler.

"Wait here, Alex," ordered Tanni. "If there seems to be any danger, run for help."

She crossed the ground to the open airlock. Strange, the ship was not even dented. Peering in, she saw the control room. No sign of Echpo or Seesis—maybe they were somewhere aft. She entered.

It struck her that the controls were in very good shape for a vessel that had landed hard enough to knock out its communication gear. On impulse, she went over to the visio and punched its buttons. The screen lit up . . . why, it was perfectly useable! She would call Mixumaxu and have a detachment of Hoka police flown here. The Private Eyes and Honest Cops could easily—

A thick, hairy arm shot past her and a long finger snapped the set off. Another arm like a great furry shackle pinned her into the chair she had taken.

"That," whispered Echpo, "was a mistake, dear lady."

For a second, instinctively and furiously, Tanni tried to break loose. A kitten might as well have tried to escape a gorilla. Echpo let her have it out while he closed the airlock by remote control. Then he eased his grip. She bounced from the chair. A hard hand grabbed her wrist and whirled her about.

"What is this?" she raged. "Let me *go!*" She kicked at Echpo's ankles. He slapped her so her head rang. Sobbing, she relaxed enough to stare at him through a blur of horror.

"I am afraid, dear Mrs. Jones, that you have penetrated our little deception," said the Chakban gently. "I had hoped we could abandon our ship here, since a description of it has unfortunately been broadcast on the subvisio. By posing as castaways, we could have used the transportation to Gelkar which you so graciously offered us, and hired another vessel there. But as it is—" He shrugged. "It seems best we stay with this one after all, using you, madam, as a hostage . . . much though it pains me, of course."

"You wouldn't dare!" gasped Tanni, unable to think of a more telling remark.

"Dare? Dear lady," said Echpo, smiling, "our poor friend Seesis is the Tertiary Receptacle of Wisdom of Sanussi. If we dared kidnap him, surely—Please hold still. It would deeply grieve me to have to bind you."

"Sanussi . . . I don't believe you," breathed the girl. "Why, you're unarmed and he must have twice your strength."

"Dear charmer," sighed Echpo, "how little you know of Sanussians. Their ethical code is *so* unreasonably strict. When Heragli and I entered Seesis' embassy office on Earth, all we had to do was threaten to fill an ancestral seltzer bottle we had previously . . . ah . . . borrowed, with soda pop. The dishonor would have compelled the next hundred generations of his family to spend an hour a day in ceremonial writhing and give up all public positions. We wrung his parole from him: he was not to speak to anyone or resist us with force until released."

"Not *speak* . . . oh, so that's why he was trying to write," said Tanni. A degree of steadiness was returning to her. She could not really believe this mincing dandy capable of harm. "And I suppose he slipped back here with some idea of calling our officials and showing them a written account of—"

"How quickly you grasp the facts, madam," bowed Echpo. "Naturally, I trailed him and, since he may not use his strength on me, dragged him into a stateroom aft and coiled him up. As long as Heragli and I abide by the Sanussian code—chiefly, to refrain from endangering others—he is bound by his promise. That is why we have no weapons; the General is so impulsive."

"But why have you kidnapped him?"

"Politics. A matter of pressure to get certain concessions from his planet. Don't trouble your pretty head about it, my lady. As soon as practical after we have reached our destination—surely not more than a year—you will be released with our heartfelt thanks for your invaluable assistance."

"But you don't need *me* for a hostage!" wailed Tanni. "You've got Seesis himself."

"Tut-tut. The Sanussian police are hot on our trail. Despite the size of interstellar space, they may quite possibly detect us and close in . . . after which, to wipe out the stain on *their* honor, they would cheerfully blow Seesis up with Heragli and myself. But their ethics will not permit them to harm an innocent bystander like you, so—" Echpo backed toward the airlock, half dragging the woman. His bulk filled the chamber, blocking off escape, as he opened the valves. "So, as soon as Heragli returns—and not finding me at the agreed rendezvous, he will surely come here—we depart."

His simian face broke into a grin as discordant noises floated nearer. "Why, here he is now. Heragli, dear friend, do hurry. We must leave this delightful planet immediately."

His voice carried to the Rowra, who had just emerged from the canebrake with Bagheera on one side and Baloo on the other. Staggering, Heragli sat down, licked one oversized paw, and began to wash his face. Peering past Echpo, Tanni saw that the General's swiping motions were rather unsteady.

"Heragli!" said the Chakban on a sharper note. "Pay attention!"

"Go sputz yourself," boomed the Rowra, and broke into song. "Oh, when I was twenty-one, when I was twenty-one, I never had lots of mvrouwing but I always had lots of fun. My basket days were over and my prowling days begun, on the very very rrnowing night when I was twenty-one—*Chorus!*" he roared, beating time with a wavering paw, and the two Hokas embraced him and chimed in: "*When we wash twenty-one—*"

"Heragli!" yelled Echpo. "What's wrong with you?"

Tanni could have told him. She realized suddenly, as she stood there with the Chakban's heavy grip on her wrist, that when she evoked thirst in Baloo and Bagheera, she had pointed them in one inevitable direction: the abandoned camp of the Black Tyrone. The phrase "take Shere Khan off and let him drink with you" could have only one meaning to a Hoka. Heragli, like many beings before him, had encountered the fiery Tokan liquor.

There are bigger, stronger, wiser races than the Hokas, but the Galaxy knows none with more capacity. Heragli was twice the size and eight times the weight of a Hoka, but his companions were just pleasantly high, while he was—no other word will do—potted. And Tanni was willing to bet that Baloo and Bagheera were each two bottles ahead of him.

The General rolled over on his back and waved his feet in the air. "Oh, that little ball of yarn—" he warbled.

"Heragli!" shrieked Echpo.

"Oh, those wild, wild kittens, those wild, wild kittens, they're making a wildcat of me!"

"*General!*"

"Old tomcats never die, they just fa-a-a-aade—huh? Whuzza matta wi' you, monkey?" demanded Heragli, still on his back, looking at the spaceship upside down from bloodshot eyes. "Stannin' onna head. Riddickerluss, ab-so-lute-ly . . . Oh, curse the city that stole muh Kitty, by dawn she'll—Le's havva nuther one, mnowrr, 'fore you leave me! Hell an' damnation," said Heragli, suddenly dropping from the peak of joyous camaraderie to the valley of bitter suspicion, "dirty work inna catagon. Passed over f' promotion, twishe. Classmate, too . . . Is this a ray gun that I see b'fore me, the handle toward muh hand? Come, lemme clutch thee. . . . Monkeys an' snakes. Gallopin' horrors, I call 'em. Never trus' a primate—" and he faded off into mutterings.

"General!" called Echpo, sternly. "Pull yourself together and come aboard. We're leaving."

"Huh? Awri', awri', awri'—" said Heragli in a bleared tone. He lurched to all four feet, focused with some effort on the ship, and wobbled in its general direction.

"Mom!" cried a boyish voice, and Alex broke into the meadow. "What's going on?" He spotted Tanni with Echpo's hand clutching her. "What're you doing to my mother?"

"Heragli!" yelped Echpo. "Stop that brat!"

The Rowra blinked. Whether he would have obeyed if he had been sober, or if he had not been brooding about other races and the general unfairness of life, is an open question. He was not a bad felino-centauroid at heart. But as it was, he saw Alex running toward the ship, growled the one word *"Primate!"* to himself, and crouched for a leap.

His first mistake had been getting drunk. His second was to ignore, or be unaware of, three facts. These were, in order:

1) A Hoka, though not warlike, enjoys a rough-house.

2) A Hoka's tubby appearance is most deceptive; he is, for instance, more than a match for any human.

3) Baloo and Bagheera did not think Shere Khan should be allowed to harm the Man-Cub.

Heragli leaped. Baloo met him in mid-air, head to head. There was a loud, hollow *thonk*, and Heragli fell into a sitting position with a dazed look on his face while Baloo did a reeling sort of off-to-Buffalo. At that moment, Bagheera entered the wars. He would have been more effective had he not religiously adhered to the principle of fighting like a black panther, scrambling onto the Rowra's back, scratching and biting.

"Ouch!" howled Heragli, regaining full consciousness. "What the sputz? Get the snrrowl off me! Leggo, you illegitimate forsaken object of an origin which the compilers of Leviticus would not have approved! Wrowrrl!" And he made frantic efforts to reach over his shoulder.

"Striped Killer!" squeaked Bagheera joyously. "Hunter of helpless frogs! Lame Thief of the Waingunga! Take that! And that!"

"What're you talking about? Never ate a frog in m' life. Unhand me—gug!" Bagheera had wrapped both sturdy arms around Heragli's neck and started throttling him.

At the same time Baloo recovered sufficiently to stage a frontal attack. Fortunately, being in the role of a bear, he could fight like a bear, which is to say, very much like a Hoka. Accordingly, he landed a stiff one-two on Heragli's nose and then, as the Rowra reared up, wheezing, he fell into a clinch that made his enemy's ribs creak. Breaking cleanly, he landed a couple of hard punches in the midriff of Heragli's torso, chopped him over the heart, sank his teeth into the right foreleg, was lifted off his feet by an anguished jerk, used the opportunity to deliver a double kick to the chin while flurrying a series of blows, and generally made himself useful.

"Run, Alex!" cried Tanni.

The boy paused, uncertain, as Rowra and Hokas tore up the sod a meter from him.

"Run! Do what Mother tells you! Get help!"

Reluctantly, Alex turned and sped for the woods.

Tanni felt Echpo's grasp shift as he moved behind her. When he pulled a Holman raythrower from beneath his tunic, the blood seemed to drain out of her heart.

"Believe me, dear lady, I deplore this," said the Chakban. "I had hoped to keep my weapon unknown and untouched. But we cannot risk your son's warning the authorities too soon, can we? And then there are those Hokas." He pinned her against the wall and sighted on Alex. "You *do* understand my position, don't you?" he asked anxiously.

Struggling and screaming, Tanni clawed for his eyes. The brow ridges defeated her. She saw the gun muzzle steady—

—and there was a shock that threw her from Echpo's grip and out onto the ground.

Dazed, she scrambled to her feet with a wild notion of throwing herself in the path of the beam . . . But where *was* Echpo?

The airlock seemed to hold nothing but coil upon coil of Seesis. Only gradually, as her vision cleared, did Tanni make out a contorted face among those cable-thick bights. The Chakban was scarcely able to breathe, let alone move.

"Sssssso!" Seesis adjusted his pince-nez and regarded his prisoner censoriously. "So you lied to me. You were prepared to commit violence after all. I am shocked and grieved. I thought you shared my abhorrence of bloodshed. I see that you must be gently but firmly educated until you understand the error of your ways and repent and enter the gentle brotherhood of beings. Lie still, now, or I will break your back."

"I—" gasped Echpo. "I . . . had . . . my duty—"

"And I," answered Seesis, swaying above him, "have my honor."

Alex fell into his mother's arms. She was not too

full of thanksgiving to pick up the fallen gun. Across the meadow, Baloo and Bagheera stood triumphant over a semi-conscious Heragli and beamed at their snaky ally.

The Cold Lairs were taken. The Man-Cub had been rescued from Bandar-log and Lame Thief. Kaa's Hunting was finished.

II.
THE NAPOLEON CRIME

The Napoleon Crime

Be it understood at the outset, the disaster was in no way the fault of Tanni Hostrup Jones. Afterward she blamed herself bitterly, but most unfairly. She was overburdened with other matters, hence unable to concentrate on this one. She had no reason whatsoever to suspect evil of Leopold Ormen; after all, he was a Dane like herself, as well as being a famous journalist. Furthermore, while Tanni was chaste, she was a full-blooded woman, her husband had been gone for days and might not return for weeks, and Ormen had a great deal of masculine charm.

Having arrived on Toka by private spacecraft and settled into the Mixumaxu Hilton, he made an appointment to see her and at the time agreed on arrived at the plenipotentiary's residence. The day was beautiful and the walk through the quaint streets a delight. Native Hokas swarmed about, their exuberance often becoming deference when they saw the human. He smiled benignly and patted an occasional cub on the head. The adults looked just as cuddly: rather like bipedal, meter-tall teddy bears with golden fur and stubby hands, attired in a wild variety of costumes, everything from a barbarian's leather and iron to the elegant gray doublet and hose of his little companion, as well as Roman, Mandarin, cowboy, and other garb. Yet with few exceptions the squeaky voices chattered in English.

Thus, when he reached his destination, Ormen was not unduly surprised to be greeted at the door by a Hoka wearing coarse medieval-like clothes, hobnailed boots, a yellow hood, and a long white false beard tucked into a broad belt from which hung a geologist's hammer, a coil of rope, and a lantern. "Hello," the man said, and gave his name. "Mrs. Jones is expecting me."

The Hoka bowed, careful to do so in a fashion that showed he was not accustomed to bowing. "Gimli the dwarf, at your service," he replied, as gruffly as his larynx allowed. "Welcome to Rivendell. The Lady Galadriel did indeed make known to me that—Ah, ha! Hold!" Both his hands shot out and seized Ormen's left.

"What off Earth?" exclaimed the journalist.

"Begging your pardon, but that ring you're wearing. You'll have to check it before you go in."

"Why?" Ormen stared down at the gold band and its synthetic diamond. "It's only an ornament."

"I doubt not your faith, good sir," declared Gimli, "but you may conceivably have been tricked. This *could* be the One Ring under a false seeming—you not even invisible. Can't be too careful in these darkling times, right? You'll get it back when you leave."

Ormen tried to pull free, but the native was too strong. Suppressing an oath, the visitor yielded. Gimli turned the ring over to an elderly Hoka who had shown up, also whitebearded but attired in a blue robe and pointed hat and bearing a staff. Thereafter the self-styled dwarf ceremoniously conducted Ormen through the door. The entry-room beyond had been hung with tapestries that appeared to have been very hastily woven; colored tissue glued on the window-panes imitated stained glass, while candlelight relieved the dimness. Elsewhere the house remained a normal Terrestrial-type place, divided between living quarters and offices.

Tanni Jones received the newcomer graciously in her parlor. She was tall, blond, and comely, as was he, and eager to see anybody from the home planet. "Please sit down, Mr. Ormen," she invited. "Would you care for coffee, tea, or perhaps something alcoholic?"

"Well, I've heard about the liquor they make here, and confess to being curious," he said.

She shuddered a bit. "I don't recommend you investigate. What about a Scotch and soda?" When he accepted, she rang for a servant, who appeared with churchwarden pipe in hand and bare feet on which the hair had been combed upward. "We'll have the happy hour usual, Gamgee," she said. "*Scotch* Scotch, mind you."

The humans began to talk in earnest. "What's happening?" Ormen inquired. "I mean, well, isn't your staff acting rather oddly?"

Tanni sighed. "They've discovered *The Lord of the Rings*. I can only hope they get over it before the fashion spreads further. Not that it would upset Alex—my husband, that is, the plenipotentiary—to be hailed as the rightful King when he returns. He's used to that sort of thing, after all our years in this post. But meanwhile—oh, for example, we get visitors

from other worlds, nonhumans, and many of them
are important—officials of the League, representatives of firms whose cooperation we need to mod-
ernize Toka, and so on." She shuddered again. "I can
just imagine the Hokas deciding some such party
must be orcs or trolls or Ring-Wraiths."

"I sympathize. You inhabit a powder keg, don't
you?"

"M-m, not really. The Hokas do take on any role
that strikes their fancy, and act it out—live it—with
an uncompromising literal-mindedness. But they're
not insane. They've never yet gotten violent, for
instance; and they continue to work, meet their
responsibilities, even if it is in some fantasy style.
In fact," said Tanni anxiously, "their reputation for
craziness is quite undeserved. it's going to handicap
my husband on his mission. I suppose you know he's
gone to Earth to negotiate an upgrading in status
for Toka. If he doesn't succeed in convincing the
authorities our wards are ready for that, we may
never in our lifetimes see them become full members of the Interbeing League; and that is our dearest
dream."

Leopold Ormen nodded. "I do know all this, Mrs.
Jones, and I believe I can help." He leaned forward,
though he resisted the temptation to stroke her hand.
"Not that I'm an altruist. I have my own living to
make, and I think there's a tremendous documen-
tary to be done about this planet. But if it conveys
the truth, in depth, to civilized viewers throughout
the galaxy—yes, and readers too, because I'd also
like to write a book—public opinion should change.
Wouldn't that be good for your cause?"

Tanni glowed. "It certainly would!"

Ormen leaned back. She was hooked, he knew;
now he must play his line so carefully that she

remained unaware of the fact. "I can't do it unless I have complete freedom," he stated. "I realize your husband's duty requires him to impose various restrictions on outsiders, who might otherwise cause terrible trouble. But I hope you—in his absence, you are the acting plenipotentiary, aren't you?—l hope you'll authorize me to go anywhere, see anything and anybody, for as long as I'll need to get the whole story. I warn you, that may take quite a while, and I'll be setting my aircar down in places where the Hokas aren't accustomed to such a sight."

As said, Tanni cannot be blamed. She did not rush into her decision. In the course of the following week, she had several meetings with him, including a couple of dinners where he was a fascinating, impeccably courteous guest. She inquired among the local folk, who all spoke well of him. She studied recordings of his previous work from the data file, and found it excellent. When at last she did give him *carte blanche,* she expected to keep track of what he was doing, and call a halt if a blunder seemed imminent. Besides, Alex should be back presently, to apply the sixth sense he had perforce developed for problems abrew.

That none of these reasonable considerations worked out was simply in the nature of Hoka things.

First she was kept busy distracting the natives, lest a Tolkien craze sweep through thousands of them. That was less difficult than it might have been elsewhere on the globe. Most of the human-derived societies were still rather isolated and naive. This was a result of policy on Alex's part. Not only did he fear the unforeseeable consequences of cross-fertilization—suppose, for example, that the Vikings came into close contact with the Bedouins—but a set of ongoing, albeit uncontrolled psychohistorical experiments gave him hints about what was best for the race as a whole. Nevertheless, it did leave those cultures vulnerable to any new influence that happened by.

As the seat of the plenipotentiary and therefore, in effect, the capital city of the planet, Mixumaxu was cosmopolitan. Its residents and those of its hinterland were, so to speak, immunized. This did not mean that any individual stuck to any given role throughout his life. On the contrary, he was prone to overnight changes. But by the same token, these made no fundamental difference to him; and therefore the Jones household continued to function well in a bewildering succession of guises.

Soon after she had headed off the War of the Rings, Tanni got caught up in the *Jungle Books* affair. Since that involved beings of status, and a scandal which must not become common knowledge lest the tranquility of the galaxy be disturbed, the sequel kept her occupied for weeks. She handled her end of the business with a competence which caused the Grand Theocrat of Sanussi, in an elaborate honors ceremony years later, to award her a cast-off skin of his.

Meanwhile a cruel disappointment arrived, in the form of a letter from Alex. Complications had developed; the delegation from Kratch was, for some reason known only to their nasty little selves, using every parliamentary trick to delay the upgrading of Toka; he must stay and fight the matter through to a successful conclusion; he didn't know how long it would take; he missed her immeasurably, and enclosed one of his poems to prove it.

Tanni refrained from weeping in front of their children. She did utter a few swear words. Afterward she plunged into work. Suddenly there seemed to be a great deal of it. Information-gathering facilities were stretched thin at best, so that she was seldom fully apprised of events on other continents; but such reports as came in were increasingly ominous. They told of unrest, strange new ideas, revolutionary changes—

No wonder that she lacked time to follow what Leopold Ormen was about. Events moved far too fast. All at once she saw catastrophe looming before her. The single thing she could think to do was send a frantic, although enciphered, message to her husband; and indeed, this was the single thing she could have done.

An airbus took Alexander Jones from League headquarters in New Zealand to the spaceport on Campbell Island. There he walked past sleek, gleaming starships to the far end of the field, where sat a craft larger than most, but battered and corrosion-pocked. Its bulbous lines proclaimed it to be of nonhuman manufacture, and its registration emblem to be a tramp freighter. Beneath the name etched on the bows was a translation into the English of the spaceways: *Thousand-Year Bird*. Alex mounted the movable ramp that led to the main personnel lock and pressed the buzzer button.

A gentle, if mechanical voice sounded from the speaker grille: "Is someone present? The valve isn't secured. Come in, do, and make yourself at home."

Alex pushed on the metal. Nothing happened. "Brob, it's me, Alexander Jones," he said into the intercom. "It won't open. The valve won't, I mean."

"Oh, dear, I *am* sorry. I forgot I had left it on manual. One moment, please. I beg your pardon for the inconvenience."

Something like a minor earthquake shivered through hull and ramp. The valve swung aside, revealing an oversized airlock chamber and the being who had the strength to move so ponderous an object. "How pleasant to see you again, dear fellow," said the transponder hanging from his neck. Meanwhile his real voice, which the device rendered into frequencies a human could hear, vibrated subsonically out of his feet and up into the man's bones. "Welcome to my humble vessel. Come in, let me make you a cup of tea, tell me how I may serve you."

The 'sponder likewise converted Alex's tones into impulses Brob sensed through his skin. On their airless world, his species had never developed ears. "I've got a hell of a request to make, and you don't really know me well enough, but I'm desperate and you seem to be my only possible help."

Eyes that were soft and brown, despite their lack of moisture, looked thirty centimeters downward to Alex's lanky height. "Sir, it has been a pleasure and an enlightenment making your acquaintance. Furthermore, I feel certain that your purpose is not selfish, but for some public good. If so, whatever small assistance I can perhaps render will earn me merit, which I sorely need. Therefore it shall be I who enter into your debt. Now do come in and tell me about this."

Brob led the way, moving gracefully despite his bulk; but then, Earth gravity was a mere one-third of his planet's. For that matter, had he been short like a Hoka, he would have been considered even more cute. He too possessed a pair of arms, his thicker than a gorilla's and terminating in enormous four-fingered hands, and a pair of stout legs, ending in feet that were a meter long and half as wide; their soles enclosed the tympani with which his race listened and spoke. The torso was so rotund as to be almost globular. The head was equally round;

though it naturally lacked a nose, it had a blunt snout whose lipless mouth was shaped into a permanent smile. All in all, he suggested a harp seal puppy. Baby-blue fur covered him, save on the hands and feet; there it was white, which gave him an appearance of wearing mittens and booties. His actual clothing consisted of the 'sponder and a belt with pockets full of assorted tools.

The saloon of the ship whose owner, captain, and crew he was seemed less alien than might have been expected, considering how unlike Earth was the planet which humans called Brobdingnag. That world had begun as a body more massive than Jupiter. A nearby supernova had blown away its gas and deposited vast quantities of heavy elements over the solidifying core. They included radioactives. Somehow life had evolved, making use of this source of energy rather than the feeble red sun. Plants concentrated isotopes which animals then ate. Brob, as Alex dubbed him for lack of ability to pronounce his real name, did not live by oxidizing organic materials like most creatures in known space, but by fissioning nuclei. His physical strength was corresponding.

The metabolism posed no hazard to anyone else. The fission process worked at a far lower level than in a powerplant, and whatever radiation it gave off was absorbed by the dense tissues around the "stomach." Brobdingnagians traveling abroad needed merely take certain precautions in disposal of their body wastes. Regardless, many beings feared and shunned them. Having delivered a cargo to Earth, Brob found himself unable to get another, and the waiting time while his broker searched for one grew lonely as well as long. Chancing to meet Alex in a Christchurch pub, where he had gone in hopes that somebody would talk to him, he was pathetically grateful when the man not only did, but pursued the acquaintance afterward.

For his part, Alex enjoyed Brob's tales of distant worlds. Sometimes he grew bored, because the alien had fallen in love with Japanese culture and would drone on for hours about calligraphy, flower arranging, and other such arts. Yet even that was better than sitting around yearning for Tanni and his children, cursing the abominable Kratch, and wondering how many more weeks it would take to complete his business.

Brob did his best to bow as he gestured his visitor to sit down on a tatami mat, politely ignoring the shoes that the human had not removed. He left Alex to meditate upon a lily and a stone, placed in a bowl of water beneath a scroll depicting Mount Fuji, while he occupied himself preparing for a tea ceremony. This was necessarily modified, since as he sipped the aqueous substance, it turned to steam. Serenely, he contemplated the white clouds swirling out of his mouth, before at last he inquired what he could do for his friend.

Alex had learned not to be boorishly direct in Brob's presence. "Let me review the situation, though you do know why I'm stuck here on Earth," he said. "The Chief Cultural Commissioner had approved Toka's advancement, the vote looked like being a pure formality, and then the Kratch delegation objected. They couldn't just be voted down, because they levelled charges of misgovernment. Nothing as simple as tyranny or corruption. I could easily have disproved that. No, they claim my entire policy has been wrong and is bound to cause disaster."

Brob nodded gravely. "You have explained to me," he replied; the teapot and cups trembled "I have admired your restraint in not dwelling upon it in conversation."

Alex shrugged. "What use would that be? The fact is, I've often had to do things on Toka that, well, played kind of fast and loose with the letter of the law. I had no choice. The Hokas are like that. You know; I've told you a bundle about them. Ordinarily no one sees anything wrong in a plenipotentiary exercising broad discretion. After all, every planet is unique. Nothing really counts except results, and I pride myself that mine have been good But how can I argue against the claim that I've created the *potential* for calamity?"

"I should think a look at your record, and a modicum of common sense, would suffice to make the legislators decide in your favor."

"Oh, yes. But you see, after they'd raised this issue, the Kratch promptly raised a host of others, and got mine postponed. It's blatant obstruction on their part. Most of the delegates recognize that and are as disgusted as I am. But the Constitution forces them to go through the motions—and forces me to sit idle, waiting for whatever instant it will be that the case of Toka is opened to debate.

"It's enough to make a paranoid out of a saint," Alex sighed. "One set of villains after another, year after year—the Slissii, the Pornians, the Sarennians, the Worbenites, the Chakbans—my wife wrote me about those—conspiring and conniving. I've really begun to wonder if some evil masterminds aren't at work behind the scenes, and I wouldn't be surprised but what they're Kratch." He sighed again. "It's either believe that, or else believe we're only characters in a series of stories being written by a couple of hacks who need the money."

"It may be sheer accident," Brob suggested.

"Mortal fallibility. There is a great deal of wisdom in the universe; unfortunately, it is divided up among individuals."

Alex ran a hand through his already rumpled brown hair. His snub-nosed countenance grew stark. "Okay," he said, "what I've come to you about is a . . . a sort of dreadful climax. I've received a letter from my wife and—Toka really is about to explode. I've got to get back at once and see if I can do anything to save the situation."

"Well, yes, I should imagine that that would be indicated," Brob murmured and rumbled. "Can you describe the problem a little more fully?"

Alex pulled the letter out of his tunic. "She sent it by message torpedo; it's that urgent. It's coded, too, but by now the words are burned into my brain. Let me give you a sample." He read aloud:

"'Somehow, our policy of keeping the different Hoka societies relatively isolated has broken down. Suddenly, they had been introduced to concepts of each other. And this hasn't been in the casual way of individuals traveling around, like that sweet little Viking you met when you'd been press-ganged onto that eighteenth-century British frigate. We've always allowed for that degree of contact. No, what's happened this time must have been deliberately caused. Besides, ideas totally new to the planet, dangerous ideas, have been appearing. I've had agents in the field collecting books, video tapes—but the damage has already been done, and the Hokas themselves don't know or care how it happened. A fire like that is fatally easy to start; then it spreads of itself.

"'For instance, right on the plains of this continent, the Wild West has been introduced to the biography of Genghis Khan. Of course the cowboys promptly went overboard for being ferocious

Mongols—' Er, Tanni ordinarily handles her figures of speech better than that; but anyway— 'So far it's been harmless. The Mongols ride around to every cow town demanding it surrender to the will of the Kha Khan, and explaining that they don't stutter but "Kha Khan" really is his title. The town is always happy to yield, because they make this the occasion of a drunken party. As one mayor said to me when I flew there to question him, it's better to bottle a place than sack it. But the potential is terrifying, because the cowboys out Montana way have decided they're European knights who must resist any heathen who invade their country.

"'And the Russian Hokas are no longer content to sit around strumming balalaikas and singing sad songs; they have elected a Czar and babble about the Third Rome. Over in the United States, Abolitionists are feverishly looking for slaves to set free—and beginning to get volunteer Uncle Tom types—while the Virginia Gentlemen talk of secession. In the South Sea, a King Kamehameha has appeared, and war clubs are replacing ukuleles, and I'm afraid they'll see use. It goes on and on around the globe, this sort of dangerous nonsense.

"'What frightens me worst, and causes me to write this, is Napoleon.'" Alex cleared his throat. "You realize, Brob, that a Hoka can be perfectly sane and still claim he is Napoleon. Um-m. . . . 'He has displaced the King of France. He is organizing and equipping his Grand Army. Even after my experience of Hoka energy and enthusiasm, I am surprised at how fast the workshops in their country are producing weapons.

"'Inevitably, those eighteenth-century British have gotten alarmed and are arming too. Their island is right across a strait from that continent, you

remember. I might have been able to calm them
down, except that lengthy biographies of humans who
lived in that period have been circulating to inflame
their imaginations. I was in London, trying to argue
them out of it, and threatening to expose them to
the ridicule of the galaxy. I couldn't think what else
to do. The Hoka who calls himself the Duke of
Wellington drew himself up to his full height, fixed
me with a steel eye, and barked, "Publish and be
damned!"

" 'Oh, darling, I'm afraid! I think these playact-
ing prophecies of wars to come will soon fulfill themselves. And once Hokas actually start getting maimed
and killed—well, I believe you'll agree that they'll
go berserk, as bad as ever our species was in the
past, and the whole planet will be drenched in blood.

" 'Alex, could you possibly return?' "

The man's voice broke. He stuffed the letter back
into his pocket and dabbed at his eyes. "You see I've
got to go," he said.

"Do you expect that you can accomplish anything?" Brob asked, as softly as he was able.

Alex gulped. "I've got to try."

"But you are compelled to remain here on Earth,
waiting for the unpredictable moment at which you
will be called upon to justify your actions as plenipotentiary and urge the upgrading of your wards."

"That's no good if meanwhile everything else I'm
responsible for goes down the drain. In fact, a horror
like that would throw the whole system of guidance
for backward worlds into question. It could open the
way for old-fashioned imperialism and exploitation
of them."

"If you departed for Toka," Brob said, "the Kratch
would doubtless seize that opportunity to bring up
the matter of your stewardship—when you are not

present to defend yourself—and win custody of the planet for one of their own, who could then work toward the end of discrediting the present protective laws, as you suggest." He made a sign. "If this hypothesis maligns the motives of the Kratch, I apologize and abase myself."

"You needn't, I'm sure." Alex leaned forward. His index finger prodded Brob's mountainous chest. "I've been collecting information about them. Their government is totalitarian, and has expansionist ambitions. It's been engaged in all sorts of shenanigans—which have been hushed up by nice-nelly types in the League who hope that if you ignore a villain he'll go away. This whole thing on Toka can't be simple coincidence. It's too well orchestrated. The likelihood of war arises precisely when I can't be on hand—Do you see?"

"What then do you propose?" asked Brob, calm as ever.

"Why, this," Alex said. "Look. Toka's a backwater. No passenger liners call there. If I left on my official ship, it would be known; I need clearance for departure, and the Kratch must have somebody keeping watch on this port. They'd immediately move to get their accusations onto the floor, and probably have their agents do their best to hasten the debacle on Toka. But if they don't *know* I've gone—if they assume I'm hanging around waiting and drinking too much as I have been—they'll let matters continue to ripen while they continue to stall. And maybe I can do something about the whole miserable affair. Do you see?"

Brob nodded. "I believe I do," he answered. "You wish me to furnish clandestine transportation."

"I don't know who else can," Alex pleaded. "As for payment, well, I have discretionary funds in my exchequer, and if I can get this mess straightened out—"

Brob swept an arm in a grand gesture which smashed the tea table. "Oh, dear," he murmured—and then, almost briskly: "Say no more. We need not discuss crass cash. I will tell my broker that I have lost patience and am departing empty. Your task will be to smuggle yourself and your rations aboard. Do you not prefer ham sandwiches?"

Despite its down-at-heels appearance, the *Thousand-Year Bird* was a speedster, power-plant equal to a dreadnaught's and superlight drive as finely tuned as an express courier's. It made the passage from Sol to Brackney's Star in scarcely more than a week. Alex supposed that Brobdingnagians had an innate talent for that kind of engineering; or maybe it was just that they could work on a nuclear reactor as casually as a human could tinker with an aircar engine, and thus acquired a knack for it.

Quite aside from the crisis, Alex had reason to be glad of such a high pseudovelocity. It wasn't so much that Brob, profusely apologizing, kept the artificial gravity at that of his home world. His health required a spell of this, in between his long stay on Earth and his prospective stay on Toka. Given a daily dose of baryol, Alex could tolerate the condition for a while, though soon his lean frame grew stiff and sore under its weight of 240 kilos and he spent most of the time stretched out on an enormous bunk. The real trouble was that Brob, having little else to do under way, spent most of same time keeping him company and trying to cheer him up; and Brob's bedside manner left something to be desired.

The alien's intentions were of the kindliest. His race had no natural enemies even on its own planet;

if he chose, he could have pulled apart the collapsed metal armor of a warcraft, rather like a man ripping a newsfax sheet in half. Hence he had no reason not to be full of love for all life forms, and—while he knew from experience that it was not always true— his tendency was to assume that all of them felt likewise.

After a few sermons on the moral necessity of giving the Kratch the benefit of the doubt, since they were probably only misguided, Alex lost his temper. "You'll find out different when they bring an end to a hundred years of peace!" he yelled. "Let me alone about it, will you?"

An apologetic quiver went through the hull. "Forgive me," Brob said. "I am sorry. I didn't mean to raise thoughts you must find painful. Shall we discuss flower arrangements?"

"Oh, no, not that again! Tell me about some more of your adventures."

The 'sponder burbled, which perhaps corresponded to a sigh. "Actually, I have had few. For the most part I have simply plodded among the stars, returning home to my little wife and our young ones, where we cultivate our garden and engage in various activities for civic betterment. Of course, I have seen remarkable sights on my travels, but you don't appreciate how outstanding among them are those of Earth. Why, in Kyoto I found a garden which absolutely inspired me. I am certain my wife will agree that we must remodel ours along similar lines. And an arrangement of our very own glowbranch, ion weed, and lightning blossoms would—" Brob was off afresh on his favorite subject.

Alex composed his soul in patience. The Hokas had given him plenty of practice at that.

❖   ❖   ❖

The ship set down on Mixumaxu spaceport, Brob turned off the interior fields, and suddenly Alex was under blessed Terrestrial-like weight again. Whooping, he sprang from his bunk, landed on the deck, and collapsed as if his legs had turned to boiled spaghetti.

"Dear me," said his companion. "Your system must be more exhausted than we realized. How I regret the necessity I was under. Let me offer you assistance." Reaching down, he took a fold of the man's tunic between thumb and forefinger, lifted him daintily, and bore him off to the airlock, not noticing that Alex's feet dangled several centimeters in the air.

After taking parking orbit around the planet, he had radioed for permission to land. He had mentioned that the plenipotentiary was aboard, but forgotten to say anything about himself; and nobody on Toka had heard about his race, whose trade lanes did not bring them into this sector. Thus the ground crew who had brought the ramp, and Tanni who had sped from her home, were treated to the sight of their man feebly asprawl in the grip of a leering, blue-furred ogre.

A native security guard whipped out a pistol. "Hold still, sir!" he squeaked. "I'll kill that monster for you."

"No, no, don't shoot," Alex managed to croak.

"Why not?"

"Well, in the first place," said Alex, making his tone as reasonable as possible under the circumstances, "he wouldn't notice. But mainly, he's a good person, and—and—Hi, there, honey."

The ramp, which had not been constructed for the likes of Brob, shivered and buckled as he descended, but somehow he made it safely. Meanwhile Alex thought the poison must have spread far and deep, if a Hoka—in sophisticated Mixumaxu, at that—was so quick to resort to a lethal weapon.

Tanni's passionate embrace proved remarkably restorative. He wished they could go home, just the two of them, at once, before the children got back from school. However, politeness required that they invite Brob to come along, and when they were at the house, Alex's fears resurged and he demanded an account of the latest developments.

Woe clouded Tanni's loveliness. "Worse every day," she answered. "Especially in Europe—our Europe, I mean," she added to Brob, "though don't confuse it with that Europe that the ex-cowboys in what used to be Montana have—Never mind." She drew breath and started over:

"Napoleon's filled the French Hokas with dreams of *la gloire*, and the German Hokas are flocking to become his grenadiers—except in Prussia, where I've heard about a General Blücher—and three days ago, the Grand Army invaded Spain. You see, Napoleon wants to give the Spanish throne to his cousin Claud. That's caused the British Hokas—the British circa 1800 A.D., that is—thank God, so far the Victorian British on their own island have kept their senses, maybe because of Sherlock Holmes—anyway, yesterday they declared war, and are raising a fleet and an army of their own for a Peninsular campaign. And we won't even be able to handle the matter discreetly. I got hold of Leopold Ormen by phone and begged him to clear his stories with me, but he refused—insisted on his right of a free press, and in such a gloating way, too. . . . I'd taken him for a nice man, but—" Her voice broke. She huddled down in her chair and covered her face.

"Leopold Ormen? The journalist?" inquired Alex. "What's this?"

Tanni explained, adding that the man had since gone elsewhere, quite out of contact.

Alex cursed. "As if we didn't have troubles enough!" Suspicion struck fangs into his spirit. "Could his presence here be simple coincidence? I wonder. I wonder very much."

"Do you imply that Mr. Ormen may have stirred up this imbroglio?" asked Brob, appalled. "If so, and if you are correct, I fear he is no gentlebeing."

Alex sprang from his seat and paced. "Well, he can scarcely have accomplished everything alone," he thought aloud. "But he can sure have helped a lot to get it started, flitting freely around with the prestige of being a human, and that glib manner I recall from his broadcasts. . . . Don't cry, darling."

"I shan't," Brob said. "My species does not produce tears. However, I am deeply moved by your expression of affection."

Tanni had not begun sobbing. That was not her way. Grimly, she raised her glance and said, "Okay, he tricked me. At least, we've sufficient grounds for suspicion to order his arrest. Though he has his own flyer and could be anywhere on the planet."

Alex continued to prowl the carpet. "I doubt that that would be any use at this stage," he responded. "Arresting him, I mean. Unless we had absolute proof that he was engaged in subversion, which we don't, we'd lay ourselves open to countercharges of suppression. Besides, our first duty is not to save our reputations, but to prevent bloodshed."

He struck fist in palm, again and again. "How *could* matters have gotten so out of hand, so fast?" he wondered. "Even for Hokas, this is extreme, and it's happened damn near overnight. Around the globe, too, you tell me, the Napoleon business is just the most immediate danger. Somebody, some group, must be at work, propagandizing, offering evil advice. They wouldn't have to be humans, either. Hokas would be ready to believe whatever they heard from members of any technologically advanced society. In fact, humans have gotten to be rather old hat. Somebody different, exotic, would have more glamour, and find it easier to mislead them."

"Yes, I've thought along the same lines, dear," Tanni said. "Naturally, I forbade the French to mobilize, but the only reply I got was something about the Old Guard dies, it does not surrender. The British—well, they ignored my countermanding of their declaration of war, but I don't think they have been directly subverted. They're simply reacting as one would expect them to."

Alex nodded. "That sounds likely. The enemy can't have agents everywhere. That'd be too conspicuous, and give too many chances for something to go wrong. A few operatives, in key areas, are better."

He stopped in midstride, tugged his chin, rumpled his hair, and decided: "Britain is the place to start, then. I'm off to see what I can do. After all, I am their plenipotentiary, whom they've known for years, and if I appear in person, they'll at least listen to me."

"Shall I accompany you?" offered Brob. "On Toka I am, if not glamorous, surely exotic. Thus my presence may lend weight."

"It will that!" Alex agreed. He supposed his aircar could lift the other being.

Numerous Georgian houses graced the city renamed London. Though the Hokas could not afford to replace every older building at once, they had decorated many a wall with fake pilasters, put dummy dormers onto round roofs, and cut fanlights into doors.

Tophatted, tailcoated Regency bucks swaggered
through the streets, escorting ladies in muslin; seeing Alex and Brob, such males would raise their quiz-
zing glasses for a closer look. Inspired by Hogarth,
the commoners who swarmed about were more vocal
at sight of the newcomers. Luckily, the dinosaurian
animals hitched to wagons and carriages were not as
excitable as Terrestrial horses. In general, this place
was more safe and sanitary than its model had been;
Alex had managed to bring that about in every society that his wards adopted.

Thus far. Today he saw a high proportion of
redcoated soldiers who shouldered muskets with
bayonets attached. He overheard a plaintive voice
through a tavern window: "Please, matey, do resist
us like a good lad. 'Ow can we be a proper press
gang h'if h'everybody *volunteers*?"

Proceeding afoot, since Brob would have broken
the axles of any local vehicle, Alex and his companion
reached Whitehall. There a guard of Royal Marines
saluted and led them to the First Lord of the
Admiralty. The man had called ahead for this
appointment; even the most archaic-minded Hokas
maintained essential modern equipment in their more
important offices, although in the present case the
visiphone was disguised as a Chippendale cabinet.
The native behind the desk rose. He had attired his
portly form in brown smallclothes and set a wig on
his head. It didn't fit well, and rather distracted from
the fine old-world courtesy of his bow, by slipping
down over his muzzle.

"A pleasure to meet you again, my dear fellow,
'pon my word it is," he said in calm, clipped accents
while he readjusted the wig. "And to make your
acquaintance, sir," he added to Brob, "as I trust I
shall have the honor of doing. Be seated and take

refreshment." He tinkled a bell. The staff were prepared, for a liveried servant entered immediately, bearing a tray with three glasses and a dusty bottle. "Fine port, this, if I do say so myself." Indignantly: "To think that Boney would cut us off from the source of supply! Infernal bounder, eh, what? Well, damme, he'll whistle a different tune, and out of a dry throat, when we've put him on St. Helena."

Alex settled down and took a cautious sip from his goblet. The drink was the same fiery distillation that was known as claret, sherry, brandy, rum, whisky, or whatever else a role might call for. "I am afraid, Lord Oakheart, that Bonaparte has no intention of going to St. Helena," he replied. "Instead—" He broke off, because the Hoka's jaw had dropped. Turning about to see what was wrong, he spied Brob. The giant spacefarer, careful to remain standing, had politely swallowed the drink given him. Blue flames gushed out of his mouth.

"Er, this is my associate, from Brobdingnag," Alex explained.

"From where?" asked Oakheart. "I mean to say, that Swift chap does have several interesting ideas, but I wasn't aware anybody had put 'em into effect . . . yet." Recovering his British aplomb, he took a pinch of snuff.

Alex braced himself. "Milord," he said, "you know why we've come. Armed conflict cannot be allowed. The differences between the governments of His Majesty and the Emperor shall have to be negotiated peacefully. To that end, my good offices are available, and I must insist they be accepted. The first step is for you people to take, namely, cancelling your expedition to Spain."

"Impossible, sir, impossible," huffed the Hoka. "Lord Nelson sails from Plymouth tomorrow. True, at present he has only the Home Fleet under his command, but dispatches are on their way to the colonies, summoning all our strength afloat to join him at Trafalgar How can we stop 'em, eh? No, the British Lion is off to crush the knavish Frogs."

Alex thought fast. A leaderless armada, milling about, would have still more potential for causing disaster than one which was assembled under its respected admiral. "Wait a minute," he said. "It'll take two or three weeks for those windjammers to reach the rendezvous, whereas Spain's only two or three days' sail from here. Why is Nelson leaving this early?"

Oakheart confirmed his guess: "A reconnaissance, sir, a reconnaissance in force, to gather intelligence on the enemy's movements and chivvy him wherever he shows his cowardly face with fewer ships than ours."

"In that case, suppose I ride along. I could, well, maybe give Lord Nelson some helpful advice. More importantly, being on the scene, I could attempt to open negotiations with the French."

Oakheart frowned. "Most irregular. Danger of violation of the Absolutely Extreme Secrets Act. I am afraid I cannot countenance—"

Alex had learned how to turn Hoka logic against itself. "See here, milord, I am the accredited representative of a sovereign state with which your own has treaties and trade relations. I am sure His Majesty's government will accord me the usual diplomatic courtesies."

"Well . . . ah . . . but if you must talk to that Bonaparte rascal, why don't you simply fly to his camp, eh?"

Alex stiffened and replied coldly: "Sir, I am shocked to hear you propose that His Majesty's government should have no part in a vital proceeding like this."

Oakheart capitulated. "I beg your pardon, sir! No such intention, I assure you. Roger me if there was. Here, I'll give you a letter of introduction to the admiral, in my own hand, by Jove!" He reached for a goosequill, imported at considerable expense from Earth. As he wrote, he grew visibly more and more eager. Alex wished he could see what was going down on the paper, but no gentleman would read someone else's mail.

The human had excellent reasons—he hoped—for taking this course. While the Hoka Napoleon himself was doubtless well-intentioned, whatever persons had inflated his vainglory until he was red for war were, just as doubtless, not. They would be prepared for the contingency of a direct approach by a League authority. A blaster could shoot his aircar down as it neared, or he could be assassinated or kidnapped after he landed, and the Hokas led to believe he had been the victim of a tragic accident.

Traveling with Nelson, he had a better chance of getting to the Emperor, unbeknownst to the conspirators. Whether or not he succeeded in that, he expected to gather more information about how matters actually stood than he could in any other fashion.

Tanni would never let him take the risk. If nothing else, she'd fly out in her own car and snatch him right off the ship. Reluctantly, he decided to tell her, when he phoned, that he was engaged in delicate business which would keep him away for an indefinite time.

Since their ancient Slissii rivals departed, Hokas had had no need of military or naval forces, except to provide colorful uniforms and ceremonies. Hence the Home Fleet gathered at Plymouth was unimpressive. There were about a dozen Coast Guard cutters, hitherto employed in marine rescue work. There were half as many commandeered merchant ships, though these, being squareriggers of the Regency period, naturally bore cannon. There were three minor warcraft, the pinnace *Fore*, the bark *Umbrageous*, and the frigate *Falcon*. And finally there was a line-of-battle ship, the admiral's pennant at its masthead and the name *Victory* on its bows.

Leaving Brob ashore, lest the gangplank break beneath him, Alex boarded the latter. Two sailors who noticed him whipped fifes out of their jackets and played a tune, as befitted a visitor of his rank. This caused crewmen elsewhere on deck to break into a hornpipe. A Hoka in blue coat and cocked hat, telescope tucked beneath his left arm, hurried across the tarry-smelling planks.

"Welcome, Your Excellency, welcome," he said, and gave Alex a firm handshake. "Bligh's the name, Captain William Bligh, sir, at your service."

"What? I thought—"

"Well, H.M.S. *Bounty* is being careened, and besides, Lord Nelson required a sterner master in wartime than Captain Cook. Aye, a great seaman, Cook, but far too easy with the cat. What can I do for Your Excellency?"

Alex realized that a fleet admiral would not occupy himself with the ordinary duties of a skipper on his flagship. "I must see His Lordship. I have an important message for him."

Bligh looked embarrassed. He shuffled his feet. "His Lordship is resting in his stateroom, sir. Indisposed. Frail health, you know, after the rigors of Egypt."

Alex knew full well. Horatio Lord Nelson's public appearances were few and short. The nuisance of having to wear an eyepatch and keep his right arm inside his coat was too much.

Bligh recovered his spirit. He lowered his voice. "Although I'd say, myself, Lady Hamilton's had a bit to do with his weariness. You understand, sir." He gave Alex a wink, a leer, and a nudge in the ribs that sent the human staggering.

Instantly contrite, he offered to convey the letter. Alex gave him the sealed envelope, wishing again that he knew just what Oakheart had written. Hoka helpfulness often took strange forms. Bligh trotted aft. Alex spent the time arranging for his luggage to be fetched from his aircar. He saw Brob standing near it on the dock, surrounded by curious townsfolk, and wondered how he could do the same for his friend.

Bligh returned, twice as excited as before. "We shall have the honor of dining with His Lordship this evening," he announced. "Meanwhile, the squadron must be off on the afternoon tide. But we've time for a tot of rum in my cabin, Commodore, to welcome you into our company.

"Commodore? Huh?" Alex asked.

Bligh winked anew, though he kept his thumb to himself and, instead, took the man's elbow. "Ah, yes, I know full well. Ashore, the walls have ears. Mustn't let the Frenchies learn Commodore Hornblower is on a secret mission in disguise, damme, no. When we're safe at sea, I'll inform the men, by your leave, sir. Brace 'em up for certain, the news will, scurvy lot though they be." Walking along, he shrilled right and left at the crew: "Avast, ye lubbers! Look lively there! Flogging's too good for the likes o' ye! Keel-hauling, aye, scuttle my bones if I don't keelhaul the first mutinous dog who soldiers on the job! Marines excepted, of course," he added more quietly.

In his quarters he poured, proposed the health of the King and the damnation of Boney, and fell into a long jeremiad about his lack of able officers. "The weak, piping times of peace, that's what's done it, Commodore." Alex listened with half an ear. If Oakheart's fantasy had appointed him Hornblower, maybe he could turn the situation to his advantage. Hornblower certainly rated more respect from Hoka mariners than any mere plenipotentiary—

A knock sounded on the door. "Come in, if ye've proper business," Bligh barked. "If not, beware! That's all I say, beware."

The door opened. A sailor in the usual striped shirt, bell-bottomed trousers, and straw hat saluted. A truncheon hung from his belt. "Bosun Bush, sir, press gang, reporting," he said. "We've caught us a big 'un. Does the captain want to see him?"

"Aye, what else?" Bligh snapped. "Got to set these pressed men right from the start, eh, Commo—eh, Your Excellency?"

The boatswain beckoned. Flanked by a couple of redcoated marines, Brob's enormous form made the deck creak and tremble as he approached. "What the hell?" burst from Alex. "How did they ever get you aboard?"

"They rigged a derrick," Brob answered. "Most kind of them, no? I had not even requested it when suddenly there they were, instructing me in what to do."

"Stout fella, this, hey, sir?" beamed the boatswain.

Captain Bligh peered dubiously at the acquisition. "He does look strong—" His ebullience returned to him. "Nevertheless, he'll soon find that aboard a King's ship is no life of ease." To Brob: "You'll work 'round the clock, me hearty, swab the planks, climb the ratlines, fist canvas along with the rest of 'em, or you'll hang from a yardarm. D'ye understand?"

Alex had a horrible vision of what would happen to the *Victory* if Brob tried to climb its rigging. His memory came to the rescue. Once he too had been impressed onto a ship out of this very England.

"Here's the first mate you said you lack, Captain Bligh," he declared in haste.

"What?" The skipper blinked at him.

"Pressed man always appointed first mate," said Alex, "in spite of his well-known sympathy for the crew."

"Of course, sir, of course," Bush chimed in happily.

"Well—" Bligh scratched his head. "Far be it from a simple old seaman like me to question the wisdom of Commodore Hornblower—"

"Commodore Hornblower!" The boatswain's eyes grew large. He tugged his forelock, or rather the fur where a human would have had a forelock. "Begging your pardon, sir, I didn't recognize you, but that's a clever disguise you're wearing, shiver me timbers if it ain't."

Bristling, Bligh turned his attention to Brob. "Well?" he snarled. "What're you waiting for, Mr. Christian? Turn out the crew. Put 'em to work like a proper bucko mate. We've the tide to make, and a fair wind for Spain."

"But, but I don't know how," Brob stammered.

"Don't try to cozen me with your sly ways, Fletcher Christian!" Bligh shouted. "Out on deck with you and get us moving!"

"Excuse me," Alex said. "I know this man of old, Captain. I can explain." He stepped forth, drew Brob aside, and whispered:

"Listen, this is typical Hoka dramatics. The crew are perfectly competent. They don't expect anything but a show out of the officers, as far as actual seamanship goes. You need only stand around, look impressive, and issue an occasional order—any order that comes to mind. They'll interpret it as being a command to do the right thing. Meanwhile I'll handle the details for both of us." Luckily, he reflected, that need not include rations. He could eat Tokan food, though it was preferable to supplement it with a few Terrestrial vitamin pills from his kit. He always carried some on his person. Brob had eaten before they left Mixumaxu, and one of his nuclear meals kept him fueled for weeks.

Bemused, the alien wandered off after Bosun Bush, rather like an ocean liner behind a small tugboat. Alex was taken to a vacant cabin and installed. It was reasonably comfortable, except that a human given a Hoka bed must sleep sitting up. One by one, the ships warped from the docks, set sail, and caught the breeze. When Alex re-emerged, *Victory* was rolling along over chill greenish waters, under a cloud of canvas like those that elsewhere covered the sea. Air sang in the rigging and carried a tang of salt. Crewmen went about their tasks— which included, ominously, the polishing of cannon as heavy as Brob himself—or, off watch, sat around telling each other how French blood would redden the ocean. Land was already low on the northern horizon.

Alex didn't stay topside long. He had had a difficult time of late, and faced a dinner with Lord Nelson, Captain Bligh, and heaven knew who else, in his role as Hornblower. Let him get some rest while he was able.

Shouts, trumpet calls, drumbeats, the thud of running feet roused him from an uneasy night's sleep. He stumbled forth in his pajamas. Pandemonium reigned, Hokas scurrying everywhere to and fro.

Aloft, a lookout cried, "Thar she blows—I mean to say, Frogs ahead, two p'ints t' starboard!"

"Stand by to engage!" yelled Captain Bligh from the quarterdeck.

Alex scrambled up the ladder to join him. Nelson was there already, the empty sleeve of his dressing gown aflap in the wind, a telescope clapped to his patchless eye. "We've the weather gauge of them," he said. "They'll not escape us, I trow. Run up the signal flags: England expects every man will do his duty."

Aghast, Alex stared forward, past the bowsprit and across the whitecaps. Dawnlight showed him three large sailing vessels on the rim of sight. Despite the distance, he identified the Tricolor proudly flying at each staff. Louis XIV had built a navy too. (The Hoka France had never had a Revolution, merely an annual Bastille Day fête. At the most recent of these, Napoleon had taken advantage of the usual chaos to depose the king, who cooperated because it would be more fun being a field marshal. The excitement delighted the whole nation and charged it with enthusiasm. Only in Africa was this ignored, the Foreign Legion preferring to stay in its romantic, if desolate, outposts.)

"No danger of their escape, milord." Bligh rubbed his hands. "See, they're coming about. They mean to meet us. We outnumber 'em, aye, but those are three capital ships. Ah, a jolly little fight it'll be."

Down on the main deck, and on the gun decks below, sailors were readying their armament. The sardonic old prayer drifted thence to Alex's ears: "For that which we are about to receive, Lord, make us duly grateful." Marine sharpshooters swarmed into the masts. He shuddered. Like children at play, the Hokas had no idea what shot and shell would inflict on them. They would find out, once the broadsides began, but then it would be too late. Nor would they recoil. He knew well how much courage dwelt in them.

Feeling ill, he mumbled, "Admiral, wouldn't it be best if we—er—avoided commitment in favor of proceeding on our mission? Preserve the King's property, you know."

Nelson was shocked. "Commodore Hornblower! Do you imagine British seamen would turn tail like a . . . like a . . . like a crew of tailturners? Egad, no! Britannia rules the waves! Westminster Abbey or victory!"

Captain Bligh smiled. "I'm sure the Commodore is no craven, but has some ruse in mind," he said cunningly. "What is it, sir?"

"I—well, I—" Desperate, Alex looked downward from the rail which his white-knuckled hands gripped. Brob stood like a rock in a surf of Hokas. "Can you do anything, anything at all?" the human wailed to him.

"As a matter of fact," Brob responded diffidently, "I believe I may see a perhaps useful course of action."

"Then for mercy's sake, do it! Though . . . we can't take French lives either, do you realize?"

"I would never dream of it." Brob fanned himself, as if the very thought made him feel faint. "You shall have to lower me over the side." He looked around him. "Possibly with one of those—er—spars to keep me afloat."

"Do you hear that?" Alex exclaimed to Nelson and Bligh. "Brob—uh, Mr. Christian can save the day." They stared blankly at him. He saw he must give them an impression of total calm, complete mastery of the situation. Somehow, he grinned and winked. "Gentlemen, I do indeed have a ruse, but there isn't time now to explain it. Please ready a cargo boom and drop the mate overboard."

Nelson grew distressed. "I do not recall, sir, that any precedent exists in the annals of war for jettisoning the mate. If we should be defeated, it would count heavily against us at our courts martial."

Bligh was quicker-witted. "Not if he's mutinied," he said. "Do you follow me, Christian, you treacherous scoundrel? Don't just stand there. Do something mutinous."

"Well, er—" With a mighty effort, against his every inclination, Brob raised a cable-thick middle finger in the air. "Up yours, sir. A rusty grapnel, sir, sideways. I do require a grapnel."

"Ah, hah! D'ye hear what he was plotting? Next thing we knew, we'd be adrift in an open boat 4000 miles from Timor. Overboard he goes!" bellowed Bligh in his shrill soprano.

A work detail was promptly organized. To the sound of a lusty chanty, Brob, a spar firmly lashed to his massive body and carrying his implement, went on high, swung above the gunwale, and dropped into the waves. An enormous splash followed. Fearful of the outcome, yet intensely curious himself, Alex watched his friend swim off to meet the French.

They were still well out of gunshot range. Windjammers can't maneuver fast. The sight of the monster nearing them alarmed the crews, who opened fire on him. Two of the cannonballs struck, but bounced harmlessly off.

Coming to the nearest vessel, Brob trod water while he whirled his hook at the end of a long chain. He let fly. It bit hard into a mast and snugged itself against a yard. Brob dived and began to haul. Drawn by the chain, the ship canted over—and over—and over—The sea rushed in through gunports and hatches.

Brob came back to the surface. A deft yank on the chain dislodged the grapnel and brought it to him again, along with a portion of the mast that he had snapped across. The warcraft wallowed low. It was not sinking, quite, and nobody had been hurt, but its powder was drenched, leaving it helpless.

Brob gave a similar treatment to the next. The third showed a clean pair of heels, followed by hoots of British derision.

Brob returned to the *Victory*, where his sailors winched him on deck to the tune of "Way, hey, and up he rises, ear-lie in the morning." Lord Nelson magnanimously issued him a pardon for his insubordinate conduct and Captain Bligh ordered an extra ration of grog for everybody.

Indeed, beneath their boasting, the Hokas seemed glad to have avoided combat. That gave Alex a faint hope.

Whether or not the entire naval strength available to France in these parts at this time had been routed, none was on hand when the flotilla from England dropped anchor two days afterward. Sunset light streamed over a hush broken only by the mildest of breezes and the squeals of leathery-winged seafowl. The bay here was wide and calm. Above it loomed the Iberian peninsula. Like its namesake on Earth, this land was rugged, though lushly green. A village, whitewashed walls and red tile roofs, nestled behind a wharf where fishing boats lay moored.

Also red were the coats of marines ashore. They had occupied the place as a precaution against anyone going off to inform the enemy of their arrival.

It turned out that there was no danger of that. These isolated local folk were unconcerned about politics. Rather, they were overjoyed to have another set of foreign visitors. They had already seen Napoleon's Grand Army pass through.

Indeed, that host was encamped about ten kilometers off, beyond a high ridge to the southeast, alongside a river which emptied into the bay. Alex supposed the Emperor had chosen that site in order to be safe from surprise attack and bombardment out of the sea. He saw the smoke of campfires drift above trees, into the cool evening air.

Standing on the quarterdeck between Nelson and Bligh, he said fervently, "Gentlemen, I thank you for your cooperation in this secret mission of mine. Tonight I'll go ashore, alone, to, er, get the cut of the Frenchman's jib. Kindly remain while I'm gone, and please refrain from any untoward action that might warn him."

His plan was to steal into yonder camp, find Napoleon, identify himself, and demand a ceasefire (not that firing had begun, except for target practice, but the principle was the same). It should be less risky than an outsider would think. Hokas would scarcely shoot at a human, especially one whom various among them would recognize as the plenipotentiary. Instead, they would take him to their leader, who if nothing else would respect his person and let him go after they had talked.

This was the more likely because he had had the sailmaker sew him an impressive set of clothes. Gold braid covered his tunic, gold stripes went down his trousers, his boots bore spurs and his belt a saber. From the cocked hat on his head blossomed fake ostrich plumes. From his shoulders, unfastened, swung a coat reaching halfway down his calves, whose elbow-deep pockets sported huge brass buttons. Borrowed medals jingled across his left breast.

The main hazard was that the subversives would discover his presence before he had had his meeting. To minimize this chance, he meant to sneak as far as he could.

He might actually make it undetected to the Emperor's tent. On such short notice as they had had, even fast-learning Hokas could not have developed a very effective military tradition. Sentries would tend to doze at their posts, or join each other for a swig of *ordinaire* and a conversation about the exploits of Brigadier Gerard.

Nelson frowned around his eyepatch. "Chancy," he said. "Were it anybody but you, milord, I'd forbid it, I would. Still, I expect Your Grace knows what he's about."

"My Grace?" Alex asked, bewildered. "But I haven't been made a lord yet—that is, I'm plain Commodore Hornblower—" Seeing the look on the two furry faces, he gulped. "I am. Am I not?"

Captain Bligh chuckled. "Ah, milord, you're more than the bluff soldier they think of when they say 'Wellington.' That's clear. You couldn't have routed 'em as you did—as you're going to do, here in the Peninsula and so on till Waterloo—you couldn't do that if your mind weren't shrewd."

Admiration shone in Nelson's eyes. "I'll wager the playing fields of Eton had somewhat to do with that," he said. "Have no fears, Your Grace. Your secret is safe with us, until you've completed your task of gathering intelligence and are ready to take command of your troops."

"Scum of the earth, they are," Bligh muttered. "Just like my sailors. But we'll show those Frenchies what Britons are worth, eh, milord?"

Alex clutched his temples. "Omigawd, no!" He stifled further groans. Whether Oakheart had included the assertion in his letter, or whether these officers had concluded on their own account, now that he was going ashore in his gaudy uniform, that he must really be the Duke of Wellington, traveling under the alias of Horatio Hornblower—did it make any difference?

To be sure, somewhere in England, a Hoka bore the same name. Tanni had mentioned him. That mattered naught, in his absence, to the elastic imaginations of the natives.

Alex struggled to remember something, anything, concerning the original Wellington. Little came to him. He had only read casually about the Napoleonic period, never studied it, for it was not an era whose re-enactment he would have allowed on Toka, if he had had any say in the matter. At one time, Alex recalled, somebody had tried to blackmail the great man, threatening to publish an account of his involvement with a woman not his wife. Drawing himself up to his full height and fixing the blackmailer with a steely eye, the Iron Duke had snapped, "Publish and be damned!" It seemed rather a useless piece of information now, especially for a happily married man who cherished no desire for illicit affairs.

Alex blanched at the prospect of being swept along by events until he in fact commanded the British army in outright combat. That would certainly put an end to his career, and earn him a long prison sentence as well.

He rallied his resolution. The thing must not happen. Wasn't that his entire purpose? Why else would he be dressed like this?

✧ ✧ ✧

"Yonder land," said Bertram kindly, "is, as you

Having reassured an anxious Brob, he went ashore in a dinghy rowed by two marines, and struck off inland. Night fell as he strode, but a moon and a half illuminated the dirt road for him. Apart from the warmth and scratchiness of his clothes, the uphill walk was no hardship; he was still young, and had always been athletic—formerly a champion in both track and basketball.

Loneliness did begin to oppress him. Save for farmsteads scattered over the landscape the coziness of whose lamplit windows reminded him far too much of home, he walked among trees and through pastures. Shadows bulked, menacing. He almost wished he had brought a firearm. But no, that might be construed as a threat, and generate resistance to his arguments. Persuasion seemed his solitary hope.

In due course he entered a forest, but soon he welcomed its darkness, when he stood looking down into a valley ablaze with campfires. Campaigning or not, Hokas liked to keep late hours. Tents, more or less in rows, lined the riverbanks; he saw fieldpieces gleam, the bulks of the "horses" that drew them, a large and flag-topped pavilion which must house Napoleon; he heard a murmur of movement down there, and occasional snatches of song. While this Grand Army did not compare with the original, it must number thousands.

Having picked a route, Alex began the stealthy part of his trip. His pulse was loud in his ears, but his feet were silent. The stalking and photographing of wild animals had long been a sport he followed.

Eventually he passed a couple of pickets, who were too busy comparing amorous notes to observe him. His limited French gave him the impression that Madeleine was quite a female—unless she was a pure fiction, which was not unlikely. Farther on, he belly-crawled around fires where soldiers sat tossing dice or singing ballads that all seemed to have the refrain *"Rataplan! Rataplan!"* Lanes between tents offered better concealment yet.

And thus he did, indeed, come to the out-size shelter at the heart of the encampment. From its centerpole a flag fluttered in the night wind, bearing a golden *N* within a wreath. Moonlight sheened off the muskets and bayonets of half a dozen sentries who stood, in blue uniforms and high shakos, before the entrance. A brighter glow spilled from inside, out of an opened windowflap at the rear. Alex decided to peek through it before he declared himself.

He did—and drew a gasp of amazement.

Luxuriously furnished, the pavilion held a table on which lay the remnants of a dinner (it seemed to have been an attempt at turning a native flying reptiloid into chicken Marengo) and several empty bottles. Perhaps this was the reason why a rather small and stout Hoka kept a hand thrust inside his epauletted coat. He stood at another table, covered with maps and notes, around which four spectacularly uniformed officers of his race were gathered. It was the alien squatting on top, next to the oil lamp, who shocked Alex.

Had he straightened on his grasshopper-like legs, that being would not have reached a Hoka chin. His two arms were long and skinny, his torso a mere lump which his black, silver-ornamented clothes did nothing to make impressive. Gray-skinned and hairless, his head was a caricature of a man's—batwing ears, beady eyes, needle-sharp teeth, and a nose ten centimeters long, that waggled as he spoke in a voice suggestive of fingernails scratching a blackboard.

He was employing English, the most widespread
language on Toka as it was throughout the spaceways.
Probably he knew less French than Alex did, whereas
Napoleon and his staff would have had abundant
contact with humanity before they assumed their
present identities.

"You must seize the moment, sire," he urged.
"Audacity, always audacity! What have we done
hitherto, we and the Spanish troops, but march and
countermarch? Not a single shot fired in anger.
Madness! We must seek them out, attack and destroy
them, at once. Else we will have them at our backs
when the English, that nation of shopkeepers, arrive
in force."

The Hoka Napoleon gestured with his free
hand. "But we don't want to hurt the Spaniards,"
he objected. "After all, they are supposed to
become my loyal subjects, under my cousin. *Du
sublime au ridicule il n'y a qu'un pas*, as my
distinguished predecessor put it, after the retreat
from Moscow."

"Nonetheless," hissed the alien, "we must take
decisive action or else undergo an even worse disaster
than that same retreat. What is the use of your military genius, my Emperor, if you won't exercise it?"
He turned to another Hoka, whose fur was red rather
than golden. "Marshal Ney, you've talked enough
about your wish to lead gallant cavalry charges. Do
you never propose to get out there and do it?"

"*Oui, Monsieur* Snith," replied that one, "although
I had, um-m, seen myself as an avenger, or better
yet a defender, and the Spanish haven't done us any
actual harm."

So, thought Alex, the alien's name was Snith. He
had already recognized whence the being hailed. As
he had suspected, this was a member of the Kratch.

Now he knew, beyond doubt, that the Universal Nationalist Party which held power on their world had begun actively to undermine the wardship system and thus weaken the entire Interbeing League. Out of discord among the stars could come war; out of war, chaos; out of chaos, hegemony for those who had anticipated events.

"Hear me," the Krat was saying. "Has not my counsel put you on the way to power and glory? Do you not want to bring your species under a single rule, and so prepare it to deal equally with those that now dominate space? Then you must be prepared to follow my plans to the end." He lowered his voice. "Else, my Emperor, I fear that my government must terminate its altruistic efforts on your behalf, and I go home, leaving you to your fate."

The Hokas exchanged glances, somewhat daunted. Clearly, Snith had instigated their grandiosity, and continued to inspire and guide it. For his part, Alex felt sickened. Well, he thought, he'd wait till the conference was over and Snith had sought his quarters, then rouse Napoleon and set forth a quite different point of view

A bayonet pricked his rump. "Yipe!" escaped from him. Turning, he confronted the sentries. They must have heard his heavy breathing and come to investigate.

"*Qui va là?*" demanded their corporal.

Alex mastered dismay. If the Hokas were reluctant to attack their fellow planetarians, they would be still more careful of a human. A face-to-face showdown with Snith might even change their minds. "Show some respect, *poilu!*" he rapped. "Don't you see who I am?"

"*Je ne suis pas—Monsieur,* I am not a *poilu,* I I am an old *moustache,*" said the corporal, offended. "And 'ere by my side is Karl Schmitt, a German grenadier lately returned from captivity in Russia—"

Alex's whirling thought was that these French could not have studied their Napoleonic history very closely either. The Emperor himself interrupted the discussion, by stumping over to the opening. *"Mon Dieu!"* he exclaimed. *"Mais c'est Monsieur Le Plenipotentiaire* Jones! Sir, is this not irregular? The use of diplomatic channels is more in accord with the dignity of governments."

Snith reacted fast. "Ah, ha!" he shrilled. "There you see, my Emperor, how the Earthlings who have so long oppressed your world despise you. Avenge this insult to the honor of France."

Alex reacted just as fast, although he was operating mainly on intuition. "Nonsense," he said. "In point of fact, I'm being—I mean I am none less than the Duke of Wellington, dispatched by none less than the Prince Regent, the Prime Minister, the First Lord of the Admiralty, Lord Nelson, and Commodore Hornblower, on a special mission to negotiate peace between our countries."

He drew himself up to his full height and did his best to fix Snith with a steely eye.

"Hein?" Napoleon gripped his stomach harder than before. "Now I am confused, me. Quick, a carafe of Courvoisier."

Snith jittered about on the table. "Where is your diplomatic accreditation, miserable Earthling?" he squealed, waving his tiny fists. "How will we be sure you are not a spy, or an assassin, or a—a—"

"A shopkeeper," suggested Marshal Ney.

"Thank you. A shopkeeper. My Emperor," said Snith more calmly, "a British ship must have brought him. Else he would have flown in like an honest plenipotentiary. Therefore he must be in collusion with perfidious Albion. Arrest him, sire, confine him, until we can discover what new threat ties in wait for you."

Under the gaze of his marshals, Napoleon could not but be strict. "Indeed," he said regretfully. "*Monsieur le Duc*, if such you are and if your intentions are sincere, you shall have a formal apology. Meanwhile, you will understand the necessity of detaining you. It shall be an honorable detention, whether or not we must afterward place you before a firing squad." To the soldiers: "*Enfermez-il, mes enfants.*"

In a kind of dull consternation, Alex realized that his image required him to go off, a prisoner, too stoic to utter any protest.

First Napoleon took custody of his sword, and under Snith's waspish direction he was searched for hidden weapons, communications devices, and anything else of possible use. If only he had had a portable radio transceiver along, he could have called Brob at the instant things went awry. The giant could gently but firmly have freed him. Why didn't he think of simple precautions like that beforehand? A fine secret agent he was! The excuse that he wasn't supposed to be a secret agent, and moreover had had a good deal else on his mind, rang false.

The squad conducted him to a nearby farmhouse. They turned the family out, but those didn't object, since the Emperor had ordered they be well paid for the inconvenience. Alex had often thought that the Hokas were basically a sweeter species than humankind. Perhaps a theologian would suppose they were without original sin. The trouble was, they had too much originality of other sorts.

The house was humble, actually a cottage. A door

at either end gave on a living room, which doubled as the dining room, a kitchen and scullery, and two bedrooms, all in a row along a narrow hall. The floor was clay, the furnishings few and mostly homemade. When the windows had been shuttered and barred on the outside, Alex's sole light would be from some candles in wooden holders.

"I give myself, me, ze honor to stand first watch outside ze south door," said the squad leader. "Corporal Sans-Souci, at Your Lordship's service. Karl, *mon brave*, I reward your *esprit* and command of English by posting you at ze north end."

"*Viel Danke, mein tapfere Korporal*," replied the little German grenadier. "If *der Herzog* Vellington vould like to discuss de military sciences vit' me, please chust to open de door."

Jealousy made Sans-Souci bristle. "*Monsieur le Duc* is a man of ze most virile, *non*?" he countered. "If it should please 'im to describe 'is conquests in ze fields of love, and 'ear about mine, my door shall stand open too."

"No, thanks, to you both," Alex muttered, stumbled on into the cottage, and personally closed it up. He knew that, while either trooper would happily chatter for hours, exit would remain forbidden. Despite their size, Hokas were stronger than humans, and these must have a stubborn sense of duty.

Alex sank down onto a stool, put elbows on knees and face in hands. What a ghastly mess! Outnumbered as they were, the British could do nothing to rescue him. If they tried, they would be slaughtered, which was precisely what Snith wanted. Brob—No, Alex's idea about that being had been mistaken. Cannon and bullets meant nothing to Brob, but Snith undoubtedly had energy weapons against which not even the spacefarer could stand.

Could he, Alex, talk Napoleon into releasing him? Quite likely he could—for example, by an appeal to the Emperor's concern for the diplomatic niceties—except, again, for the everdamned Snith. The Krat had the edge; he could outargue the man, whose position was, after all, a bit dubious in the eyes of the French (and in his own eyes, for that matter). Thus, if Alex was not actually shot, he would at least languish captive for weeks, probably after being moved to a secret locale. Meanwhile Snith would have egged Napoleon into an attack on the Spanish army, and shortly thereafter Nelson's assembled fleet would begin raiding the coasts and landing British troops, and before the League could do anything to prevent it, there would have been wholesale death and devastation. No doubt it would also occur elsewhere on Toka. Snith might be the leading Kratch agent, but obviously he had others doing the same kind of dirty work in chosen societies around the planet.

Wearily and drearily, Alex decided he might as well go to bed. In truth, that was his best course. Sometimes in the past, when he slept on a problem, his subconscious mind, uninhibited by the rationality of his waking self, had thrown up a solution crazy enough to work. The trouble now was, he doubted he could sleep.

He rose to his feet, and stopped cold. His glance had encountered an object hanging on the wall. It was a small leather bag, stoppered and bulging. This being a Spanish home, it must be a *bota*, and that word translated as "wineskin."

Alex snatched it to him, opened it and his mouth, and squeezed. A jet of raw, potent liquor laved his throat.

✧   ✧   ✧

A deep buzz wakened him. Something brushed his nose. Blindly, aware mainly of a headache and a raging thirst, he swatted. The something bumbled away. Its drone continued. Soon it was back. Alex unlidded a bleary eye. Light trickled in through cracks and warps in the shutters across his bedroom window. A creature the size of his thumb fluttered clumsily, ever closer to him. Multiple legs brushed his skin again. *"Damn,"* he mumbled, and once more made futile swatting motions.

The insectoid was as persistent as a Terrestrial fly. Maybe an odor of booze on his breath attracted it. Alex would get no more rest while it was loose.

He forced himself to alertness. Craftily, he waited. The huge brown bug hummed nearer. Alex remained motionless. His tormentor drew within centimeters of him. He kept himself quiet while he studied its flying pattern. Back and forth it went, on spatulate wings. Uzz, uzz, uzz it went. Alex mentally rehearsed his move. Then, pantherlike, his hand pounced. Fingers closed on the creature. "Gotcha!" he rasped. A sorry triumph, no doubt, but better than no triumph at all.

The bug fluttered in his grip. He was about to crush it, but stopped. Poor thing, it had meant him no harm. Why must he add even this bit to the sum of tragedy that would soon engulf Toka? (What a metaphor! But he was hung over, as well as oppressed by the doom he foresaw.) At the same time, he was jolly well not going to let it disturb his sleep any more.

He could carry it to a door, have that door swung aside, and release *his* prisoner. But then the sentinel would be eager to talk to his prisoner, and that was just too much to face at this hour.

Alex swung his nude body out of bed. A cham-

ber pot stood nearby. He raised the lid, thrust the
bug inside, and dropped the lid back in place. The
bug flew about. Resonance made the vessel boom
hollowly. Alex realized he had not done the most
intelligent thing possible, unless the house contained
another chamber pot.

He looked around him. Daylight must be very
new, at sunrise or before, since it was weak and gray.
In a while someone would bring him breakfast. He
hoped it would include plenty of strong black coffee. Afterward he would insist on a hot bath. Damnation, here he was, unwashed, uncombed, unshaven,
confined in a peasant's hovel. Was that any way to
treat the Duke of Wellington?

As abruptly as the night before, Alex froze. Now
his gaze did not stop at a leather flask, which in any
case lay flaccid and empty. Figuratively, his vision
pierced the wall and soared over valley and hills to
the sea. Inspiration had, indeed, come to him.

It might be sheer lunacy. The chances were that
it was. He had no time for Hamlet-like hesitation.
Nor did he have much to lose. Seizing the pot, he
hurried out of the room and down the hall to the
north end of the cottage. He had changed his mind
about conversation with his guards.

None the worse for a sleepless night, Karl flung
wide the door when Alex knocked, though his
muscular little form continued to block any way out.
Mist had drenched his uniform, and as yet blurred
view of the camp below this farmstead, but reveil-
les had begun to sound through the chill air.

"Gut Morgen, gut Morgen!" the grenadier greeted.
"Did de noble captiff shlumber vell? Mine duty ends
soon, but I vill be glad to shtay and enchoy discourse
am Krieg—"

He broke off, surprised. M-m-uzzz, oom, oom went the jar that Alex held in the crook of an arm.

"Mine lord," Karl said after a moment, in a tone of awe, "you iss a powerful man, t'rough and t'rough. I vill be honored to empty dot for you."

"No need." Alex took the lid off and tilted the vessel forward. The bug blundered forth. As it rose higher, sunrise light from behind the fog made it gleam like metal. Karl's astounded stare followed it till it was out of sight.

Thereafter he scratched his head with his bayonet and murmured, "I haff heard dey feed dem terrible on de English ships, but *vot* vas *dot*?"

Alex smiled smugly, laid a finger alongside his nose, and replied in a mysterious voice, "I'm afraid I can't tell you that, old chap. Military secrets, don't y' know."

Karl's eyes grew round. "*Mein Herr*? Zecrets? But ve gafe you a zearch last night."

"Ah, well, we humans—for I am human, you realize, as well as being the Duke of Wellington — we have our little tricks," Alex answered. He assumed a confidential manner. "You're familiar with the idea of carrier pigeons. Before you became a German grenadier, you may have heard about our Terrestrial technology—miniaturization, transistors—but I may say no more. Except this, because you're stout and true, Karl, whether or not you're on the wrong side in this war. No matter what happens later today, never blame yourself. You could not possibly have known."

He closed the door on the shaken Hoka, set the mug aside, and sought the south end of the house.

"*Bonjour, monsieur,*" hailed Sans-Souci. I 'ope ze noble lord 'as slept well?"

"Frankly, no," said Alex. "I'm sure you can guess why."

The soldier cocked his ears beneath his shako. "*Eh, bien*, ze gentleman, 'e 'as been lonely, *n'est-ce pas*?"

Alex winked, leered, and dug a thumb into the other's ribs. "We're men of the world, you and I, corporal. The difference in our stations makes no difference. . . . Uh, I mean a man's a man's for a' that, and—Anyhow, if I'm to be detained, don't you agree I should have . . . companionship?"

Sans-Souci grew ill at ease. " 'Ow true, 'ow sad. But Your Lordship, 'e is not of our species—"

Alex drew himself up to his full height. "What do you think I am?" he snapped. "I have nothing in mind but a lady of my race."

"Zat will not be so easy, I fear."

"Perhaps easier than you think, corporal. This is what I want you to do for me. When you're relieved, pass the word on to your lieutenant that, if the Emperor is virile enough to understand, which he undoubtedly is, why, then the Emperor will order a search for a nice, strapping wench. There are a number of humans on Toka, you recall—League personnel, scientists, journalists, lately even an occasional tourist. I happen to know that some are right in this area. It should not be difficult to contact them and—Well, corporal, if this works out, you'll find me not ungrateful."

Sans-Souci slapped his breast. "Ah, *monsieur*," he cried, "to 'elp love blossom, zat will be its own reward!"

A couple of new soldiers appeared out of the fog and announced that they were the next guards. Sans-Souci barely took time to introduce them to the distinguished detainee—a stolid, though hard-drinking private from Normandy and a dashing Gascon sergeant of Zouaves—before hastening off. Alex heard a clatter from behind the house as Karl departed equally fast.

Returning inside, the man busied himself in preparations for that which he hoped would transpire. Whatever did, he should not have long to wait. Any collection of Hokas was an incredible rumor mill. What the sentries had to relate should be known to the whole Grand Army within the hour.

Excitement coursed through his blood and drove the pain out of his head. Win, lose, or draw, by gosh and by golly, he was back in action!

He estimated that a mere thirty minutes had passed when the door to the main room opened again, from outside. At first he assumed a trooper was bringing his breakfast, then he remembered that English aristocrats slept notoriously late and Napoleon would not want his guest disturbed without need. Then a being stepped through, closed the door behind him, and glared.

It was Snith.

"What's this?" the Krat screamed. The volume of the sound was slight, out of his minuscule lungs.

"What's what?" asked Alex, careful to move slowly. Though he towered a full meter above the alien, and probably outmassed him tenfold, Snith carried a dart gun at his belt; and his race was more excitable, impatient, irascible than most.

"You know what's what, you wretch. That communication device of yours, and that camp of your abominable co-humans somewhere close by. Thought you'd sneak one over on me, did you? Ha! I'm sharper than you guessed, Jones. Already scouts have brought back word of those English in the bay and the village. We'll move on them this very day. But first I want to know what else to expect, Jones, and you'll tell me. Immediately!"

"Let's be reasonable," Alex temporized. While he

had expected Snith to arrive alone, lest the Hokas learn too much, he could not predict the exact course of events—merely devise a set of contingency plans. "Don't you realize what harm you're doing on this planet? Not only to it, either. If ever word gets out about your government's part in this, you can be sure the rest of the League will move to have it replaced."

The Krat sneered upward at the human's naked height. "They won't know till far too late, those milksop pacifists. By then, Universal Nationalism will dominate a coalition so powerful that—Stand back, you! Not a centimeter closer, or I shoot." He touched the gun in its holster.

"What use would that be to you?" Alex argued. "Dead men tell no tales."

"Ah but you wouldn't be dead, Jones. The venom in these darts doesn't kill unless they strike near the heart. In a leg, say, they'll make you feel as though you're burning alive. Oh, you'll talk, you'll talk," responded Snith, obviously enjoying his own ruthlessness. "Why not save yourself the agony? But you'd better tell the truth, or else, afterward, you'll wish you had. How you'll wish you had!"

"Well, uh, well—Look, excuse me, I have to take a moment for nature. How can I concentrate unless I do?"

"Hurry up, then," Snith ordered.

Alex went to the chamber pot. He bent down as if to remove its lid. Both his hands closed on its body. Faster than when he had captured the bug, he hurled it. As a youth in the Naval Academy, he had been a basketball star. The old reflexes were still there. The lid fell free as the mug soared. Upside down, it descended on Snith. Too astonished to have moved, the Krat buckled beneath that impact. Alex made a flying tackle, landed on the pot and held it secure.

Snith banged on it from within, boomlay, boomlay, boomlay, boom. "What's the meaning of this outrage?" came his muffled shriek. "Let me go, you fiend!"

"Heh, heh, heh," taunted Alex. He dragged the container over the floor to a chair whereon lay strips of cloth torn off garments left by the dwellers here. Reaching beneath, he hauled Snith out. Before the Krat could draw weapon, he was helpless in the grasp of a far stronger being. Alex disarmed him, folded him with knees below jaws, and began tying him.

"Help, murder, treason!" Snith cried. As expected, his thin tones did not penetrate the door.

He regained a measure of self-control. "You're mad, insane," he gabbled. "How do you imagine you can escape? What will Napoleon do if you've harmed his . . . his Talleyrand? Stop this, Jones, and we can reach some *modus vivendi.*"

"Yeah, sure," grunted Alex. He gagged his captive and left him trussed on the floor.

Heart pounding, the man spread out the disguise he had improvised from raiment and bedding. Thus far his plan had succeeded better than he dared hope, but now it would depend on his years of practice at playing out roles before Hokas, for the costume would never have gotten by a human.

First he donned his Wellingtonian greatcoat. Into a capacious pocket he stuffed the weakly struggling Snith. Thereafter he wrapped his hips in a blanket, which simulated a skirt long enough to hide the boots he donned, and his upper body in a dress which had belonged to the housewife and which on him became a sort of blouse. Over all he pinned another blanket, to be a cloak with a cowl, and from that hood he hung a cheesecloth veil.

Here goes nothing, he thought, and minced daintily, for practice, through the cottage to the farther door. It opened at his knock. An astonished Sergeant Le Galant gaped at the spectacle which confronted him. He hefted his musket. *"Qui va là?"* he demanded in a slightly stunned voice.

Alex waved a languid hand. "Oh, sir," he answered falsetto, "please let me by. I'm so tired. His Grace the Duke is a . . . a most vigorous gentleman. Oh, dear, and to think I forgot to bring my smelling salts."

The Hoka's suspicions dissolved in a burst of romanticism. Naturally, he took for granted that the lady had entered from the side opposite. *"Ah, ma belle petite,"* he burbled, while he kissed Alex's hand, "zis is a service you 'ave done not only for *Monsieur le Duc,* but for France. We 'ave our reputation to maintain, *non? Mille remerciments. Adieu, et au revoir."*

Sighing, he watched Alex sway off.

The mists had lifted, and everywhere Hoka soldiers stared at the strange figure, whispered, nudged each other, and nodded knowingly. A number of them blew kisses. Beneath his finery, Alex sweated. He must not move fast, or they would start to wonder; yet he must get clear soon, before word reached Napoleon and made *him* wonder.

His freedom was less important than the prisoner he carried, and had been set at double hazard for that exact reason. This, maybe, was the salvation of Toka. Maybe.

When he had climbed the ridge and entered the forest, Alex shouted for joy. Henceforward he, as a woodsman, would undertake to elude any pursuit. He cast the female garb from him. Attired in greatcoat and boots, the plenipotentiary of the Interbeing League marched onward to the sea.

At his insistence, the flotilla recalled its marines and sought open water before the French arrived.

Nelson grumbled that retreat was not British, but the human mollified him by describing the move as a strategic withdrawal for purposes of consolidation.

In Alex's cabin, he and Brob confronted Snith. The diminutive Krat did not lack courage. He crouched on the bunk and spat defiance. "Never will I betray the cause! Do your worst! And afterward, try to explain away my mangled body to your lily-livered superiors."

"Torture is, needless to say, unthinkable," Brob agreed. "Nevertheless, we must obtain the information that will enable us to thwart your plot against the peace. Would you consider a large bribe?"

Alex fingered his newly smooth chin and scowled. The ship heeled to the wind. Sunlight scythed through ports to glow on panels. He heard waves rumble and whoosh, timbers creak, a cheerful sound of music and dance from the deck; he caught a whiff of fresh salt air; not far off, if he flew, were Tanni and the kids. . . . Yes, he thought, this was a lovely world in a splendid universe, and must be kept that way.

"Bribe?" Snith was retorting indignantly. "The bribe does not exist which can buy a true Universal Nationalist. No, you are doomed, you decadent libertarians. You may have kidnapped me, but elsewhere the sacred cause progresses apace. Soon the rest of this planet will explode, and blow you onto the ash heap of history."

Alex nodded to himself. A nap had done wonders for him akin to those which had happened ashore. Pieces of the puzzle clicked together, almost audibly.

Conspirators were active in unknown places around the globe. They must be rather few, though; Snith appeared to have managed the entire Napoleonic phase by himself. They must, also, have some

means of communication, a code; and they must be
ready at any time to meet for consultation, in case
of emergency. Yes. The basic problem was how to
summon them. Snith knew the code and the recog-
nition signals, but Snith wasn't telling. However, if
you took into account the feverish Kratch
temperament.

A slow grin spread across Alex's face. "Brob," he
murmured, "we have an extra stateroom for our
guest. But he should not be left to pine in isolation,
should he? That would be cruel. I think I can get
the captain to release you from your duties as mate,
in order that you can stay full time with Mr. Snith."

"What for?" asked the spacefarer, surprised.

Alex rubbed his hands together. "Oh, to try persuasion," he said. "You're a good, kind soul, Brob.
If anybody can convince Mr. Snith of the error of
his ways, it's you. Keep him company. Talk to him.
You might, for instance, tell him about flower
arrangements."

The planet had barely rotated through another of
its 24.35-hour days when Snith, trembling and blub-
bering, yielded.

It was necessary to choose the rendezvous with
care. The conspirators weren't stupid. Upon receiving
their enciphered messages, which bore Snith's name
and declared that unforeseen circumstances required
an immediate conference, they would look at their
maps. They would check records of whatever intelligence they had concerning human movements and
capabilities at the designated spot. If anything
appeared suspicious, they would stay away. Even if
nothing did, they would fly in with such instruments
as metal detectors wide open, alert for any indications of a trap.

Accordingly, Alex had made primitive arrangements. After picking up a long-range transmitter in Plymouth, he directed *Victory* alone—to an isolated Cornish cove, whence he issued his call. Inland lay nothing but a few small, widely scattered farms. Interstellar agents would think naught of a single windjammer anchored offshore, nor imagine that marines and bluejackets lurked around the field where they were supposed to land—when those Hokas were armed simply with truncheons and belaying pins.

Night fell. All three moons were aloft. Frost rings surrounded them. Trees hemmed in an expanse of several hectares, whereon haystacks rested hoar; the nearest dwelling was kilometers off. Silence prevailed, save when wildfowl hooted. Alex shivered where he crouched in the woods. Twigs prickled him. He wanted a drink.

Ashimmer beneath moons and stars, a teardrop shape descended, the first of the enemy vehicles. It grounded on a whisper of forcefield, but did not open at once. Whoever was inside must be satisfying himself that nothing of menace was here.

A haystack scuttled forward. It had been glued around Brob. Before anybody in the car could have reacted, he was there. His right fist smashed through its fuselage to the radio equipment. His left hand peeled back the metal around the engine and put that out of commission.

"At 'em, boys!" Alex yelled. His followers swarmed forth to make the arrest. They were scarcely necessary. Brob had been quick to disarm and secure the two beings within.

Afterward he tucked the car out of sight under a tree and returned to being a haystack, while Alex and the Hokas concealed themselves again.

In this wise, during the course of the night, they

collected thirty prisoners, the entire ring. Its members were not all Kratch. Among them were two Slissii, a Pornian, a Sarennian, a Worbenite, three Chakbans; but the Kratch were preponderant, and had clearly been the leaders.

A glorious victory! Alex thought about the administrative details ahead of him, and moaned aloud.

Two weeks later, though, at home, rested and refreshed, he confronted Napoleon. The Empire was his most pressing problem. Mongols, Aztecs, Crusaders, and other troublesome types were rapidly reverting to an approximation of normal, now that the sources of their inspiration had been exposed and discredited. But Imperial France not only had a firmer base, it had the unrelenting hostility of Georgian Britain. The Peace of Amiens, which Alex had patched together, was fragile indeed.

Tanni was a gracious hostess and a marvelous cook. The plenipotentiary's household staff, and his children, were on their best behavior. Candlelight, polished silver, snowy linen, soft music had their mellowing effect. At the same time, the awesome presence of Brob reminded the Emperor—who was, after all, sane in his Hoka fashion—that other worlds were concerned about this one. The trick was to provide him and his followers an alternative to the excitement they had been enjoying.

"Messire," Alex urged over the cognac and cigars, "as a man of vision, you surely realize with especial clarity that the future is different from the past. You yourself, a mover and shaker, have shown us that the old ways can never be the same again, but instead we must move on to new things, new opportunities— *la carrière ouverte aux talents*, as your illustrious namesake phrased it. If you will pardon my accent."

Napoleon shifted in his chair and clutched his stomach. "Yes, *mais oui*, I realize this in principle," he answered unhappily. "I have some knowledge of history, myself. Forty centuries look down upon us. But you must realize in your turn, *Monsieur le Plenipotentiaire*, that a vast outpouring of energy has been released in France. The people will not return to their placid lives under the *ancien régime*. They have tasted adventure. They will always desire it."

Alex wagged his forefinger. Tanni's glance reminded him that this might not be the perfect gesture to make at the Emperor, and he hastily took up his drink. "Ah, but messire," he said, "think further, I beg you. You ask what will engage the interest of your populace, should the Grand Army be disbanded. Why, what else but the natural successor to the Empire? The Republic!"

"*Qu'est-ce que vous dites?*" asked Napoleon, and pricked up his ears.

"I comprehend, messire," Alex said. "Cares of state have kept you from studying what happened to Terrestrial France beyond your own period. Well, I have a number of books which I will gladly copy off for your perusal. I am sure you will find that French party politics can be more intricate and engaging than the most far-ranging military campaign." He paused. "In fact, messire, if you should choose to abdicate and stand for elective office, you would find the challenge greater than any you might have encountered at Austerlitz. Should you win your election, you will find matters more complicated than ever at Berezina or Waterloo. But go forward, indomitable, *mon petit caporal!*" he cried. "*Toujours l'audace!*"

Napoleon leaned over the table, breathing heavily. Moisture glistened on his black nose. Alex saw that he had him hooked.

✧   ✧   ✧

At Mixumaxu spaceport, the Joneses bade Brob an affectionate farewell. "Do come back and see us," Tanni invited. "You're an old darling, did anybody ever tell you?" When he stooped to hug her, she kissed him full on his slightly radioactive mouth.

The couple returned to their residence in a less pleasant mood. Leopold Ormen had appeared at the city and applied for clearance to depart in his private spaceship.

Tanni begged to be excused from meeting him again. She felt too embarrassed. Alex insisted that she had made no mistake which he would not have made himself under the circumstances, but she refused anyway. Instead, she proposed, let her spend the time preparing a sumptuous dinner for the family; and then, after the children had gone to bed—

Thus Alex sat alone behind his desk when the journalist entered at the appointed hour. Ormen seemed to have lost none of his cockiness. "Well, Jones," he said, as he lowered himself into a chair and lit a cigarette, "why do I have to see you before I leave?"

"We've stuff to discuss," Alex answered, "like your involvement in the Kratch conspiracy."

Ormen gestured airily. "What are you talking about?" he laughed. "Me? I'm nothing but a reporter—and if perchance you get paranoid about me, that's a fact which I'll report.'

"Oh, I have no proof," Alex admitted. "The League investigation and the trials of the obviously guilty will drag on for years, I suppose. Meanwhile you'll come under the statute of limitations, damn it. But just between us, you were part and parcel of the thing, weren't you? Your job was to prepare the way for the Kratch, and afterward it would've been to write and televise the stories which would have brought our whole system down."

Ormen narrowed his eyes. "Those are pretty serious charges, Jones," he lipped thinly. "I wouldn't like your noising them around, even in private conversation. They could hurt me; and I don't sit still for being hurt. No, sir."

He straightened. "All right," he said, "let's be frank. You've found indications, not legal proof but indications, that would cause many of my audience and my readers to stop trusting me. But on my side—Jones, I've seen plenty on this planet. Maybe somehow you did pull your chestnuts out of the fire. But the incredible, left-handed way that you did it— not to mention the data I've gotten on your crazy, half-legal improvisations in the past—Let me warn you, Jones. If you don't keep quiet about me, I'll publish stories that will destroy you."

From his scalp to his toes, a great, tingling warmth rushed through Alex. He had nothing to fear. True, in the course of his duties he had often fallen into ridiculous positions, but this had taught him indifference to ridicule. As for his record of accomplishment, it spoke for itself. Nobody could have bettered it. Nobody in his right mind would want to try. Until such time as he had brought them to full autonomy, Alexander Jones was the indispensable man among the Hokas.

He could not resist. Rising behind the desk, he drew himself to his full height, fixed Leopold Ormen with a steely eye, and rapped out: *"Publish and be damned!"*

III.
STAR PRINCE CHARLIE

Prologue

Seen from Earth, the sun of the planet which men have named New Lemuria lies in the southern constellation of Toucan. Of course, it is not seen from Earth except through powerful telescopes, for it lies more than 200 light-years away. A Sol-type star is nowhere near bright enough to reach the naked eye across such a distance.

Nevertheless, New Lemuria is especially interesting to humans, not only because the world is quite similar to Earth, but because its natives are quite similar to them. It was only natural for the Interbeing League to make humans its agents for the guidance of this race. Although the League was organized for the mutual benefit of all starfaring creatures, one must admit that—for example—an eight-tentacled Zaggerak, breathing hydrogen at minus 100 degrees, would be at somewhat of a disadvantage here.

And guidance, education, development have long been recognized as a duty which the civilized owe

101

to the primitive. Glamorous though a preindustrial society may look, it is nearly always overburdened with handicaps and horrors which modern science and technology can eliminate. Furthermore, every new planet which joins the League is one more contributor to its strength and prosperity.

At the same time, the greatest care is essential. Development must not go too fast. Only imagine atomic bombs in the possession of Stone Age savages! More seriously, imagine natives becoming dependent on the products of an industry which they are unable to operate themselves. Still more seriously, consider the chaos and heartbreak that a sudden breakdown of ancient institutions always causes. Finally, by far the most important, is the right of every people to freely choose their own destiny.

Thus guidance may not be thrust on a race. It may only be offered. If the offer is accepted, the agents of the League must operate with extreme care, never letting their actions run ahead of their knowledge. They must enforce severe restrictions both on themselves and on any visitors from space. Often the natives will object to such a policy of making haste slowly. But it is for their own long-range good.

At first the case of New Lemuria looked fairly typical. League representatives contacted the leaders of its most advanced society. To be exact, they contacted the rulers of the Kingdom of Talyina, the largest, strongest, and most influential country on the planet. It had reached an Iron Age level of development. Socially it was backward, being a kind of feudal monarchy. But the Talyinan lords were willing to let the League establish a base, if only for the sake of the trade goods this would bring in.

From the League viewpoint, that was just a means to an end—the gradual introduction of the ideas and *ideals of civilization. It would take generations, perhaps centuries before New Lemuria was ready for full status and membership in the commonalty of the starfaring worlds. But the program looked straightforward.*

Until, early in this particular game—

WILLIAM RUPERT,
New Lemuria: A Study of the Random Factor,
thesis submitted in partial fulfillment of the
requirements for a master's degree in socio-
technics at the University of Bagdadburgh.

1

The Innocent Voyage

For once the Honorable Athelstan Pomfrey, Pleni-potentiary of the Interbeing League to the Kingdom of Talyina and (in theory) the planet of New Lemuria, had met somebody more pompous than himself.

"But," he sputtered, "but I am not convinced you understand, yes, comprehend the situation. The, ah, exigencies. Underdeveloped autochthons of warlike thought patterns, having lately undergone political upheaval—"

"Quite," interrupted Bertram Cecil Featherstone Smyth-Cholmondoley.

So far he had replied to Pomfrey's booming pro-nouncements, admonitions, and citations with four-teen "quites" and eight "indeeds." As he stood aside, Charlie Stuart found himself enjoying the spectacle.

He began to feel hopes of getting some fun, as well as instruction, out of his daily sessions with Bertram.

Not that he wasn't fond of his tutor. But why had bad luck decreed that the Hoka would seize on the one particular model he did? Surely the cosmos held more colorful possibilities than an Oxford don.

Now his father was chuckling, too. That made Charlie happier still. Dad had seemed glum for quite a while, and Charlie knew the reason. Malcolm Stuart, captain of the space freighter *Highland Lass*, was worried about his only son. Charlie felt it but didn't know what to do about it. Somehow, in the last few years, an invisible wall had risen between them. Each realized how much the other wanted to break through, but neither was able.

"You will be well beyond the treaty zone where League police may travel," Pomfrey was saying for about the twentieth time. "If you get into trouble, we can't send a rescue party after you. Can try to negotiate, but if that fails, my hands are tied."

"Quite," said Bertram Smyth-Cholmondoley.

The two of them were worth traveling far to watch, Charlie thought. They stood with their rotund stomachs almost touching; the paunch of the human Plenipotentiary overhung the middle bulge of the Hoka. Pomfrey was balding and jowly. He gained little from his fashionable purple jacket, lacy white shirt, yellow bell-bottom trousers, and red slippers. They simply added to his respectability.

Bertram's quieter garb gave a wild contrast. For one thing, it was hundreds of years out of date, belonging to the nineteenth or early twentieth century on Earth. Faultless morning coat, old school tie over starched linen, striped trousers, spats, top hat, and monocle in one eye—which didn't actually need any help—would have been suitable in a museum.

They most certainly were not suitable on a living teddy bear whose round head reached to the chest of an adult human.

"Oh, your persons should be safe," Pomfrey intoned. "I wouldn't let you go at all if they weren't used to visitors in Grushka and if the local baron didn't keep this entire island well pacified."

"Indeed," said Bertram in his shrill voice and clipped accent. He waved a languid hand which, except for the stubbiness of the fingers, was very humanlike. The rest of him was less so. His moon face, crowned by upstanding semicircular ears, consisted of two beady black eyes and a blunt muzzle with a moist black nose. Though he walked erect on two legs, those were short and thick, even in proportion to his tubby body. Soft golden fur covered his skin.

"My apprehensions principally concern unpredictable effects you yourselves may have on the citizenry," Pomfrey declared. "Remember, they underwent a revolution a few years ago. Unrest is prevalent. Banditry is on the increase through most of the kingdom. It is not inconceivable that some random influence may touch a nerve, spark an explosion."

"Quite," said Bertram.

"Should adverse effects ensue, you would be liable to punishment," Pomfrey continued. "We, the fully civilized, are responsible for the welfare of our underdeveloped brothers, or at a minimum for not provoking unnecessary trouble among them. Indeed—"

Bertram gave him a mildly indignant look, as if to accuse him of stealing that word.

Charlie's gaze wandered. How long must this argument go on?

The Commission dwelled in a walled compound. The buildings were prefabricated on Earth, therefore uninteresting to a visitor who had spent most of his eighteen years on that planet. The flower beds between them did hold gorgeous, strangely colored and shaped native blossoms, whose perfumes blended with the sea salt in a gentle breeze. Above one side of the compound towered the spaceship he had come in. But his eyes went from that metal spear to tree-tops glimpsed across the stockade. Their green was subtly different from any he had ever seen back home. They rustled and shimmered beneath a few white clouds which walked through a dazzling day.

How he longed to be off!

"I frankly wish you and young Mr. Stuart had not taken an electronic cram in the Talyinan language," Pomfrey was droning. "A number of islanders, including your guide, speak English. If you, with only the sketchiest knowledge of the psychopolitical situation, of this entire culture and its mores, if you should ignorantly say something which disturbs one of those turbulent warriors—"

Bertram must have been getting impatient too, for he was finally stirred to a new reply. "Tut-tut!" he said, and tapped Pomfrey in the stomach.

"What?" The Plenipotentiary gaped at him.

Bertram reached up, hooked Pomfrey's elbow, and pulled the human down toward him till their heads were at a confidential distance. He did this without effort. In spite of being short and chubby, Bertram, like any Hoka, had astounding strength and speed. He would have been more than a match for three or four full-grown men in good shape, let alone an aging and overweight diplomat. Casually, he yanked the other down so that the chief representative of the Interbeing League was forced to stand on one foot and flail his free arm to keep balance.

"Yonder lad," said Bertram kindly, "is, as you have

observed, my pupil. I've been engaged to tutor him during his travels. He must be prepared to enter college when we return. *Ergo*, in the absence of his father, Captain Stuart, I stand *in loco parentis* to Master Charles Edward. On this little jaunt of ours into the hinterland, I myself shall be responsible. Hence you may set your mind at rest. *Quod erat demonstrandum.*" After a second he added, "Your mind is at rest, isn't it?"

"Guk!" gargled Pomfrey, striving to escape from the iron grip upon him, regain his lost balance, and reassert his dignity. "It is! It is!"

Bertram released him. He gasped and wiped sweaty brow.

"Then pip-pip, old chap." The Hoka beamed. "Best we be off now, if we're to make Grushka by nightfall, eh, what? I've studied those jolly old maps of yours." He bowed to the space skipper. "Sir, I feel confident our junket will prove most educational for my charge." In a whisper that could be heard for meters: "Enlightening. Psychologically salutary. Right?" To Charlie: "Come, my young friend, say your farewells in proper style and let's be gone. We've already kept our chauffeur waiting an unconscionable time. Mustn't abuse the lower classes."

Charlie first offered Pomfrey a polite, formal, good-bye. The Plenipotentiary wasn't a bad man. He seemed too fussy and rule-bound, perhaps not the ideal choice for a medievallike country. But he had been hospitable enough and had actually raised no serious objection to the proposed tour. To shake his father's hand was more difficult for Charlie. Except for red hair, blue eyes, and freckled, sharply cut features, they hadn't a great deal in common. Both wished it were otherwise. Captain Stuart was tall and rawboned, hearty of manner, as intelligent as a space officer must be, but fonder of sports than study. Charlie would never match his father's height. In plain blue tunic and trousers, his frame showed wiry rather than muscular.

"So long, Dad," he said, in a low voice.

"Take care," Captain Stuart answered softly. Louder: "A good orbit to you! Enjoy yourself!"

"Th-thanks." Charlie turned about fast and hurried off with Bertram.

Captain Stuart stared after them till they were out of sight. Pomfrey cleared his throat. "Ah-hum!" said the Plenipotentiary. "I hope my cautionings don't have you worried. Simply my duty, to reinforce proper procedures in their minds. They should encounter no hazard whatsoever. And it's merely for a week."

In fact, the jaunt was scheduled for less than that, since New Lemuria rotates in twenty hours.

The tall man shook himself. "Oh. Sure," he said.

"Merely a trip to Grushka, to inspect native architecture, folkways, historic sites, et cetera," Pomfrey continued. "Scores of people have made it, mostly spacehands but not infrequently passengers, when a vessel which called there has had to layover like yours. The inhabitants are used to tourists."

Stuart nodded absently. He had reviewed the situation in detail before he gave his own permission.

His ship had brought a consignment of off-planet wares and was supposed to pick up local products in exchange—dried seafood, vegetable oils, exotic furs, and handicrafts. Because of the current troubles, these goods were not waiting for him, but delivery was promised soon. In such cases, the rule was that a freighter delayed liftoff. Native merchandise was seldom especially valuable to a far-flung civilization.

But the encouragement of those natives to deal with that civilization was important.

The Kingdom of Talyina occupied no continent, but rather a group of islands. Shverkadi was neither the greatest nor the least of these. It lay near the western edge of the archipelago. The League Commission wanted to remain a little off side, so as not to get too closely involved with a monarchy that was often oppressive. It established its base at the thinly populated north end of Shverkadi. The harbor town of Grushka was at the south end.

"I would have avoided the lecturing altogether," Pomfrey said—Stuart privately doubted that—"except for the recent political unrest, which may not be finished yet. But given reasonable discretion, no outsiders should meet serious problems."

"Anyhow," the captain replied in a rough tone, "you can't keep a young fellow tied down forever. You've got to let him try his wings, never mind the risk."

Pomfrey stroked a double chin. "The, ah, circumstances do appear a trifle unusual," he remarked.

Stuart couldn't help blurting, "Maybe not. Spacemen spend long stretches away from home. It makes for strains in the family."

"You wish to, ah, become closer to your son, and therefore took him along on this trip?"

"Yes. He's always been . . . well, bookish. Too much by himself, I think; living too much in his imagination, not the real universe. Oh, don't get me wrong. I'm all for learning. If Charlie becomes an artist or a scientist or whatever, that's fine. But hang it, he ought to live more. Finally my wife and I agreed he should come on a voyage with me. A swing through the frontier worlds might stimulate him to be more active, more sociable. That's why I haven't opposed, have even pushed, his idea of visiting Grushka. And I'm deliberately sending no one along except Bertram. Let's start Charlie coping with things by himself, instead of daydreaming while somebody else manages for him."

Pomfrey raised his eyebrows. "I must say, Captain, that sophont who accompanies him is, mmm, unique."

Stuart relaxed a bit and laughed. "Isn't he!"

Pomfrey grimaced. "A Hoka, did you call him?"

"Yes. Native of the planet Toka. I'm surprised you haven't heard of it. It's still under guidance, but moving fast toward full status. A good many individuals of that race already have jobs or scholarships that keep them on other worlds. Bertram studied in Great Britain. It's affected him."

"It certainly has!" Pomfrey huffed. "Though why he should imitate a classical rather than a modern Englishman is beyond me."

Stuart laughed again. "That's the Hoka character. They're extremely bright and quick to learn. But they have absolutely overriding imaginations. Any role that strikes a Hoka's fancy he'll play to the hilt, till he hits on a different one that he likes better." He paused. "Or is 'play' the right word? 'Live' might be more accurate. Oh, a Hoka doesn't get confused about identity or anything like that. But apparently he's so single-minded, so thoroughgoing, that his new personality *becomes* the true one, for him or for his entire society. I've been on Toka myself and seen complete replicas of the Wild West, Camelot, the French Foreign Legion—things Earth forgot long ago, but the Hokas found in books or tapes. Somehow, our Bertram decided to be an old-time Oxford don."

"And still you hired him for a tutor?" Pomfrey asked.

"By and large, I'm well pleased. Bertram may slouch about smoking a foul old pipe and quoting tag ends of Latin. But he knows what he's supposed to know, and he gets the information into Charlie's head. I can't even guess how much miscellaneous learning he carries around besides. And then he's physically powerful. We might someday be glad he is."

Pomfrey winced at that reminder. Stuart saw, and decided to be gentle to his host. "Why not come aboard ship?" he invited. "I've stuff you haven't seen yet, from any number of planets, that ought to interest you. Frankly, I admire you for sticking it out in this backwater where nothing important ever happens."

2
Stranger in a Strange Land

As he left the compound, Charlie lost what sadness he had felt at bidding his father good-bye. He was off for adventure! He all but pranced in sheer glee. Gravity on New Lemuria is 90 percent that of Earth—no great difference, but he could feel that he was several kilos lighter than at home. And the sun stood at early morning; wind whooped off the sea and brawled in the trees; overhead soared winged creatures that were snowy against a sapphire sky.

The vehicle in which he and Bertram were to ride stood beyond the main gate. Its driver lifted his right arm in salute.

He was a typical New Lemurian of this region,

which is to say he looked rather like a man whose legs were a trifle too long for the stocky torso. In fact, all his proportions were noticeably though not extremely nonhuman. His hands bore six fingers apiece. On his blocky head, the eyes were large and green, with no whites showing; the nose flat; the ears pointed and movable. His blue hair grew in a crest over the top of his scalp. His skin was bright yellow. He had no beard but, being a male, sported catlike whiskers, which he had dyed red.

For clothes he wore a bolero jacket of scaly leather, green trousers tucked into floppy boots, a scarlet sash, and a pouch. Sheathed at one hip was a knife, at the other a curved sword.

"Greeting!" he hailed in English. The shape of his speech organs added an indescribable overtone to his Talyinan accent. "I am Toreg, your friendly guide. Please to go aboard."

While Charlie had seen a yachina before, this was his first chance to travel in one. It ought to be an unusual experience, to say the least. The conveyance vaguely resembled a wooden Ferris wheel. Around its rim were six platforms. On each of these stood a yachi—the chief beast of burden on New Lemuria, suggestive of a giant kangaroo, though with a larger head and a blue pelt. The yachis were tethered, not harnessed, in place. At the hub of the double wheel hung a gimbal-mounted open box with benches inside.

Toreg helped carry their baggage up one of the spokes. These were also ladders, being twinned and having rungs between their halves. After stowing the gear, the three took their places, Charlie on the rear bench, the two others side by side in front. "Please to hang on tight till we have speed," warned the native. "I, Toreg, require this." He took a long whip from a socket and cracked it behind the yachi directly ahead of him.

Well trained, the beast leaped upward. Obedient to the third law of motion, the yachina began rolling forward. The next yachi bounded likewise, and the next, until they were all rhythmically hopping. Six gongs of varying tones, beaten by a cam-driven arrangement, directed them.

At first progress was in shuddering jerks. But as the yachina accelerated, the ride became smoother. Soon they moved at what Charlie estimated was an even ten kilometers per hour. It seemed like an utterly mad design for a vehicle, before he reflected that New Lemuria had no horses, oxen, or indeed any large and steady-gaited domestic animals.

Feet thumped on planks; gongs resounded; gravel in the dirt road rattled; the whole structure creaked and groaned. Above the noise, Toreg said, "We stop at village called Push for lunch and change team. Next we push on. Is joke. Is to go ha-ha."

"Well, actually, old egg," replied Bertram in fluent Talyinan, "considering the meaning of 'Push' "—which was the name of a variety of seafowl—"I am forced to admit that your otherwise miserable pun includes winged words."

"Hai!" exclaimed Toreg in the same language. "You talk good Peoplespeak!"

Bertram's nose rose slightly in the air. "Come, come, my dear fellow," he said, in English so he could employ certain technical terms. "I speak not good but perfect Talyinan. You will find Master Stuart equally proficient. True, we did not acquire a bally native lingo just for the sake of a week's touring. It was to initiate my pupil in the use of the electronic language inductor."

Toreg's crest and whiskers bristled. His lips curled

back, revealing formidable teeth. "Seek you to make fun of me?" he growled in his own tongue. "If so, declare it like an honest male, that we may duel and I cut you in half."

"Oh, piffle." Bertram adjusted his monocle. "I couldn't allow that. Not when I'm responsible for the scion of the Stuart house. Fine sort of guardian I'd look, cut in half. Eh, what? No offense intended, I assure you. Here, have a drop of sherry and let us revel in the good old rustic scene, what, what, what?" From beneath his coat he produced a silver hip flask uncapped and offered it.

Toreg took the container and sniffed. A broad grin made his mustache tips quiver. No doubt his threat had not been seriously meant, Charlie decided. In a violent culture, a male of warrior stock had to be touchy or at any rate act like it.

Charlie turned his attention from Toreg to the landscape about them. And indeed the landscape was delightful. Tall feather-leaved trees, full of rich fragrance, bright-winged insects and caroling birds, confronted a grassy slope which led down to sparkling sea waters. Afar he glimpsed a fishing boat, high-prowed beneath a red fore-and-aft sail.

Of course, he thought, he probably should avoid words like "insect," "bird," or "grass." Though life on New Lemuria had close parallels to that on Earth, any biologist could point out innumerable differences. However, for ordinary purposes it was easiest to use unscientific language—for instance, to say "fish" instead of "ichthyoid."

"Ho!" Toreg was exclaiming happily. "Shmiriz!"

"No—" Bertram began. He was too late. Toreg put the flask to his mouth and poured down a healthy swig of the contents. Then he choked. He dropped the liquor and clutched at his throat.

"Ee-ee-aa-aaroo-ooh!" he howled. "I burn! I am on fire! Poisoned! Help!"

Bertram caught the flask in midair and turned around to Charlie. "Now there, young Stuart," he said gravely, "let that be a lesson to you. Note well the effects of a limited education. This disgraceful hullaballoo over a simple drop of sherry."

"That's what you call it," Charlie retorted. "It's really that awful rotgut nobody but a Hoka can drink without ruining himself inside."

"Tut-tut," said Bertram. "I see I must coach you in logic. A gentleman drinks sherry. I am a gentleman. Therefore, what I drink is sherry."

Meanwhile Toreg's wails had diminished to grunts, which gradually developed a pleased note. At last he paused, looked at Bertram, and licked his lips. "More sherry?" he asked.

"Within strict limits, old chap," said the Hoka. "You must remain fit to drive, what? And you're accustomed to nothing stronger than that, ah, shmiriz you mentioned." The metabolism of his own race gave him an incredible capacity for alcohol before he was much affected by it.

"Ha, little you know!" Toreg grabbed the flask and took a more careful gulp. "I am a warrior—a household trooper of Lord Dzenko of Roshchak—as mighty at the flowing bowl and the steaming trencher as I am on the field of battle."

Bertram grew interested. "Say on, old bean," he urged.

For an alarmed instant, Charlie wondered if his tutor might decide to switch roles and become a barbaric Talyinan. But no, that would scarcely happen. However volatile on the surface, Hokas kept steadfast in what counted. Besides, they usually adopted characters from human history or literature.

A warrior's life had always tempted Charlie.
Everyone seemed to like him well enough, but he
had no close friends and often felt lonesome. He
would then imagine himself with a wholly changed
personality—a man of action, who led other men on
great feats of derring-do. . . .

He came back to reality with a start. He must
have been daydreaming for quite a while. Toreg had
been nipping and talking and had gotten maudlin.

"I *was* a warrior, a household trooper of Lord
Dzenko, mighty at the laden board and on the clang-
ing battlefield. Today I am but a servant of the
humans."

"Dear me." Bertram clicked his tongue in sympathy. "Cashiered, eh? Drumhead court-martial, no
doubt. Stripped your buttons off."

"Huh? What're you hooting about? I was sent away
in honor, I was. My good Lord Dzenko—may he live
prodigiously—had to reduce the size of his guard. He
had to let me go, 'mong a lot of others. But he didn't
want to." Toreg waggled a forefinger. "As a matter of
fact, fuzzy one, my good Lord Dzenko pers'nally
found me the job I've got. He knows the Plenipotentiary. I've heard him more'n once, asking the Plenipotentiary to help us here in his province. He could,
you know—the Plenipotentiary, I mean. He could
whistle up flying ships and, uh, guns and everything,
and make an end of Olaghi. But no, he won't. Keeps
quacking about, uhn, noninterference . . . the law of
the League—"

"Well, why did Lord Dzenko have to dismiss most
of his fighters?" Bertram asked. "High cost of living, perhaps?"

"No," Toreg growled. "Olaghi made him. Olaghi
the accursed."

Charlie listened, fascinated, while Bertram got the

story. It took hours. Not only was Toreg a little incoherent by now, but centuries of history needed explaining.

However, basically the past of Talyina paralleled many countries on Earth. A conquering warlord had created the kingdom by bringing less powerful chieftains under him, throughout the islands. But while those magnates had to swear service to the king, they kept a great deal of local authority and their own troops of warriors. These they used against bandits, pirates, and foreign enemies. Occasionally this feudal system broke down, but hitherto order had always been restored after a period of chaos.

At last few bandits or pirates were left, and no foreign enemies within ready sailing distance. About that time the League established its Commission. Pomfrey hoped for social progress, the gradual evolution of barons into squires and their councils into a true, democratic Parliament. But he was only allowed to encourage that, not take any direct hand in affairs.

Several years ago, the last head of the old royal house died without heirs. Pomfrey had been preparing for this, urging the barons to elect a new king but limit his powers. Unfortunately, a strong noble, Olaghi, had been preparing, too. With the help of several of his fellows, he seized the capital and proclaimed himself the ruler. After some fighting, the lords of the islands yielded.

Olaghi thereupon proceeded to make social changes of his own. He replaced as many barons as he was able with his favorites. He forced the remainder to reduce their private troops to mere guardian corps. Besides collecting tribute from them, he imposed high new taxes directly on the common people.

Yet Talyina did not revolt. Apart from the fact that Olaghi had taken care to make a successful revolution look impossible, there was the fact that no Talyinan could really imagine doing without a king. And he was on the throne, however dubious his claim to it.

"Bad to worse, bad to worse," Toreg mumbled. "Time indeed for the Prince of the Prophecy to arrive, if ever he does. . . ."

Sad though the tale was, Charlie didn't let it spoil his enjoyment. The countryside was picturesque, and the natives he saw didn't look unhappy. When he pointed this out, Toreg insisted it had a double cause. First, Shverkadi Island was in the fief of Lord Dzenko, who managed to protect his subjects somewhat, especially since the capital was far from here. Second, more important, the League outpost was on Shverkadi, and Olaghi was too cunning to let the representatives of the stars see daily wretchedness.

What Charlie spied seemed prosperous in a primitive fashion. After a stretch of forest, broken by an occasional camp of charcoal burners, cultivated clearings began to appear. South of Push, the coastal land was nothing but farms.

The stop at the village was a diverting spectacle. Toreg pulled on a brake lever with one hand while he disconnected the gongs with the other. Lacking a beat to guide them, the yachis jumped out of phase, until they stopped altogether. Thus the wheel jerked to a halt. Charlie and Bertram nearly lost their seats. This was at the inn, a long thatch-roofed wooden house near the waterfront. Behind it, a few similar buildings sprawled along dusty irregular streets, where animals wandered about among females, who nearly all carried heavy burdens of one sort or another. In front lay the dock. Most boats were out fishing. Most males not aboard them were

in the fields, toiling with hoes and spades. Charlie
had thought the Middle Ages atmosphere romantic,
but now he started to see why the League felt that
everybody had a right to modern machinery as soon
as he could safely use it.

In the dirt-floored common room stood a plank
table and benches. The travelers sat down and had
lunch, paying for it in brass coins of the kingdom,
of which they had an ample supply. They were served
by the landlord's wife and daughters. New Lemurian
females lacked the cat whiskers of the males and
indeed looked still more human except for being
completely bald. Their customary dress was a one-
piece gown, ankle-length, ornamented with tie-dyeing
or beadwork, caught at the waist by a belt from
which dangled small tools for their endless tasks.

The food was coarse black bread, cheese, meat,
and fruits, accompanied by ale or milk. Again he
realized he was using English words for things which
were never of Earth. Everything had a taste, smell,
and texture alien to him, usually flavorful but
strange—like the milk, which reminded him of
nutmeg and dill pickles. The basic biochemistries
were so similar that a human or a Hoka could eat
most New Lemurian dishes and get ample nourish-
ment. Yet the variations were such that no native
germ could live in their bodies. The Talyinans had
barely begun to learn about sanitation—one of
Pomfrey's more successful programs—but Charlie and
Bertram need not fear getting sick on this planet.

The landlord's sons released the tired yachis. When
the moment came to put a fresh team on the wheel,
Toreg did the job himself. Charlie soon saw why. It
took special skill.

Apparently yachis were not very sharp-witted.
Their normal reaction upon being startled or

displeased was to leap three or four meters straight up. Twice Charlie had the entertainment of seeing Toreg carried along, clinging to a tether and swearing a blue streak till he thumped back down, rolled over, and sprang erect.

Under the circumstances, it was surprising how kindly he treated the animals. Aside from sulfurous language, he did not force but coaxed them onto their platforms, working the monster wheel forward so as to bring each position near the ground. In spite of Toreg's bloodthirsty talk about his military prowess, Charlie decided the Talyinans could not be as simple or as brutal as they might appear.

The yachina got going again and rolled south. The road was broader and better. Traffic increased. Regular wagons trundled their loads, drawn by their owners or hirelings. Charlie also saw a few mules at work, another benefit of interstellar trade. An occasional rider bounded by on his yachi, cloak flapping off his shoulders, midriff tightly swathed, and jaws bandaged shut against the continual jolting. Peasants in the grainfields, children herding tame fowl or meat animals, unimpressed when they saw a human go by, gawked at sight of the Hoka. Slowly on the left, at the edge of the sea horizon, grew the dim vision of a neighbor island, and in the channel between, trawlers dragged their nets.

At midsummer in Talyina the days are long. Yet the sun had dropped low when Charlie reached Grushka and his destiny.

3

A Night at an Inn

This town had a population of a few thousand. As at Push, they lived in thatched timber houses, gaudily painted. But these narrow, twisty, littered and evil-smelling streets were cobbled, which made the last part of the yachina ride teeth-rattling, and the docks accommodated quite a number of boats and small ships. The hostel which Toreg had chosen fronted on a market square. Opposite stood the League's gift to a combustible community, a fire station, with horse-drawn wagons and hand-operated water pumps. At their present stage, the Talyinans would have gotten little good from motorized equipment. Where would they find energy charges, replacement parts, or skilled mechanics?

A plump landlord bustled out to greet the arrivals. When he saw Charlie, he rubbed his hands

together. The youth suspected that prices went up a
hundred percent for a "rich Earthling." The landlord
wasn't too surprised by Bertram; a few nonhuman
spacefarers had already visited New Lemuria.

"Ah," he burbled in English, "welcome, lovely folk,
to your every-modern-convenience lodgings at the
Sign of the Ritz! Immediate reservations. A gong boy
will bring your baggage. Wash off the stench of travel
while my wives prepare delicious dainties for your
gorging and swilling. How eager are we to listen to
your boasts! How few our bedbugs! How silent our
fowl in the dawn!"

Inside was a wainscoted rough-raftered taproom,
fronds strewn on its clay floor, dimly lit by
sconced candles and the flames on the hearth. A
chimney conducted away most smoke, another
innovation from the stars. The rest of the
"modern conveniences" amounted to a compartment
where guests were required to check lethal weapons, a bath whose cold-water shower was fed by
a cistern, and a couple of overstuffed leather arm-
chairs beside the central table and its benches.
Upstairs were bedrooms, on whose straw pallets
visitors usually spread their own sleeping bags.

Having cleaned himself, Charlie joined Bertram
and Toreg at dinner. This was a thick stew, plus
abundant drink served in carved wooden flagons.
Word of the newcomers was getting around, and
townsmen were coming in to meet them. The landlord beamed at the extra trade. Charlie was hard put
to answer the questions which poured over him. With
scant organized entertainment, and most of them
illiterate, these people were happy to meet outsiders. Charlie's opinion of the Middle Ages went down
another notch.

He was tired, however. It had been a lengthy and

exciting day. After his meal he curled into one of the big chairs. Nobody followed him. They clustered around Bertram, who was the real novelty as well as the inexhaustible talker. Charlie was glad of that. He decided he'd just sit and listen for a bit, then go to bed.

The sight before him was exotic, he thought: rude chamber, leaping, sputtering flames and weaving shadows, Talyinan males crowded on benches or squatting on the floor. Bertram sat at the end of the table across from Toreg. His short golden-furred form, now clad in a tuxedo, seemed appealingly helpless among these burly fishers and artisans.

"More sherry?" he invited.

The guide, who had already had some of it, shook his head. "No. You try shmiriz." He thumped a pot of the local brew down onto the planks.

"Tut-tut," reproved Bertram. "A gentleman prefers sherry." He stopped to think. "Or should it be port, at this hour? Yes, by Jove, port. Forgetful of me. Must make a note." His monocle caught a fire gleam as he took forth a penstyl and scribbled on his cuff. "Right-o. Would you care for a spot of port, my good fellow?"

"No," growled Toreg. "You try our shmiriz. Not to insult us."

"Oh, very well," agreed the Hoka. He emptied the pot into his flagon.

"Shmiriz got power," Toreg bragged. "Turns your ears purple."

A gasp of awe rose from the crowd when Bertram drained his huge cup in a single swallow.

"Nonsense," he said. "Do my ears look purple?"

Toreg squinted blearily. "Too much fur on them to tell," he complained.

Charlie's eyelids drooped. . . .

A racket brought him awake. Through the door swaggered half a dozen more Talyinans. They made the rest appear meek. Above their trousers and boots they wore coats of jingling ring mail. Above their scarred faces rode spiked conical helmets with noseguards and chain coifs. Over their backs were slung round shields on which the emblem of a fire-breathing snake had been painted. Besides their swords, two carried battle axes, two crossbows, two pikes whose butts they stamped on the ground. Every belt held at least four knives.

The leader bulked enormous, a full two meters in height. His shoulders filled the doorway. His whiskers, each dyed a separate color, reached nearly as wide.

Toreg stared, leaped to his feet, and shouted in joy, "Mishka! My dear old boss!"

"Toreg!" bawled the giant. "Why, you flop-eared flap-tongue, welcome back!" His green glance fell on Bertram; Charlie, off in the shadows, escaped notice. "Hai! Doom and hurricanes, what pretty doll have you fetched us?"

The group tossed their weapons a-clatter toward the checkroom, for the landlord's family to pick up. When Mishka strode to the table, Charlie felt the earth quiver a bit. Bertram rose. "Lemme . . . inner-dooshe you." Toreg hiccupped. "Uh, Bertram Smyth-Chum-Chum . . . Chum-m-m . . . from, uh, where's it you said? Meet muh former boss." He got control over his tongue. "Mishka, Sergeant in Chief of House-hold Guards to Dzenko, dread Lord of Roshchak! Mishka, first warrior of the West, equal to forty in combat, man of unquenchable thirst and appetite!"

"'D'je do," said Bertram politely.

"Let's shake hands like humans," Mishka proposed, not to be outdone in courtesy. Or did he wish to test strength? Muscles rippled and knotted; he must be squeezing hard. Bertram smiled and squeezed back. Astonishment came over Mishka's countenance. He let go at once. His left hand surreptitiously fingered the right.

Still, he held no grudge, simply regarded the Hoka with sudden respect. "Drink!" he clamored while he shucked his helmet. Civilians on the benches scrambled to make room before the warriors should pitch them off.

"And what brings you here, Sergeant, if I may ask?" Bertram inquired.

"Oh, patrol against bandits," Mishka said. "Didn't find any. Plague and shipwreck, what a dull tour! Going home tomorrow. Rather hear about you, fuzzy sir."

Charlie's lids fell down again. . . .

He must have slept for a couple of hours. A roar wakened him. Blinking, he saw that the fire had guttered low and most of the guests had departed. Their work started at sunrise, after all. Mishka's squad and Toreg snored on the floor or, heads on arms, across a table shiny from spilled liquor. Only their outsized chief and the small Hoka had stayed the course, and both of them were finally showing its effects.

"Olaghi!" Mishka trumpeted. He crashed his flagon down. "I'll tell you 'bout King Olaghi, may the Great Ghost eat his liver! Olaghi the Tyrant! Olaghi the Cruel! Olaghi the Meat-Stingy! Woe to the world, that Olaghi rules over Talyina!"

"Not the best sort, I take it?" Bertram asked.

"*Best?* Worst—worst usurper—"

"Usurper?" Bertram's ears pricked up. According to Toreg's account during the day, Olaghi had as much hereditary right to the throne as anybody, little though that might be.

"Usurper!" Mishka snarled, and pointed his own

ears forward like horns. "Not is he from Bolgorka, the capital, whence th' ol' royal house sprang. He's bloody foreigner—from Nyekh. Not really part of Talyina. Just got dual monarchy with us. And now they've shoved their man onto our backs!"

"Ah." The Hoka nodded. "Of course. I understand. Rather like the first Georges."

"The whats?"

"Quite. Kings of England on Earth. In the eighteenth century of our reckoning, but not English— a Hanoverian line—"

Bertram went on to relate the history. Carried away by it—and, no doubt, liters of shmiriz—he waxed more and more indignant at the wrongs inflicted by the Hanoverian kings, especially on Scotland, after that brave country had risen to restore the rightful dynasty—the Stuart dynasty, from which in fact his own companion could claim descent. . . .

Charlie dozed off. . . .

When next he woke, it was to the sound of singing. Bertram stood on the table. Gone were his monocle, bow tie, and coat. Rolling his r's in an accent which had nothing of Oxford about it, he bellowed, in his reedy voice, a Jacobite song hastily translated into Talyinan.

"Charlie is my darling, my darling, my darling—"

Down on the bench, Mishka regarded him glassy-eyed and openmouthed.

"—The young Chevalier!" finished Bertram, and added a few steps of the Highland fling. Bouncing back to his seat, he refilled both cups. "Beautiful, is it no? Aye, beautiful!"

Since the translation had necessarily involved phrases like "the young yachi rider," the present Charles Edward Stuart felt doubts about that. Mishka didn't.

"Beautiful." The guardsman wiped a tear from an eye. "Reminds me—you listen now." He began to chant rather than sing:

Woe is the world, when for Talyina's weal
Reigns no true ruler, but only a rascal.
Sorrow and sadness make sour the shmiriz.
Weary are Westfolk who wobble 'neath burdens—

"Wobble? I dinna ken the trope, lad," Bertram said, or the native equivalent thereof.

"Shut up," Mishka grunted. "You listen. This is the Holy Prophecy. Hun'erds o' years old."

He went on at some length, describing a period during which a murrain was on the yachis and eggfowl, cooking pots stood empty everywhere, and the hearts of warriors were grieved, for a false king had brought down the anger of the gods upon the realm. But then—his basso rose in volume, causing a few of the sleepers to stir and mutter—then came hope.

When all feel forsaken, and fell is the hour,
Wildly and welcome from out of the west,
Royally red-haired, and riding in leaps,
The Prince of the people comes pounding
        to save them—

"Red hair, aye, aye!" shouted Bertram. "Like my ain young Chevalier yonder!"

Charlie shook his head in bewilderment. The entire scene had taken on an eerie, dreamlike character.

Mishka chanted relentlessly:

Five are the Feats that his followers wait for.
Many will meet then to marvel and join him,

The wonders he worked having proven him worthy.
Hear, under heaven, the hero's five doings!

It took concentration to sort out, from interminable verses loaded with elaborate figures of speech, just what was supposed to happen. But Charlie gathered that this prince would establish his identity by accomplishing five things impossible for anybody else.

First, with a crossbow, in a fog and at fifty paces, he would shoot a bellfruit off the head of his best friend. Next, he would slay something unspecified but dreadful known as the Sorrow of Avilyogh. Thereafter he would sail ("Singing and swigging while other lie seasick") to Belogh, where he would fight and overcome three invincible warriors, brothers, whom that town maintained. His fourth deed, on the island of Lyovka, was of a more intellectual type. It seemed that three Priests of a certain god dwelled there, who challenged all comers to answer three riddles. Those who tried and failed, as everyone did, were cast into a fiery furnace. But the prince gave the correct replies with scornful ease. His last feat was to enter the Grotto of Kroshch, wait out the high tide which completely submerged it, and emerge unharmed—even playing his horpil, whatever that might be.

When he had thus proved himself, warriors would flock to his standard. Mishka concluded triumphantly:

In terror, the tyrant who caused all the trouble,
The false king, goes fleeing, unfollowed, in shame.
Tall over Talyina towers the mighty.
Righteous, the red-haired one rules us forever!

He slammed his flagon back down on the table. It broke, while a fountain of shmiriz leaped up over him. He didn't notice. The landlord did and made a notation on his score.

"There!" Mishka exclaimed, thick-voiced. "Wha'd 'you say to that, hai?"

The equally befuddled Hoka leaped to the floor and struck a pose, right arm flung outward, left hand clutching breast. "I say rise for the Young Prince!" he piped. "Ride, mon! Ride, and carry the wor-r-rd that Bonnie Prince Charlie has come back to his ain!"

With a whoop that shook the rafters, Mishka also sprang erect. "I go! Take rowboat . . . cross channel . . . rouse m'Lord Dzenko—for freedom!" He snatched his helmet off the table. The padded lining was still within the outer coif of mail, and he clapped the whole unit over his head. Unfortunately, he clapped it on backwards and spent a minute choking and blundering about until he got it right.

Enthusiasm undimmed, he grabbed a sword from the checkroom and staggered off into the night. His war calls echoed among the darkened houses.

Bertram was not much steadier on his feet as he approached Charlie. "Hoot, mon," he said in English, "are ye awake the noo?"

"I—gosh, I don't know," Charlie faltered.

"Aweel, 'tis time ye waur abed." The Hoka scooped him up in strong but gentle arms and bore him away, while crooning:

Speed, bonnie boat, like a bird on the wing.
"Onward!" the sailors cry.
Carry the lad who is born to be king
Over the sea to Skye. . . .

4
Kidnapped

Charlie woke late and alone. Having donned undergarments, tunic, trousers, and stout shoes, he went downstairs in search of breakfast. Toreg sat brooding over the remnants of his. "Good morning," the human said in Talyinan. "I'm sorry I overslept."

"Oversleep all you want," mumbled his guide. "Oo-ooh, my head! Worst is, that fuzzy demon was up at dawn—*cheerful*."

"Where is Bertram?" As Charlie seated himself, a wife of the landlord brought him a dish of scrambled native eggs (they had green yolks) and a cup of hot herb tea.

"I know not," Toreg answered. "He asked me where to find a tailor and a swordsmith and bounced off. Never did I get back to sleep."

"That's too bad," Charlie said. "Uh, we will go for

that ride you mentioned yesterday, won't we?" Toreg
had promised a trip into the hills behind town, to
see their forests and wildlife.

The guide nodded. Immediately he clutched his
brow and groaned.

The fresh cup of tea seemed to make him feel
a trifle better. When Charlie had eaten, they went
outside. Hitched to a rail stood three saddled horses.
"I didn't know there were any of these here, except
for the fire department," said Charlie.

"It rents them to tourists," Toreg explained.

"What? But suppose a fire broke out!"

"Which is more important, some smelly fishermen's
cabins or the mayor's treasury?"

Charlie's view of the Middle Ages sank still
further. To be sure, he thought, these simple
wooden houses probably weren't too hard to
replace, while off-planet money could buy modern
tools and materials of improvement. But did the
mayor spend it on his community? Nothing in sight
suggested that he did.

"Gr-r-reeting, my Prince!" resounded behind him.

Charlie jumped at the unexpected, squeaky burr.
Turning, he saw Bertram. The Hoka was not
dressed in the outdoor clothes he had brought
along, tweed jacket, plus-fours, deerstalker cap, and
so forth. Instead, he must have commissioned the
tailor and smith he found to do hurry-up jobs for
him.

Upon his head was a flat tam-o'-shanter sort of cap
with a long feather in it. From his shoes, heavy stockings of native wool rose to his knees. Upon his body
he wore a great piece of coarse red-green-and-black
plaid cloth, pleated, folded, bunched, and belted to
form a kilt whose end draped across torso and left
shoulder. Below his stomach dangled a furry pouch.

Various sizes of daggers were thrust under belt or stocking tops. Slung scabbarded over his back was a broadsword nearly as long as he was tall. This type was not unknown in Talyina, though curved sabers were generally preferred, but he had added to it a basket hilt.

"Bertram!" Charlie cried.

"Bertram?" said the Hoka. "Nay, Hieness, nae Sassenach I, but your ain Hector MacGregor—a rough, untutored Hieland mon, 'tis true, but loyal to my Prince, aye, loyal to the last wee drappie o' bluid. Ah, Charlie, 'tis lang and lang we've awaited' your coming, lad."

Struck by a dreadful suspicion, Charlie tried to bring the Hoka back to his senses. "Bertram Cecil Featherstone Smyth-Cholmondoley," he said in as stern a tone as possible, "you were supposed to come along on this trip in case of trouble—"

"Aye!" With a bloodcurdling yell, the little being whipped out his sword and whirled it till the air whistled. "Let any dar-r-re lay hand on my Pr-r-rince, and the claymore o' Hector MacGregor wull cleave him for the corbies!"

Charlie leaped back. The blade had almost taken his nose off. Toreg was unimpressed and still in a sour mood. "Come along, if we're to finish our ride ere nightfall," he grumbled. "Or like you the thought of riding in the dark when ilnyas prowl?"

The Hoka sheathed his weapon and scrambled to the saddle, whose stirrups had been adjusted for him. "Aye, come, my Prince," he chirped. "And ne'er fear for your back whilst Hector MacGregor rides to guard it."

Numbly, Charlie mounted too. Toreg did likewise, doubtless glad in his present condition to be on a horse instead of a jolting yachi. Hooves clopped on cobblestones, and the group rode out of town, followed by the stares of passersby.

It was another beautiful day, breezes full of the scents of green growth, brilliant sunlight, warbling birds. The road through the countryside soon became a mere trail, left farmsteads behind, and wound into ever steeper, wooded hills. From these Charlie had magnificent views across the island and the blue-glittering strait to its neighbor. On a headland there he spied the walls and towers of a castle. That must be Roshchak, the seat of Lord Dzenko.

As he rode, Charlie figured out what had happened to his companion. Inspired by warlike company and that curious folk poem which Mishka rendered, the typical Hoka imagination had flared up. It had seized on the coincidence of Charlie's name—well, not entirely coincidence. Captain Malcolm Stuart was of Scots descent and he named his son after the Bonnie Charlie of romantic memory, the prince whose Highland followers had tried to restore the Stuarts to the throne. The soldiers of Hanoverian King George defeated them, and Charles Stuart was forced into exile. His supporters—Jacobites, they were called—could do little more than compose sentimental songs about their Prince.

Yes, of course that part would appeal to a Hoka. Away with dull old Bertram! Up with the wild clansman Hector MacGregor!

No appeal to common sense would reverse Bertram's change. The Hoka knew perfectly well that this wasn't the eighteenth century or even the planet Earth.

Charles Edward Stuart decided not to waste breath denying his royalty. Let him play along with Bertram's—no, Hector's—fancy. It could do no harm, he supposed, and might even be fun. When they got back to the ship, his father could doubtless find some way to straighten matters out.

He had spent a couple of hours in these meditations while the horses plodded onward, Toreg nursed his hangover, and Hector recited endless border ballads. The gloomier they were, the happier the Hoka got. Charlie had almost settled down to enjoy his outing, when they met the warriors of Dzenko.

They were passing through a ravine. Its brush-covered walls blocked off vision away from the trail. Rounding a bend, the travelers confronted half a dozen armed New Lemurians.

Charlie recognized the patrol from last night. Now they were yachi-mounted. The horses shied when a couple of the kangaroolike chargers bounded past them, to cut off retreat.

"Good day. May all your enemies welter in gore," Sergeant Mishka said in conventional politeness. "How pleasant to meet you here."

Toreg, who knew them, snapped, "Belike not by chance. Methinks you waited for us, having asked in Grushka about our plans."

"Well, yes, after I returned from Roshchak before dawn and shook my squad awake," Mishka admitted. he smiled at Charlie. "When my lord Dzenko heard of you, who are red-haired and a prince—"

"I'm not really."

"Aye, Bonnie Prince Charlie and none ither!" cried Hector. "And who are ye to question the Royal Per-r-rson?"

"I question him not," Mishka replied. "I do but bear word that my lord would be honored did his Highness pay a call."

"Why, uh, I, I meant to," Charlie stammered.

He did not like the way these armored males crowded near or the set expressions on their faces. "Later."

"Today," Mishka said. "We have a boat ready."

"Thanks," Charlie said. "but I'd rather—"

"I must insist."

Hector sprang from the saddle. Down on the ground, he put one foot on a boulder which protruded from the soil, drew his sword, and swung it in whining arcs. The nearby yachis edged away.

"Inseest, do ye? Nae mon shall force the Prince tae any place whaur he doesna weesh tae gae, ne'er whilst Hector MacGregor lives."

Mishka growled. His own sword flew free. His men lifted weapons.

"Hold it!" Charlie screamed. "I—I do want to see Lord Dzenko. Very much. I can't wait." To Hector he added, "Take it easy, clansman. I, uh, I will honor Lord Dzenko with my presence."

"Weel, weel," muttered the Hoka as he sheathed his blade. "But 'tis nae true Scots name, yon Dzenko."

"Oh, he's a Lowlander, I'm sure," Charlie improvised.

"Lowlander?" For a second the Hoka frowned, as if he were about to be Bertram and declare that Dzenko was not a name from anywhere on Earth. Luckily, however, he recalled that he was Hector, who didn't know any better. "Aye, nae doot, syne your Hieness says so."

The Talyinans relaxed. "Come," snapped Mishka. "We ride."

An hour's stiff travel downhill brought them to a cove, a notch in the wilderness where nobody dwelled. A large rowboat or small galley lay beached. They shoved it off and climbed aboard. One soldier stayed to tend to the animals. These were seldom transported across water; yachts bounced too much.

Mishka had spoken little. Now he ordered Charlie and Bertram into the cabin. The boy knew the reason. It explained his having been accosted in the ravine, rather than openly in town. Lord Dzenko must want everything kept secret.

Oars creaked and splashed. The boat drove forward at a good pace. Charlie wished he could look out, but the cabin had no portholes. "Ah," said Hector shrewdly, "noo I see! Yon laird be a closet Jacobite, and ye're aboot tae conspire wi' him against the usurper." He sighed. "If ainly I'd wits tae help ye twa plot! I'm nobbut a rough, unlettered Hielander, though, wi' naught tae offer save his steel and bluid." He fumbled in his pouch. "And, aye, my sporran holds money, and a sandwich, and"—he drew out his flask—"a wee bit whisky, should my prince hae hunger or thirst."

"No, thanks," Charlie whispered.

The boat docked at a village below the castle. Mishka gave hooded cloaks to the human and the Hoka, and his guardsmen surrounded them closely while they went up the path to the stronghold.

In spite of his worries, Charlie was gripped by what he saw. Here was no medieval ruin or restored museum piece. This was a working fortress.

Gray stone blocks were mortared together to form a high wall. On its parapets tramped men-at-arms in mail, archers in leather jerkins. At intervals rose turrets. From flagpoles on their tops blew banners which were not merely ornamental, but which told who the owner and his chief officers were and identified battle stations for each member of the garrison.

Behind a main gate of heavy timbers and strap iron, a flagged courtyard reached among several stone

buildings. Greatest of these was the keep, a darkling pile whose windows were mere slits. Wooden
lean-tos edged the curtain wall, wherein the mani-
fold workaday activities of the castle went on.

Porters carried loads; grooms tended yachis; black-
smiths and carpenters made the air clamorous; bakers
and brewers filled it with odors which blended with
woodsmoke and the smell of unwashed bodies.
Females and children were present, too, as well as
small domestic animals and fowl walking freely and
messily about. Everybody seemed to have a task,
though nobody seemed in a hurry about it. Voices
chattered, laughed, swore, shouted, sang snatches of
song; wooden shoes thumped on stones.

Mishka dismissed his troopers at the entrance to
the keep and himself conducted Charlie, Hector, and
Toreg inside. The walls of an entry room bore tapestries and hunting trophies. The floor was carpeted
with broad-leaved plants, whose sweetness relieved
the reek of smoke from a gigantic feasting chamber
where an ox-sized carcass was roasting.

By the dim interior light, Mishka pointed to a spiral
staircase off the entry. "Follow that, if it please you."

At the fourth-floor landing, he received the salutes
of two guards and opened the door "Come," he said,
"and meet my lord Dzenko."

5
The Redheaded League

Within, the stone of a fair sized room was relieved by rugs and by plastered walls whose frescoes depicted battle scenes. The scarlet pigment used for blood did much to brighten things, for otherwise there was only a shaft of sunlight through a narrow window. A few carved chairs were placed at irregular intervals. In one of them, sat a gaunt middle-aged New Lemurian, his face deeply lined, the blue of his crest sprinkled with gray. He wore a flowing rainbow-striped robe and silver necklace, and his whiskers were gilded.

Mishka clicked heels. "Lord Dzenko, here have brought you, unbeknownst to others as you bade, the fiery-topped person who may be the Deliverer of the

Prophecy. Also, for good measure, his guide—my lord will remember Toreg—and, er—"

"Sir Hector MacGregor," said Charlie in haste, before the Hoka could declare himself a commoner. It might be protection against indignities.

Hector was quick to pick up the cue. "Aye," he declaimed, striking a pose, "an ancestor o' mine was ennobled after the Battle o' Otterburn. Let me tell ye. 'It fell aboot the Lammas tide, when the muir-men win their hay—' "

Charlie shushed him, "My name is Charles Edward Stuart. My father is captain of the ship which lately flew in from the stars. He expects me back soon."

Dzenko smiled. "I trust we can oblige him. Pity that the strange law of your folk—or perhaps their weakness—binds him from coming after you in force."

Charlie gulped. Living so close to the League's enclave, this baron must be more sophisticated about it than most.

"But do be at ease," Dzenko urged. "My only wish is to welcome you, the Prince of the Prophecy, our rescuer from oppression."

"Huh?" exploded from Toreg. "But, but, Lord—him? Why, he's not even one of our kind!"

"Does the Prophecy anywhere say he must be?" Dzenko purred. "Indeed, have you ever heard of a dweller on our world who has red hair?"

"N-no, Lord," Toreg admitted. Excitement seized him. "Could it really be? Could Olaghi in truth be overthrown, and I get my rightful job back?"

"The councils of the mighty are not for common ears," Dzenko said. "You may go, Toreg, and greet your old comrades." The guide bowed and rushed out. "You stay, Mishka," continued the baron. The gigantic guardsman placed himself at parade rest in a corner.

"You know I'm nothing of the sort," Charlie protested. "This is only a, a coincidence."

"Conceivably. Though a wise saw has it that 'Chance is the hand of heaven which hauls us.'" Dzenko rose, to take the human's arm in a confidential manner and lead him across the room. "Upon receiving the news, I, ah, did feel it my duty to investigate further. If nothing else, your presence might cause unrest among the populace."

"Maybe," Charlie admitted. "I suppose I'd better go straight back to the compound."

Dzenko's grasp tightened on his elbow. "On the other hand, perhaps you had better not."

To and fro they paced. Hector stumped behind them. "See you," Dzenko went on, low-voiced, "I say no word against our beloved King Olaghi. He would demand my head on a pikeshaft did I call him aught but a good ruler. Yet is any ruler ever as good as he might be? There are even some who call him a tyrant. Mind you, I say this not myself, but some do. When rumors start flying, a prudent man wants to know whether or not they hold the truth, so he can advise the people who are dependent on him. Now naturally, I don't imagine there's aught to this talk about your being the young Prince who'll perform the Five Feats and dethrone the wicked ruler of legend, but still, at the same time—"

He talked in that vein for several minutes. Charlie got the impression he was really stalling. Meanwhile, a clamor grew below them, shouts, running feet, occasional blasts on the crooked Talyinan trumpets.

"Mishka!" said Dzenko at last. "See what that noise is about and shut them up."

Though sharply spoken, the order had a false

sound in Charlie's ears, as if rehearsed well in advance. But the guardsman clattered out at once and down the stone steps.

"The commoners are quite impetuous, you know." The baron sighed. "Get them overheated, and bloodshed is apt to follow."

Mishka reappeared, hustling Toreg along in front of him. The racket from below pursued them, louder than ever, hardly muffled when the door closed.

"Well, Sergeant, what goes on?" Dzenko demanded.

"This clown here went right out and told them the Prince has come," Mishka snarled. He gave Toreg a shake.

"What?" Dzenko's anger seemed more deliberate than genuine, but the guide quailed.

"Y-you didn't tell me not to, lord," he stammered.

"I *didn't*?"

"Did you? I, I—"

"Stupid lout!"

"Yes, my lord." Toreg cowered.

"Be quiet!" barked Dzenko. He turned on Mishka. "What do they want? And make sure you get things straight."

Stung in his pride, the officer flushed and responded stiffly, "I hope my lord does not confuse me with this yachi-brain."

"Fry and sizzle you, numbwit!" roared Dzenko. "Will you answer a simple question or will you not?"

"Yes, my lord," said Mishka, sulkier yet. "They want to see the Prince shoot the bellfruit off the head of his friend."

Dzenko relaxed. "Well, well," he said. "I was afraid of something like this. That's why I was anxious to handle matters discreetly, Charles. Take an old legend, and the commoners will believe every word of it. Now what is our wisest course?"

"If you sent me away—" Charlie began.

Dzenko shook his head. "No, I fear that won't do."

"Won't do?" asked Charlie, dismayed.

"Won't do," Dzenko emphasized. "I appreciate your not wanting to have any truck with a foolish folk tale. But I have my people to think of. They're wildly agitated. Nought will calm them down again until they see you shoot at the bellfruit. I hate to ask you—"

"I hate to refuse—" Charlie tried.

"But, as I was saying," proceeded Dzenko, "if you do it not, they'll suppose it's because you are an impostor, and the custom around here is to roast impostors over a slow fire. Of course, my guard and I would do our best to defend you. But on Olaghi's orders, they are so few these days that I much fear the peasantry would overwhelm them and take you from us. And really, it's not such a stiff request, is it? All you are asked to do is shoot bellfruit off the head of your best friend, using a crossbow, in the fog at fifty paces."

Charlie's stomach felt queasy. He seized after an excuse. "But my best friend isn't here! He's far off on Earth."

"Come, come," chided Dzenko. "We see your best friend, right at your back. I'm sure he'll be willing to help. What say you, Sir Hector?"

The Hoka's bearlike head nodded vigorously. "What mon dares say Hector MacGregor doesna trust the aim o' his ain true Prince?" he snorted. "Aye—I'll stand target wi' a bellfruit, or an apple, or a walnut, where noo sits my bonnet."

"Tell me, my lord," Charlie asked. "As long as I try to do it, will that satisfy them? I mean, even if I miss?"

"Oh, yes. Should you miss, they will indeed be saddened, to know you are not the Deliverer after all. But none can fairly say you refused to try. What few complainers remain will not be too many for my guardsmen to handle."

"And . . . once I've taken this shot, Sir Hector and I are free to leave? Go back to the compound if we want?"

"My dear boy! Leave? Go back? After shooting the bellfruit off your best friend's head? Certainly not! You must continue to do the other four Feats and liberate the kingdom."

"Sure, sure," said Charlie. "But that's if I shoot the way the legend tells. Suppose I miss."

Dzenko waved his hand. "Why, then you can go wherever you like, do whatever you wish," he replied airily. "Except for their disappointment, it won't matter much to anyone."

"Okay, I'll do it."

"Good!" Dzenko beamed. "I knew we could count on you."

It was necessary to wait for the evening mists to blow in off the sea, in order that every condition of the poem be fulfilled. Charlie and Hector were kept in the upstairs room meanwhile, under guard of Mishka. But servants brought them a sumptuous lunch. And to his surprise, Charlie found that the sergeant was, in his way, both intelligent and decent. He actually apologized for the trouble he had caused.

"In a tide of shmiriz, I roused my lord from slumber," he explained. "Later I bethought me how foolish I had been. Think of my astonishment when I got orders to bring you hither. As my lord's sworn man, I must needs obey." He sighed. "Ah, 'twould be wondrous were you in truth he who shall cast the yoke off us. But though you deny it, I wish you well."

"Dzenko doesn't seem to take the legend seriously," Charlie said. "So why did he want me brought here in the first place?"

"He told you 'twas to make certain matters will not get out of hand."

"Is that the whole truth?" Charlie asked, thinking how calculated the scene this afternoon had appeared.

"Well, he's a deep one, my lord is," Mishka admitted.

"We've need o' craftiness, if we're to avenge Culloden," Hector declared. Charlie knew he referred to the battle in 1746, when the last Jacobite force was defeated, but it seemed late to do anything about that.

Near sunset, an honor guard fetched them. They tramped out of the castle through an awed silence. Every native in the neighborhood had gotten the word and come to watch—close-packed lines of amber-skinned beings in mostly drab clothes, held back by armed troopers in ring mail or jerkins. The procession went to the north shore of the island, where a course had been marked on the beach.

Surf boomed, nearly invisible in a chill, thick fog which tolled over the waters. That mist smelled of salt and seaweed, but the low sun turned it golden. Solemnly, Lord Dzenko removed Hector's cap and placed on the furry round head a purple fruit the size of a clenched fist. The Hoka stood unflinching, nothing but love and encouragement in his beady gaze. Mishka took Charlie's arm and, just as gravely, strode fifty huge paces over the sand before he stopped and turned.

A few trusted warriors accompanied them. Nobody was allowed near Hector and Dzenko. Spectators along the strand were dim blurs in the mist.

"May the gods guide your aim," said Mishka as he put a cocked crossbow in Charlie's hands.

Another soldier whispered, "How sure our baron is of the Prophecy's fulfillment, that he stands right beside the target!" For at this distance, both of them were lost to sight.

Charlie hefted the weapon. Its wooden frame was cold and damp. He was astonished at the weight. The cord that powered it had been wound tight. The short quarrel rested in a groove in the stock. Its razor-sharp steel head would go clear through Hector if it struck him.

The human hesitated. Mishka was standing close, able to see what he did entirely too well. Charlie tried moving the crossbow around, but these warriors were made of stern stuff. Although the deadly quarrel swung past their noses, none of them blinked.

Abruptly a gust of wind brought a streamer of fog which turned everything hazy. Charlie swung the weapon to his shoulder. He had to miss but dared not be obvious about it. Yes, he thought, this must be the right aim, to put his shot safely out into the waves. He squeezed the trigger. The crossbow twanged, banged, and slammed back against him.

For a moment, only the surf spoke. Then to his stupefaction, cheers began to lift from the crowd he could barely see.

"Struck! Struck fair and square! . . . Cloven through the core! . . . A wondrous firing, nay, incredible, miraculous! He is the Prince of the People! Rejoice, rejoice!"

Through the fog loomed the lean figure of Dzenko and the stocky one of Hector. The baron held in his left hand the halves of a bellfruit, in his right a crossbow quarrel.

"Congratulations, my Prince!" he shouted.

"We didna doot ye for a meenute," Hector added.

Night brought clear air and a nearly full moon. The moon of New Lemuria is smaller than that of Earth, but also closer. It shows larger and brighter in the sky and raises higher tides.

Charlie looked out the window of the upstairs room, upon a castle turned to silver and shadows. The hush of night contrasted with the din of evening's celebrations. Charlie was alone with Dzenko.

The nobleman sat near a brazier which glowed to fight off the chill. He toyed with a knife such as every Talyinan carried. Candle flames made the blade shimmer against gloom.

"You faked that test," Charlie accused him. "You knew I'd aim wide and out to sea. You arranged for nobody to be near enough to see what happened. As soon as you heard my bow go off, you palmed the bellfruit on Hector's head and let a split one fall from your sleeve, along with a quarrel."

Dzenko smiled. "Sir Hector believes you struck truly, Prince," he answered.

"A Hoka will believe anything, if it suits his fancy!" The adulation lavished on Charlie the past hours had emboldened him. "Why did you do it? You've visited the League compound often. You know I'm not allowed to meddle in your politics."

"But you are allowed to travel," Dzenko pointed out. "If the natives choose to interpret your actions in special ways, that's scarcely your fault, is it?"

"Do you really mean for me to do those silly Feats—or rig them for me the way you did this one?"

Dzenko stroked his whiskers. "We can but try."

"I *won't*!"

"I fear you must." Dzenko's tones stayed low and smooth. "The whole of Roshchak has the news. Already boats must be bearing it elsewhere. I warned you what the reaction would be to an impostor. Well, what of the reaction when hopes are blasted? Besides your own life, Charles, think of the other lives that would be lost, as people rose in rebellion and, lacking proper military guidance, got cut down by Olaghi's army. No, face the fact: You have a destiny."

"To do what?"

"To help overthrow a cruel tyrant. I know you Earthlings want to see more freedom in this world. Well, for years Olaghi has been taking away what there was."

"I, well, I have heard—from Toreg and Mishka— some complaining about you barons having to pay heavy tribute and reduce the size of your armed forces. But that's just your class and the professional warriors who feel hurt."

Dzenko shook his head sadly. "Prince, consider. Where can we barons get the means to pay off Olaghi, except out of our commoners? And in addition, his tax gatherers squeeze them directly— heartlessly. Those who are ruined by it must go either into beggary or into Olaghi's immediate service. I suspect that is the real purpose behind the new taxes, not any need of the kingdom. And as for whittling down the household troops of the barons, it does more than make them unable to revolt. It means they can no longer patrol their fiefs well. Thus bandits and pirates are again rising up to prey on the people." He lifted his knife. "Prince," he said, and his voice rang, "by this, my steel, I charge you to help me right these grievous wrongs. If your spirit be true, you cannot refuse."

Charlie understood that he had no real choice. Unless he could somehow give Dzenko the slip, he was in the baron's power. If he didn't cooperate, he could be quietly murdered—or maybe tortured till he yielded.

Yet was Dzenko's cause an evil one? Charlie harked back to various unhappy remarks which Pomfrey had let drop. The Plenipotentiary frankly wished that Olaghi had never been born.

Suppose he, Charles Edward Stuart, did play out this charade of the Five Feats. As clever a leader as Dzenko would find ways to make them come out right. Afterward, Dzenko could be left in charge of the kingdom. He was said to govern his own province effectively, and he should be far more agreeable to suggestions from the League than Olaghi was.

As for Charlie, he saw himself as a liberator, a man on a white horse—no, yachi—riding down the streets of Bolgorka, capital of Talyina, while crowds cheered and threw flowers. Later they would erect statues to him. . . .

"My father will be frantic," Charlie protested weakly.

"I will send him a message that you have decided to accept my offer of a guided tour through the whole realm," Dzenko answered. "He can proceed on his voyage. I have League funds available, to buy passage home for you and your companion after you have completed your mission."

"My father will be furious," Charlie said, but without force. When he heard the facts, Captain Stuart would have to admit that his son could not have behaved otherwise.

6
Songs of Experience: The Tiger

For the sake of discretion and, he said, the youth's personal safety, Dzenko sent Charlie off before dawn, in care of Mishka, to a hunting lodge he owned in the woods. There the two of them spent four days. Mishka taught his charge the rudiments of the knightly arts—yachi riding, the use of weapons, the correct forms for boasting of one's own prowess. Charlie declined to study shmiriz guzzling.

In the evenings they talked. Far from being an ignorant roughneck, Mishka was widely traveled and had many stories to tell. He had been born in another province to a poor fisher family. After an adventurous career as a sailor, he enlisted in Dzenko's guard largely because he wanted to be near the

League compound and learn more about the strangers from the stars. In a few years he had risen to the top. He had been saving his pay and hoped before long to retire to his birthplace and marry.

He in his turn asked eager questions. When Charlie remarked that he must be exceptional, Mishka said not. Though most Talyinans were illiterate, respect for learning was ingrained in the peasantry, as well as the aristocracy.

"Then you can't believe this nonsense about my being the Prince," Charlie said.

"M-m, I don't know," the trooper responded. "My father always taught me the Prophecy was a direct revelation from one of the gods. You wouldn't want me disrespectful of my father, would you? Of course, maybe *you're* not the Prince."

"I know I'm not."

"Do you? Nothing in the Prophecy says he'll be aware of it himself till after the Five Feats have been performed, any more than it says he'll've been born on this world. We just took for granted he would be. Let's wait and see how things go, hai?"

Charlie almost blurted forth how the first deed had been faked but stopped himself in time. Mishka's code of honor would not let him admit his lord might have acted less than ethically—not without much better proof than was available here. Such an accusation would only lose Charlie his friendship, and the human felt very alone.

Hector could have come along but had elected to stay behind and supervise some craftsmen in the construction of a set of bagpipes. In addition, he had weavers prepare an ample supply of cloth in different tartans.

At the end of the waiting period, Toreg arrived to fetch Charlie and Mishka. The human asked

about the message to the League compound, and
Toreg said he wasn't supposed to deliver that till
the end of the week's absence originally planned.
For the same reason, they would travel by night
to Avilyogh. That was a tricky stretch of water,
where no master of a sailing vessel dared move
after dark, but Dzenko was commandeering a motor
ferry.

The motor, Charlie discovered, was a treadmill in
a well amidships of the big craft, geared to a pair
of paddle wheels. Ordinarily, it was powered by
steerage passengers, while the wellborn took their
ease topside. Now Dzenko put to work the members of his retinue. These were a couple of dozen
soldiers, a personal servant or two, and a court
minstrel named Hasprot, whose duty would be to
commemorate Charlie's actions in a suitable epic
poem. The baron's grown sons were left on the
separate islands which he had given them the admin-
istration of. It would not have been wise to go in
a large, conspicuous company. The king might hear
of that and look into the matter.

Despite his excitement, Charlie slept well in the
bunk assigned him. Soon after dawn, they entered
the harbor of Vask, chief town on the steeply rising,
thickly forested island of Avilyogh.

The community resembled Grushka in both size
and architecture, except for being dominated by a
huge circular building of rough stone. Dzenko said
that was the Councilhouse, where the adult males
met to consider public business. It was also the home
of Igorsh, baron of this province, who presided over
meetings, though he could vote only in case of a tie.
"Why, that sounds kind of, uh, democratic," Charlie
said.

"Avilyogh is backward," Dzenko answered. "Its

lords never have managed to put the commoners in their place and run things efficiently."

Startled, Charlie gave the master of Roshchak a long stare. But events moved too fast for him to ponder. In minutes the party had docked, disembarked, and were trampling through the streets. Females and children stared; some cheered, probably because newcomers broke the monotony. Few males were about. Dzenko had sent word ahead to Igorsh that he had a vital matter for discussion. So most of the local electorate were assembled to hear it.

At the center of the Councilhouse was a great circular chamber, its flagstone floor surrounded by tiers of benches. Above, a ring of windows admitted light and drew off some of the smells which the crowd of seated fishermen and farmers bore with them even when they were dressed in their dull-colored best. Nevertheless, wealthier males held burning sticks of incense.

Lord Igorsh occupied a massive chair in the middle. It was mounted on a revolving platform, so that his guardsmen could turn him to face anyone speaking from the benches. He was a stout person, who, instead of a robe like Dzenko, wore ordinary jacket and trousers. His sole finery was a shabby red cloak and a gold chain of office.

Local courtesy did not require him to rise. Instead, he lifted an arm and boomed, "Greeting, excellent colleague. As head of the Grand Council of Avilyogh, I welcome you and your folk to our sacred gathering place. We are honored by your visit—" Having run out of set, formal phrases and being as bewildered as his people—who had uttered a gasp when Charlie and Hector appeared—he began to flounder. "But I must say this is . . . is rather sudden and . . . um . . .

mysterious? Yes, mysterious. My lord of Roshchak must forgive us that we have had no time to prepare a reception suitable to his dignity."

Dzenko laid his hand on the hilt of the sword he bore, raised the other palm, and posed with knees bent, right foot forward. It looked ridiculous to Charlie, but evidently had a solemn meaning in Talyinan culture. The buzz of talk among the encircling commoners died out.

"What says the ancient wisdom?" belled Dzenko. "'Haste is a weapon to harry foes home. He who moves swiftly escapes the springing of traps.'"

"True, true," replied Igorsh. "Well is it written: 'Wise are the words of the war-skilled among us.'"

Dzenko twitched his whiskers and waggled his ears in acknowledgment of the compliment. "But also," he said, not to be outdone either in urbanity or learning, "'Knowing is he who draws nigh to good neighbors.'"

"Indeed." The other nodded. "'Friends are the fiercest of weapons 'gainst foemen.'"

"'Alliance is bound to be better than battle.'"

"Yet 'Shunned is the ilnya by all other animals.'"

"However, 'Causes in common make curious partners.'"

"'Greatest are gains that in goodwill are shared.'"

"'The first and the foremost of profits is fame.'"

"Well, well," said Igorsh, rubbing his hands together, "if that's settled, no doubt we can work out the details at leisure. Ah . . . your message hinted at a possible arrangement between our fiefs, for mutual benefit . . . something warlike, you implied?"

"Yes," Dzenko drew his sword and waved it flashing aloft. He pointed to Charlie. "Behold our Deliverer, the Prince of the Prophecy!"

Another gasp turned into a roar. Igorsh himself

needed a few minutes to recover from amazement and shout for order. He had no gavel, but his guardsmen beat weapons on shields until at length there was silence again.

Dzenko told the story with skilled oratory, taking a good half hour about it. Part of that was due to interruptions. The members of this parliament behaved—to Charlie's mind—like large-sized children, jumping up and down at dramatic moments, howling forth proverbs, slogans, and deep-sea oaths. But doggedly, Dzenko made his point clear. He emphasized the presence of many witnesses when the first of the Feats had been performed.

Charlie felt guilty at going along with the fraud. But the enthusiasm of the Avilyoghans was genuine. Why should they take the risks and make the sacrifices of rebelling against Olaghi, were the king not in truth a despot who ought to be overthrown?

Finally—"Well told, Lord Dzenko!" cried Igorsh, and rose to flourish his own blade. "I think I may speak for a general consensus, that this land will fully support the Prince once he has done us the honor of slaying that curse under which we have suffered since time immemorial, the Sorrow of Avilyogh!"

Cheers thundered between the walls. Charlie forgot how tired his feet were from standing. It struck him that he had no idea what he was supposed to do.

"What says the Council?" called Igorsh, sweeping his gaze around the benches. "Would three days hence be a good time to hold the slaying?"

The males applauded. But Dzenko raised his blade to call for attention.

"May I remind the distinguished Council of the reason for my own speed in coming hither?" he said. "It were well for the Prince and those who follow him that they be far from here long before the tyrant

Olaghi learns about the miracle. He will not sit idle, you know."

"True," said Igorsh doubtfully. "Still, anything less than three days is rather short notice. After all, the town will want to raise the head tax on people coming in to see the slaying. Our food vendors will want to lay in extra supplies to sell. Besides the inns, many private households will want to prepare rooms for rent. Not to mention manufacturers of souvenirs—"

"I propose for your consideration," said Dzenko, "that the advantages of such activities be weighed against the possibility of Olaghi sailing into Vask Harbor with his battle fleet and reducing the town to ashes."

"Hm, yes, there is that," agreed the Council chief. "Day after tomorrow, then?"

"This afternoon," said Dzenko firmly.

"But really, my dear colleague—"

Dzenko nudged Charlie. Since the baron of Roshchak must have some plan, the human could only pipe up, "Today. I've got to do it my own way, don't I?"

Igorsh sighed. "Ah, well. A sad thing it is, to think upon the many folk who would wish to see this event and meanwhile enjoy the sights and cooking of our town. But if they must miss it, they must. Tell me, 0 Prince, how do you mean to slay our Sorrow?"

"Why, uh, that is—" Charlie stuttered.

"The Deliverer keeps his own counsel," Dzenko said smoothly.

"He can use my boat!" cried a voice from the stands.

"No," shouted others. "Mine! . . . Mine! My boat, I say—"

A barrel-chested individual in leather clothes stood

up and roared hoarsely, "What need has the Prince for a boat? Can a boat fare on dry land?"

Another large person, whose knitted garments smelled of fish, bounced to his feet and retorted, "Dry land? Show me dry land at the bottom of Grimsa Deep!"

"Grimsa Deep? Who said anything about Grimsa Deep?"

"Where else?" demanded the second male. "Do you suppose the great decapod—the gods rot his tentacles for the nets he has torn and the catches he has stolen—do you suppose he lives anyplace else?"

"What babble is this?" bawled his opponent. "Dare you pretend some mere sea monster is the Sorrow of Avilyogh? Nay, what can it be save the Rookery of Tetch?" He directed his words at Charlie. "From those unclimbable heights descend huge flocks of xorxa birds. to ravish the grainfields of every farmer for three days' journey around. What could be sadder?"

"Decapod! Xorxa birds!" A plump male in a fur-trimmed robe stood erect. "Have you lost your wits, men, to even hear such maunderings? What was ever the Sorrow of Avilyogh but the bandits who lurk in the Hills of Nitchy, robbing the caravans till no honest merchant can send a consignment overland from one end of our island to, another? Know you how exorbitant sea freight has become?"

The clamor grew with more candidates offered. Just before people came to blows, Igorsh had shields beaten again. And Dzenko's voice cut through, crying, "Hold! Hold! I speak for the Deliverer!" until the assembly was seated and quiet.

"Enough of this," said the baron scornfully. "Did you think the Prince himself knows not what is the Sorrow of Avilyogh?"

He paused for effect. "Well, what is it?" Igorsh asked at length.

"Why!" Dzenko spread his arms wide. "What but the Giant Demon Ilnya which has prowled your hills throughout the centuries? What but its accursed existence has spoiled your luck and brought these other misfortunes on you? Now no more! Today the Prince will seek out the Demon and slay him, and a golden age will come to Avilyogh!"

Males stared at each other. Charlie caught some of the puzzled murmurs: "Demon? . . . Giant Ilnya? . . . I never heard . . . Well, at least it isn't that decapod 'Tisn't your fool Rookery, either. . . ."

Meanwhile Igorsh inquired plaintively, "But where is this creature? I, ah, I must admit my own memory is somewhat hazy on the subject. It's, ah, not ordinarily discussed."

"Of course it isn't," Dzenko said. "Doesn't that prove how cunning the Demon is? But fear no more. In the interests of expediting things, esteemed colleague, I took the liberty of dispatching huntsmen of my own to your island. They landed secretly and, armed with magical knowledge given them by the Prince, scouted out the lair of the ogre. I have a map they made. According to it, the Prince should be able to get there in a mere few hours."

Many people shuddered to think the fiend had been so near them for lifetimes, and they never aware of it. They drew signs against evil. There was no further argument.

It wasn't that New Lemurians were stupid, Charlie thought . . . they were by nature as intelligent as humans. But they were brought up in an environment where countless superstitions were believed. Nobody had ever taught them to ask for scientific evidence before accepting a story.

If any did suspect this was being staged, they must be keeping quiet for the sake of getting rid of the hated King Olaghi.

A party left Vask before noon. It consisted of Dzenko's following, plus Igorsh and some of the more prominent citizens of his baronry. Conversation was impossible while bouncing along on a yachi, and Charlie had much time to brood. He hardly noticed the woodland scenery as he climbed the heights of the island.

When they stopped for lunch, he drew Dzenko aside into a thicket; a nearby waterfall helped cover their low words. The noble had beckoned a certain member of the troop to come along. This was a weather-beaten sly-eyed male who, while equipped like a soldier, was actually the huntmaster of Roshchak.

"Hadn't you better tell me what's what?" Charlie proposed.

"You do need instructions," Dzenko agreed. "Boraz, are you sure everything is in order?"

"As of yesterday morning, it was, Lord," the hunter replied. To Charlie he added, "I stayed behind when the rest of my gang returned, to care for the ilnya, and got back barely in time to catch the ferry."

"Care . . . for . . . the ilnya?" Charlie spoke in a daze.

Through his mind passed what he had heard about beasts of that kind. An ilnya was a carnivore, the size of a tiger and not unlike one in appearance, save for blue fur, short tail, and enormous hind legs which helped it run down its prey. The distribution of such species throughout the islands meant there had been land bridges in the past.

Fear chilled him. "I don't know anything about ilnya hunting," he said thinly.

"You need not," Boraz said. "My men and I captured this brute and chained him in a cave. You will go in alone. How declares the Prophecy? 'Swiftly, then, merrily, swinging his swordblade, Slays he the scarer called Sorrow of Avilyogh.' All you have to do is stand out of reach and hack away. When he's dead, cut off his head to slip the chain free, and bury it. The chain, I mean; you'll need the head to show."

The time grew unbearably long as they traveled on—and then, when they dismounted at mid afternoon, it was as if no time had passed whatsoever.

Nothing appeared real to Charlie. He felt his own trembling and smelled his own sweat. The sunlit greenness around him seemed infinitely far away.

Boraz pointed. Uphill from the animal trail which they had been following, barely visible between trunks and leafy boughs, a cave mouth gaped black in a bluff. "Yonder lairs the Demon," said the hunter. "Can you not smell his nearness?" Indeed a rank odor lay beneath the forest fragrances.

Awed, the natives stood mute. Mishka drew blade. "Take you my sword," he bade Charlie, "and would that I might be with you!"

"The Prince fares alone to his destiny," Dzenko said fast.

"What's this?" exclaimed Hector. "Alone? Ne'er whilst breath moves a MacGregor breast!"

All eyes went to the Hoka. He planted his feet firmly and glowered defiance. Small though his teddy bear form was amid the big New Lemurians, they were too shaken to attempt force on him. "Whaur Bonnie Prince Charlie fights, there fight I," he told them.

"Order him to stay," Dzenko snapped.

It was the wrong tone to take. "Why should I?" Charlie flared. "I am the Prince. Remember?"

"But," said Igorsh reasonably, "*you* must slay the Sorrow of Avilyogh. You're not supposed to have assistance."

The wily Dzenko saw a way out. "Our Deliverer's faithful servant can leave his steel behind," he said. "And . . . ah . . . things may happen when one is dealing with a demon, things not fit to be related in public. You will keep silence about whatever you witness, will you not, Sir Hector?"

"If the lad asks it, I wull." The Hoka nodded.

Dzenko gave Charlie a meaningful glance. "Silence may be to your best advantage, Prince," he reminded.

"Yes," whispered Charlie. "Please, Hector."

"I swear, then, by the honor o' my clan, nae wor-r-rd s'all e'er pass my lips," promised the Hoka. "Aye, twill not e'en get as far as my teeth."

Quickly he divested himself of sword and miscellaneous knives. He kept his bagpipes, maintaining that these were a military necessity. Igorsh was dubious; bagpipes were completely unknown in Talyina, and this might be a weapon of some kind. Hector defied him to find any sharp edges in the apparatus, and he gave way.

Mishka wrung Charlie's hand and clapped his shoulder. No one had words. Boy and Hoka trudged uphill to the cave.

Quietness hung heavy. Shivering, Charlie entered. For a second he stood blind in damp, strong-smelling gloom. Then his eyes adapted and he could see.

The cave was about ten meters deep. Its floor was soft dirt, easily movable to hide the chain, collar, and staple that held the ilnya captive. When first he made out the beast, at the far end, Charlie strangled on a cry. It was truly a giant.

But it lay so quietly. He decided it was asleep. Step by step he moved closer, until he realized that this was an old animal—oh, very old. Its great body was bone-thin, its coat faded and in many patches fallen out. As he watched, it began to snore. The mouth curled back, and he saw that the fangs were snags or altogether gone. Once it had been proud and beautiful, but now—no wonder Boraz's men had been able to lay nets and ropes around it and drag it here to await its death!

"Och," said Hector eagerly, "ye've nobbut to stab whilst yon cat snarks, and your second Feat is done."

Dread washed out of Charlie, leaving only a huge compassion. "I, I can't," he protested. "That'd be like shooting somebody's old pet dog."

"Pet? I dinna think yon claws are for decoration, laddie." Hector considered. "Aweel, gi'en the size o' him, I doot one stab wad sairve anyhoo. So, if you wish, I'll rouse him." He tucked the bag under his arm, put one of the pipes to his muzzle, and blew. The bag inflated.

A grisly vision rose before Charlie—the butchery he was supposed to carry out. It might take hours to end the torment.

"No!" he cried. "Stop! I won't! I don't care what they do to me—"

He was too late. Hector had begun playing.

A screech such as New Lemuria had never heard before erupted in the cave. Echoes blasted Charlie's eardrums and rattled around in his skull. The ilnya came awake. By sheer reflex, it bounded upward. Its head struck the roof. It fell with an earthshaking thud and lay still.

Slowly, in eerie wails and moans, the bagpipes deflated. Hector goggled through the dusk. "What . . . what— 'Tis dead!"

Charlie took his courage in both hands and approached the ilnya. He knelt, prodded it, felt for any breath. There was none. "Yes," he said.

"What happened?" Hector asked.

Charlie rose. "I think," he said in a hushed voice, "I'll never know for sure, but I think— It was so old and feeble, and it could never have heard anything like that racket of yours before. I really think it died of a heart attack. Thank God for His mercy."

"A heart attack?" For an instant, Hector was dumbfounded. Then he brightened. "Ah, the bra' notes o' Hieland music! Ever hae Caledonia's foes withered and fallen awa' at the pure and powerful sound o' it!"

7
Man and Superman

Now Charlie must remove the head of the ilnya and hide the evidence. "I hate being dishonest like this," he said.

"Statecraft, lad," Hector reassured him. "Turning his ain guile again' the Sassenach." He inflated his instrument once more. "Yet 'twas a gallant beast here, desairving o' meelitary honors." And while Charlie did the job, the Hoka skirled forth a coronach.

Thus Charlie emerged from the cave with his ears numb and ringing. Mishka whooped and sobbed for joy as he ran to embrace the human. "Why, where've the others gone?" Charlie wondered.

"They fled from the Demon's shrieks and roars," Mishka answered. "I can't really blame them, either. 'Twas all I could do to stand my ground while those gruesome noises shook my very liver."

"Shrieks?" Hector tilted his bonnet in order to scratch his head. "Roars? I heard naught. Naught the least. Did ye, lad?" He snapped his fingers. "Och, but o' coorse, I was playing the pipes. Naught could reach me but yon sweet melodies."

And, Charlie realized, those were precisely what had stampeded the Talyinans. Mishka didn't draw that conclusion, fortunately—or unfortunately, since the tears on the guardsman's cheeks made the human feel guiltier than ever. He got no chance to think further about that. The sergeant lifted a horn slung at his side and winded it to summon the rest of the party. They hadn't gone far and made their yachis take huge leaps while they shouted forth their happiness.

Charlie couldn't resist twitting Dzenko: "I never thought you would flee from a being you understood so well."

The baron looked embarrassed. "It was . . . unexpected . . . that noise. I almost thought the Prophecy spoke truth—" He caught himself. "That is," he snapped, "my men were departing, and naturally they needed me to lead them."

Entering the cave, the Talyinans murmured in awe. Charlie wondered why. Admittedly the ilnya was of uncommon size, but weren't the signs plain that it had also been of uncommon age? Besides, they had never had a legend about an ogre in such a shape till Dzenko invented it for them this morning. Yet they solemnly offered prayers and poured shmiriz on the ground to the gods before they began skinning the animal. The carcass they would leave for a sacrifice, the head they would mount in the Councilhouse, but the hide they would cut up into tiny squares for distribution among the folk as prized relics.

Hasprot, minstrel of Roshchak, took the word after they started home. He was a short and skinny male, his gray crest of hair dyed with the blue juice of berries and his whiskers waxed to keep them from drooping. He affected polka-dotted trousers, bells on his boots, and a jacket not of leather but of fluorescent pink neolon from Earth. However, he did have a good voice, and he was among the few who could speak—not needing his jaws tied shut—while bouncing along on a yachi. He could even play a horpil as he rode. That was an instrument not dissimilar to an ancient Greek lyre, except that it was tuned to a different scale and had a rattle built into the frame which was shaken at suitable points in a recital.

Hark [he intoned] to the tale that I have
    of the hero,
The Prince of Prophecy prancing among us—

Charlie listened in amazement. The part about the shooting of the bellfruit was fairly straightforward, if a trifle florid. ("Piercingly peering through fog stood the Prince.") You couldn't blame Hasprot for having been taken in by Dzenko's trick. But when he came to the Sorrow of Avilyogh, the minstrel gave his imagination free rein. For example, there was the moment in the fight when the Demon had turned itself into a raging fire and threatened to burn them all to a crisp. Still more outrageous, Charlie thought, were the forty-seven Demon kittens which had been about to rush from the cave and lay waste the whole province when the sight of the valiant lords Dzenko and Igorsh sent them wailing back belowground. Hasprot's diplomatic narration extended to the rest of the group. According to him, they had not fled. No.

Raging, they ran where they reckoned the foe
Starkly might strike, did he stretch the Prince dead.

This section of the epic chanced to be composed
during a rest stop, and Charlie saw heads nod and
heard self-satisfied voices rumble, "Ah, yes. . . . Just
so. . . . Indeed, indeed. . . . How well he captures
the essence. . . . Hasprot, would you mind repeat-
ing that bit about how I personally challenged the
Demon?"

Because their lives were hard and usually dull
when not disastrous, these people needed brightly
colored visions. When suddenly it seemed that these
might become real, they were bound to seize on that
hope and to gloss over any flaws in the evidence—
not even aware that they were doing so. Likewise,
they unconsciously edited their eyewitness memories in order to save their pride.

The same thing had happened over and over on
Earth.

Charlie glanced at Hector. Was that kilted teddy
bear really very different from the natives . . . or
from man?

He was too tired to think further. When they
reached Vask, well after sunset, he stumbled directly
to bed. Hector had to be restrained from playing him
a lullaby on the pipes.

With a fair wind to fill gaily striped sails, two dozen
ships plowed eastward. They included not only the
combined naval forces of Roshchak and Avilyogh, but
volunteers that had arrived after Dzenko's couriers,
and ordinary folk in boats, had spread the news of the
Prince through the western islands. Charlie found it
fantastic that he should be aboard the flagship of a
war fleet, a mere three days after he landed.

The vessels varied in size and appearance. But a typical fighting ship was about thirty meters long, broad in the beam, high in prow and stern, gaudily painted, and decorated with a fierce-looking figurehead. The two masts were square-rigged, apart from a fore-and-aft mizzen sail. The steersman used a wheel to control a central rudder and a primitive magnetic compass for guidance. Down on the main deck, a few peculiar cannon poked their snouts through the bulwarks on either side. However, the principal armament was catapults and mangonels. A hundred males were crowded aboard. Few were professional warriors, just ordinary fishers, farmers, laborers, or sailors, who had no armor except perhaps a shield or a kettle helmet and whose weapons had been in their families for generations.

The sea danced and sparkled. Foam went lacelike over the sapphire and emerald of its waves. They whooshed when they made the ships rock. From horizon to horizon, islets were scattered green—here and there a cottage or village visible—as if a jewel box had burst open. Surf broke upon reefs in a blinding purity of white. The sun was warm, but the wind was cool and brisk; it smelled of freshness and distance. Seafowl cruised and cried against an enormous heaven.

From the staff of the lead ship flew a tartan banner which Hector had supplied. Charlie and Dzenko stood alone on the foredeck, gazing down across a mass of crewmen and fighters. It was a conference which the human had demanded. He was tired of being put off with vague promises or distracted with sports and excursions, while the baron handled everything that mattered.

"Have no fears," Dzenko said. "Our cause advances as if the gods had greased it. We proceed openly now, because the king is bound in any case to get word soon of what's happening. But he will need time to investigate and still more time to gather in his strength, from those provinces whose masters support him. Meanwhile, the rest will be flocking to us. Especially after you have accomplished the third of the Feats."

"Yes, what about that?" Charlie fretted. "To fight the Three Brothers of Belogh—" He regarded his own slight frame.

Dzenko twirled a whisker. "Have no fears," he repeated. "All is arranged. I've not been idle since the first we met."

"But do the Brothers—well, I mean, suppose they admit afterward that they threw the fight with me."

"They won't," Dzenko promised, "because they are quite sincere. My agents went to a good deal of trouble there.

"See you, young friend, in olden years—when the Prophecy was composed—the city-state of Belogh was powerful. And ever it maintained three of its doughtiest fighters, who were supposed to be brothers, as champions. They took the lead in battle, and they represented the city in trials by combat.

"When Belogh was brought into the kingdom, this custom died out. But it was never officially abolished, and traditions about it survive. The task of my agents was to find three, ah, suitable brothers and persuade them and the local government that they be proclaimed heirs to the post. These three believe it's strictly honorary, a credit to their family and, ah, an assertion of Beloghan spirit in our era of despotism. When you land and challenge them, they will have to accept. But I trust they will get no advance warning. If they knew who you are, they might decline the engagement, and then how could you prove your identity?"

He stared at the main deck. "Yes," he continued, "we must always be careful."

His glance fell on Hector, who stood in earnest talk with Mishka. "For instance," he mused, "that associate of yours has seen a shade too much and may let slip information best kept from the public. It would not be overly distressing, would it, if he . . . ah . . . suffered an accident?"

Horror smote Charlie. "What?" he yelped.

"Oh, nothing cruel," Dzenko pledged. "Brawls will happen, you know, when armed males are crammed together. If several of them simultaneously took offense at something he said— Do you follow me?"

"*No!*" Charlie shouted. "If, if anything . . . like that—well, if you want my help, you'd better keep Hector safe! Otherwise," he choked forth, "you may as well kill me too . . . because I'll be your enemy!"

"Hush," urged Dzenko. Eyes were turning forward, attracted by the noise. "If it will make you happy, I hereby swear that"—he grimaced—"that creature will be safe as far as I am concerned. Are you satisfied? Perhaps we ought not to talk further this day." In a swirl of his robe, he strode off.

Charlie took awhile to calm down before he also descended the ladder. Hector and Mishka met him. "Prince," the sergeant declared, "we have discussed your forthcoming ordeal—"

"Aye, hear him oot, lad," said the Hoka.

"And we have decided—" Mishka went on.

"He has wisdom in his words," Hector stated.

"That you should get instruction in yakavarsh—" Mishka said.

"E'en though he be nae Hielander," Hector added.

"Which is the art of unarmed combat—" Mishka continued.

"So leesten to him most closely," Hector advised.

"Whereby the wrestler may turn the opponent's own strength against him," Mishka said, and waited for the next interruption. When there was none, he waxed enthusiastic. "Not only is yakavarsh an excellent means of self-defense, Prince; it is in truth an art, yes, a philosophy, a way of life. Consider the lovely curve as a body soars through the air! Create an infinity symbol when you elegantly dislocate his arm! See a gateway to eternity in the angle of his broken neck!"

Charlie was willing and spent some hours trying to learn Talyinan judo. He failed. New Lemurians are proportioned too unlike humans for any of the holds to work very well for him. But at least the open-air exercise kept him from growing queasy when the wind stiffened and a chop set the ship rolling. That might not have been a problem in itself, had the Prophecy not said he would cross the water "Singing and swigging while others lie seasick." The warriors kept bringing him rich food and drink and then expected him to give an a capella concert.

8
Soldiers Three

After Belogh had lost its independence, it dwindled to a small fishing port. The great stone amphitheater had stood unused for generations. Though Dzenko's following was added to the townspeople and farmers, the audience filled less than half the available space. When Charlie left the room given him to arm in and trod out into the arena, his feet scuffed up clouds of fine white dust.

The day was bright and hot. He sweated in the underpadding of the ring mail coat which had been hastily altered to fit him. Still more did he sweat in the conical noseguarded helmet, for it needed twice as much lining as it was meant to have, were it not to cover his head like a candle snuffer. A drop ran into one eye and stung. The smell and taste of the dust were acrid. The round shield hung heavy on his left arm.

He looked about. Spectators, made splashes of subdued color on gray tiers. He sensed their excitement before they started shouting. Dzenko had forbidden his men to breathe any word of Charlie's identity. The newcomer had been introduced cloaked, cowled, and masked by a scarf, as a noble faring incognito, who had heard the institution of the Three Brothers was being revived, disapproved of it, and challenged them to fight the matter out with him. Nevertheless, the circumstances were bound to start talk buzzing among those who knew the Prophecy, and now everybody could see that the stranger was human.

Hector, his second, patted Charlie on the back. "Guid luck to ye, lad," he breathed. "Stand steady and strike hard. Remember Otterburn. Remember Bannockburn. And Killiecrankie. And the Scots wha hae wi' Wallace bled. Noo I maun be off." Likewise armored, his tubby form tramped to where a yachi stood tethered for him, a lance beside it. The observer for the Brothers was already mounted, a husky person in full warlike panoply. Afoot, Hasprot, the minstrel, strummed his horpil and doubtless composed in advance many of the lines which would describe this event.

Charlie's glance searched after Dzenko. It found him in a box favorably positioned for viewing, along with Igorsh of Avilyogh, the lord mayor of Belogh and his family, and other dignitaries. The baron threw the boy a stark smile. More heartening was Mishka, who rose and clapped vigorously at sight of his friend.

A roar lifted from the crowd. Out of their own door came the Three Brothers.

Charlie swallowed. He hadn't expected them to be so *big*. They towered close to two meters. He hoped some of that impression was due to the plumed and visored helmets and the plate armor rather than ring mail which they wore. The sheen off the metal hurt his eyes. He prayed the billowing dust would soon dull it.

As per instructions, they clanked and Charlie jingled across the arena to stand beneath the official box. The lord mayor blinked at them. He was an aged, wrinkled, shaky male whose best clothes, seen at close range, bore countless darnings and patches.

"Ah . . . greeting, greeting, gentlemen," he quavered. "Obedient to the, ah, the ancient law of Belogh . . . looked it up yesterday evening in the archives, I did, while everybody else was reveling . . . hard to concentrate in that racket, but I persisted, I did, and . . ." His voice trailed off. "Where was I? Oh, yes. The ancient law of a challenge—I think—bugs have eaten a lot of it— I think in case of a challenge, I have to try and make peace before it's fought." He stared at Charlie. "Surely you, a—did I hear somebody say 'Prince?'—well, I regret I have no more daughters to offer in marriage—"

"I should hope not," snapped a stout middle-aged female in his party, "seeing I'm the youngest and it's been twenty-three years—"

"Ah, yes." The mayor nodded. "Granddaughters, I meant to say. I'm completely out of marriageable granddaughters, my dear Prince, so I'm afraid—but perhaps—"

Under Dzenko's warning scowl, Charlie replied as boldly as he was able: "Sir, I came here not to marry but to fight."

"Eh? What? Well, well. But why not? Not much difference anyway."

Impatiently, Dzenko plucked the lord mayor's sleeve and hissed in his ear. "Very well, very well, let the combat begin," agreed the latter. "I believe you're supposed to salute me. And it really would be quite nice if you saluted each other. On your honor, gentlemen, begin."

The Brothers lifted swords above shields. Charlie did the same, while taking the chance to study the others. Their armor fitted as poorly as his helmet. Doubtless it was a set of heirlooms.

Yet when all were back in the center of the arena and politely raised blades, and a trumpet sounded, and they strode forward to the encounter, Charlie's pulse fluttered. His three opponents were like remorseless robots grinding down on him.

They ground very slowly, however. Meanwhile, their second started to bounce his yachi around and around the contestants. This inspired Hector to imitation. Dust fountained up. The Earthling heard Hasprot chant:

The bugle has blown and the battle will start
The south is the side of the city combatants.
Towering, totaling more than a ton,
Brutally armed are the Brothers of Belogh—

The minstrel had to compete with Hector, who was singing "Charlie Is My Darling" at the top of his own lungs.

The dust was getting thick as a seafog, a dry mist which clogged nostrils and throat. He could barely make out his rivals a few meters off. Why in the name of sanity did that yokel have to create such a cloud?

Wait! Could it be that he wanted to hide the

engagement so that nobody could see how easily the local team was overcome?

The fact was, Dzenko had told the human, his agents had taken care to pick the three oldest brothers of acceptable ancestry that they could find and persuade these to set up as the Warriors Advocate of former times. (The appeal had been to their civic spirit. Besides asserting its cultural identity, if Belogh revived picturesque customs, it might attract tourists, especially starfarers.) The agents had assured Dzenko that the group consisted of dodderers like the lord mayor. Charlie should be able to wear them out and make them surrender with no danger to himself or any need to harm them.

What was that terrible clangor which broke loose in the whiring grayness? It gave believability to Hasprot:

Heavily hewing, the heroes are met.
Singing, the sword of the Prince now descends
In a left to the head that would lay most men low,
And a right to the ribs that rocks his foe back—

Perhaps his imagination compensated the audience for its inability to see what went on, though Charlie did hear boos.

A shape loomed out of chaos. The human recognized the yachi-mounted native in bare time to jump aside from the lance aimed at him.

"Wait!" he screamed. "Hey, wait! You're not supposed to—" The yachi bounded past, stopped, spun around. The rider dropped his spear, drew his sword, and chopped downward. Somehow Charlie caught the blow on his shield, but it staggered him. In sick terror, he knew that the dust had been raised not to blur view of the defeat of the Brothers but to hide his own murder by their second. Afterward the trio would claim they had legitimately slain him. "Honor" demanded that they win.

Though how honorable, really, were Dzenko's wiles?

Again the sword smote from above. Charlie's blade met it, and was nearly torn from his grasp. Hasprot declaimed:

I chant of a champion's challenge anew.
Sir Hector will have quite a hand in the fight.
Calm and courageous, he couches his lance—

The Hoka must have guessed what was going on. Ablaze with indignation, he bounced into sight on his own yachi. "Defend y', blackguard!." He squeaked.

Charlie thought he saw contempt on the face of the hulking Beloghan as that rider turned to meet the little alien. But Hector's first blow nearly cast him from his saddle. Smiting, they disappeared into the dust. "Crimson the field is, as carnage grows common," reported Hasprot.

Charlie felt dizzy with relief. Yet he dared not stop. He groped his way ahead. The frightful noises of battle he had heard were silenced. Instead, as he neared his opponents, he caught sounds of—what?— yes, wheezing and panting.

Vaguely before him appeared the Three Brothers. They leaned on each other for support. "No, Moach," one said in a high-pitched, thready voice, "I can't whang my shield any longer, no more than you or Chekko can. I must have a rest."

"What's the matter with that grandson of yours?" the second demanded of the third. "He should have taken care of that . . . that upstart . . . by now . . . shouldn't he?"

In grim glee, Charlie entered their view. "He
didn't," he announced, and lifted his blade.

Unable to move their own weapons, the Brothers wailed, "Mercy! Mercy! We yield! Only get us
out of these confounded bake ovens—" One of them
fell backward in a great clatter and lay feebly waving his arms and legs like an overturned insect.

Charlie heard Hasprot:

Blow-struck and bleeding his body, the Prince
Waits what may well be the wound that
     will slay him.
Skyward goes soaring the sword of a Brother.
Down the edge drops—

But the dust did not settle. The minstrel saw
Charlie stand triumphant and, not missing a beat,
continued:

And disarms the Brothers.
Yare are the Three to yield to the youth,
Who graciously gives them their lives as a gift,
Though fully well able to flick them to flitches—

Across the arena, Charlie saw Hector stand above
a prostrate warrior who himself pleaded to be spared.

He had won! He was safe! In the glory of that,
Charlie knew he would, indeed, show pity on his
antagonists, not only let them go but forbear to tell
of their plot. After all, whispered a part of his mind,
his own role in this wouldn't bear the closest exami-
nation.

"Prince of the Prophecy," Dzenko shouted, "reveal
yourself!"

As Charlie bared his red head to a cooling breeze,
the crowd went wild.

❖   ❖   ❖

Belogh was under the sway of a baron who dwelled at the far end of Vletska, the large island on which this town stood. That powerful but cautious lord had hung back from making a commitment to the revolution. Dzenko sent new messengers to him. The word they bore was that the Prince had truly come; that already he had performed three of the Five Feats, and the rest were mere technicalities; that therefore everyone who loved freedom—and, it was added, wanted to be on the winning side—should immediately join the cause.

"I am certain he will," Dzenko told Charlie, "but he'll take a few days yet to make up his mind. In the meantime we must lodge here, before we go on to Lyovka." The island where the Riddling Priests lived was more strategically placed for fighters to rendezvous who came from all over the kingdom.

Belogh had few accommodations. Most of the travelers had to sleep outdoors or on shipboard. Charlie and his entourage would actually have preferred that to the lord mayor's drafty palace. But etiquette demanded they accept the proffered hospitality.

"Good show, good show," the elderly leader had congratulated the boy. "Yes, good show, Garamaz—er, I mean—whatever your name is—oh, yes, Prince. Ah . . . I told you I was all out of marriageable granddaughters. But I've since been reminded that a, ah, third cousin's child is just about your age, and I ought to mention her to you. Take my advice, though, and don't have anything to do with her. Temper like an ilnya's—eh, what?"

He broke off as a buxom female jerked at his arm and whispered in his ear.

"No, I am not talking out of turn!" said the lord

mayor crossly. "I believe in calling a spade a spade. No more than that. Give a man fair warning. I simply stated she has a temper like— Oh, very well." He allowed himself to be led away.

Charlie had been astounded that the subject was ever brought up. Didn't these Beloghans understand that humans and New Lemurians were different species? There was no possibility of such a couple having children. Perhaps they were anxious enough to make the alliance that they didn't mind too much.

Not that Charlie dreamed of going along with them. No doubt someday he would get married. But that would be to a proper girl, not a bald, misshapen female of a barbarian race!

Thinking about the matter later on, he grew ashamed of himself. He had no right to feel superior. He looked just as peculiar to the New Lemurians as they did to him. And as for culture, they knew less science and engineering, true. But only a short time ago, historically speaking, no country on Earth had been further along. And how much did the Talyinans know—arts, trades, crafts, traditions, the ways of nature—of which he was totally ignorant?

Really, it was incredible that these people were even friendly to him, let alone idolized him as their Prince. Few nations in the past of Earth would have been so broad-minded.

He found that being a legendary hero is a full-time job. Everybody wanted to tell him his troubles, enlist his aid in his pet projects, give him his advice, build himself up in hopes of winning his favor, or beg him to heal him of sickness by his surely magical touch. After two days of this, he felt he had to get out or explode.

Dzenko raised no objection. In fact, the baron

made a public speech explaining that the Prince must depart for a while from his worshipful followers, in order to plan the next move in his campaign, and that their cooperation in not disturbing him was essential. Charlie suspected Dzenko was glad to get rid of him; he knew his questions annoyed the Lord of Roshchak.

Thus Charlie came to be driving along the north coast of the island, accompanied only by Hector. That was an uninhabited stretch, treeless, begrown with stiff gray-green bushes, beset by a chill wind under a leaden overcast. He thought it desolate. The Hoka waxed eloquent about the bonnie heather o' the muirs.

This time they had a real wagon. Inspired by thirdhand accounts of human piston engines, some local genius had adapted the principle to yachi-drawn transportation. Four animals on either side of a long tongue leaped in a rhythmic succession which, with the help of a spring coupling, gave a fairly smooth ride. They were timed by a device cogged to the front axle, which snapped a whip behind the ears of each one in turn.

Charlie gazed across the sea rolling gunmetal on his left. "What I hate most," he said, "is the idea of war. Is Olaghi so bad that overthrowing him is worth hurting and killing people?"

"Freedom is aye dearly bought, lad."

"And what about the League law?" Charlie fretted. "I'm afraid I *am* violating the noninterference rule. Maybe Mr. Pomfrey will believe I had to do it to save my life. But maybe he'll decide I didn't make enough of an effort to— What's that?"

The wagon jolted and jerked as the yachis got out of step. Hector snatched the reins and halted them. Jumping to the ground, he hunched down to examine the whip-timing device.

"Aye," he nodded sagely, "'tis the distreebutor."

"The distributor?" Charlie asked, climbing down to join him.

"Aye. Dinna ye ken, lad, we Scots are a' engineers? Look here." A stubby yellow-furred finger pointed. "A nut on yon bolt has been replaced wi' anither a wee bit too large, which has noo worked its way doon the shank. Hm-m-m, I think the rate could hae been estimated, so we must aye break doon richt hereaboots. . . ."

He began to tinker. His work ended in less than a minute.

From the crest of a nearby hill where they had lain in wait, five large New Lemurians, armed and armored, came dashing. Hector went after the sword and shield he had along. The newcomers halted in a semicircle, a few meters from the wagon, and Charlie saw wound-up crossbows leveled at him.

His palms prickled. His stomach revolved. "Hold it, Hector," he said dully. "They've got the drop on us."

A tough scar-faced warrior called in a sarcastic tone, "Greeting, Prince. I have the honor to invite you aboard the flagship of his Majesty Olaghi, High King of Talyina."

"What?" croaked Charlie.

"His fleet lies out to sea," the officer explained. "We have a swift shallop to transport you thither, beached a short walk hence. You will accept, will you not?"

Charlie looked again at the crossbows, gulped, and nodded.

"No, Captain Stuart," said Athelstan Pomfrey, "I much regret the necessity, but I cannot let you or any of your spacemen leave this compound. Not unless and until you leave this system altogether, under appropriate escort."

"You've got to be joking," exploded Charlie's father, "and this is no damn time for it!"

"I am not," said the Plenipotentiary. "I am doing my duty." He tried to soften the atmosphere. "Since you have obtained permission from your owners to wait for the return of your son, you are entirely welcome to stay. I will endeavor to make the time pleasant."

"While he's disappeared—and we keep hearing about some kind of trouble brewing out there, maybe a civil war—*pleasant?*" Stuart struggled for self-control. "I never believed that message from Duke Whosis over on the next island. Running off like that just isn't Charlie's style. Something's rotten for sure. All I want is to take a few men and rayguns in an aircar and go fetch him back from wherever he is."

"Would you use violence if you could not recover him peacefully?"

"Of course I would! He's my son!"

"I deeply sympathize," Pomfrey said. "However, such actions would constitute interference and imperialism within the meaning of the act. The principle must always be that we venture beyond our treaty zones at our own risk, while remaining bound to respect the rights of natives." He paused. "You may use my subspace radio to appeal this ruling to headquarters, though I guarantee you it will be upheld. For safety's sake, I must restrict you and your men to the compound." He paused anew. "You realize, I trust, that I have the personnel and weapons at my disposal to enforce this."

Captain Stuart shook his head, dazedly. "You mean we're under arrest?" he whispered.

"If you insist on so regarding it," Pomfrey replied, "you are."

9
A Midsummer Night's Dream

Several hours' sail to the north was an islet, high and steep, its barren slopes populated only by seabirds. Behind it lay anchored the ships of Olaghi. Their presence was unlikely to be discovered; should a fishing vessel chance by, it could be captured. The flotilla was no larger than that which Dzenko had led to Belogh. The bulk of the king's far-flung navy must still be on its way to join him here.

His flagship was twice as big, complex, and formidable as any other vessel Charlie had seen on New Lemuria. Besides sails, it boasted a treadmill motor, which turned not paddle wheels but a propeller. Cannon muzzles bristled from double rows of ports. The main deck was broad and unencumbered, with the two masts set far forward and aft. Thus a wheel-house on the poop overlooked a wide flat surface where six curious objects rested. Though their wicker bodies were almost hidden by furled fabric, Charlie decided they must be lighter-than-air flying craft. He got that idea from a captive balloon bobbing astern at the end of a long Jacob's ladder, a sphere with a basket where a lookout kept watch.

As he climbed aboard, disguised in a hooded cloak, he encountered warriors. They mostly resembled Dzenko's force, scantily equipped commoners. Very few could have been volunteers, to judge from the way their officers cursed, struck, and kicked them for the least reason. The sailors fared still worse. Most of those wore merely loincloths, and Charlie saw marks of the lash on more than one back. He witnessed a mate club a pair with a belaying pin when they stopped work for a moment's wonder at sight of Hector.

"Are they really forced into service?" he asked the chief of his kidnappers.

"Yes, scum that they are," the other replied. "Would you believe, instead of being grateful for a chance to die for our beloved Olaghi, they'll often as not try to hide from his recruiters? Caught, they'll whine about their families going hungry without them to bring in food. Liars, every last wretch of them. I've personally ransacked the cottages of some and found stuff that could be sold to buy groceries for months. Good, warm clothing, well-made tools, dishes, furniture, things like that. My wife's going to rejoice."

"You mean the king's men rob his own people?"

"Watch your language," huffed the native. "Fines, that's what we collect, fines levied on a bunch of draft dodgers." He glowered. "Not that we'd have had to draft many, if your gang of traitors hadn't started this trouble. March along."

Hector bristled to see Charlie hustled sternward. The boy frantically signaled the Hoka to keep quiet. They were surrounded by sharpened steel.

A door in the poop led to a guarded entry room. Beyond, across a hall, another door gave on a cabin whose spaciousness, broad glass windows, and luxurious outfitting could only be regal. A female strummed a horpil and sang for the male who sat there otherwise alone. He made a rugged contrast. His big frame was clad simply, apart from golden necklace and bracelets. His face, while battlescarred and weather-beaten, looked fairly young. Charlie strove not to cringe beneath his hard stare. This must be Olaghi.

He jerked a thumb at the female. The speed with which she left the chamber showed how frightened she was of him. The officer saluted him and announced, "Your Majesty, we bring you the Earthling who claims to be the Prince of the Prophecy, and his, um, er, co-conspirator."

"So you've told me," Olaghi said in a deep, hoarse voice. On the way here, Charlie had seen his catcher use a miniaturized sun-battery-powered radio transceiver, and he noticed a similar unit on a table here. "Don't repeat yourself. Get back and see about the other rebel leaders."

The officer was obviously surprised that the king wished to be alone with two enemies, but saluted, and the door closed behind him and his men.

Charlie was even more astounded when Olaghi smiled and invited, "Sit down, you two. Let's talk."

"Sir?" Charlie whispered. He was quick to obey, because suddenly his knees wouldn't hold him up. Hector took a stance, arms folded, behind his chair.

"You have nothing to fear if you cooperate, that is. Of course, if you're stubborn—" Olaghi touched the knife at his waist. Yet he smiled on. "Nothing personal, understand."

"I— I—" Charlie's tongue felt drier than in the arena.

"Frankly," Olaghi drawled, "I'm more curious about this funny little attendant of yours than I am about you. I'll want details on what you've been doing, but I know the general pattern already." He drew breath. "You see, I'm not at all the kind of reactionary your Pomfrey thinks. No, I'm the most progressive ruler Talyina's had since the Founder. Look how I've been reforming our institutions— breaking down feudalism, building an up-to-date absolute monarchy. And I'm interested in modernizing material things, too. I've gotten scientific books from other planets, and my engineers are designing cannon, shrapnel, aerial fighter-bombers, motorships that can take our armies clear across the ocean for making conquests. Yes, I mean to go down in history as the Great Civilizer." He scowled. "It'd be easier if the League would sell us what we need. As is, I've only managed to get some radio sets like this one, which was smuggled out. I've put secret agents, radio-equipped, in the less trustworthy provinces. They keep me alerted on what's happening and carry out jobs for me. Dzenko counts on weeks, while couriers go back and forth to rally my loyal supporters. In fact, they're already bound my way. Tell me," he asked chattily, "what do we suggest we do with Dzenko? I favor bronzing him—alive, of course— to keep with my children's baby shoes."

Charlie shivered. While Olaghi was brilliant in his fashion, he remained a lord of the wild marches of Nyekh, whose career grew from fighting tribesmen as savage as himself, until he concentrated his power and seized the throne.

"But don't be afraid," he repeated. "I'm aware you were only Dzenko's tools, you two. You owe him nothing. Besides, I'd much rather have the goodwill of your League than irritate it by harming you . . . unnecessarily, that is." He waved at a carafe and some crystal goblets. "Would you care for a slug of shmiriz while we talk? Or I can send after fruit juice if you want."

Heartened, Charlie related the entire tale of what, had happened since he left the compound. Olaghi listened intently, often asking a shrewd question. In an hour, the king had a full grasp of the situation.

"A-a-ah," he rumbled at last. "As I thought. Dzenko's been restless for years. I'd have done him in a long time ago, if there hadn't always been trouble elsewhere. Now he's been quick to use the happenstance that you fit the Prophecy, or, rather, he made it fit you. He's a smart devil, no denying that. But he's overreached himself. Without you for a sign to them, his followers will melt away like dawn dew. Panic, you see, when their godling fails. I shouldn't need more strength than I've already got here, to destroy the few who try to fight.

"So all we need to do, Charles Stuart, is keep you aboard for a six-day or two. Afterward I'll personally convey you home; might as well collect whatever reward may be offered. And you, why, you'll be clear as far as your League law is concerned. How's that sound? Good, ha?"

Charlie nodded. He ought to be jubilant. He was out of danger, freed of a role he had never wanted; his parents' anxieties about him would soon be relieved; meanwhile, he could relax in better quarters than any he had yet enjoyed on this ill-starred trip.

Then why did he feel miserable? Why did he keep thinking of people like Mishka, Toreg, and the impressed soldiers and sailors around him?

Olaghi did not want his men reminded of the Prophecy, which they also cherished. He decided Charlie must be confined to a cabin near his own, a comfortable one to which attendants would bring meals. Just outside its door, a companionway led from the hall up to the poop deck. That was officer country. The prisoner could visit it if he kept his red hair well covered and was accompanied by a guard.

Hector, who amused Olaghi, at first got the freedom of the ship, "provided," the king warned, "you breathe no hint of your master's identity. I'd soon know if you did, and neither of you would like what came next. Remember, I don't *have* to keep you alive."

"I'll be the dourest Scot ye e'er did meet," snapped the Hoka, "commencing wi' ye."

Offended or perhaps ultra-cautious, Olaghi clapped down restrictions. Hector would sleep in the forecastle, and he and Charlie must never be together.

As he stood at a rail next morning and looked across the flight deck, Charlie saw his friend pass beneath in company with a petty officer, talking. He heard: "—nay, I canna tell ye what we're aboot, save that 'tis a matter o' state secrets on the soomit level—" The Hoka broke off for a moment to shout upward in English, "Courage, lad! Stout hearts and true remain to save ye!"

Charlie didn't venture to reply. Undramatic practical politics wouldn't suit Hector MacGregor's taste. But the fact was, no matter how ruthless, Olaghi would lean backward *not* to harm them. He had too much to gain by returning such a distressed traveler—including a chance at more of the technology which fascinated him.

Certainly the royal engineers had accomplished marvels on the basis of what scant information they had been able to get about advanced machinery. Their most ambitious, if not quite their most successful, work thus far was the cannon. Charlie had observed the same devices aboard a few of Dzenko's craft, but in negligible numbers. Olaghi's flagship carried a full battery of them.

The League forbade the sale of explosives to warlike societies, and the Talyinan islands had no sulfur deposits for the manufacture of gunpowder, should anyone learn the formula. Hence Olaghi, early in his reign, had commissioned, the development of artillery fired by compressed air. The missiles were necessarily light—thin-walled globes full of oil ignited by a fuse or glass balls which broke on impact into showers of "shrapnel." Considering their inaccuracy and feebleness, their medieval types of counterparts remained more effective. But Olaghi hoped for gradual improvement. Charlie had watched crews at practice, ten males at once on a long lever, pumping up a gun while they sang:

> What'll we do with a leaky air tank?
> What'll we do with a leaky air tank?
> What'll we do with a leaky air tank,
> When the order's for a broadside?
> Way, hay, the gauge is rising—

Both lyrics and melody suggested that somebody had once heard a visiting human translate an old Earth sea chant.

No matter how ludicrous these efforts, they showed New Lemurians to possess intelligence. What might these people accomplish if they were free to work for peaceful progress rather than a belligerent tyrant?

Moonlight faded in the cabin windows as Charlie tossed and drifted into sleep. He was slow to rouse when a soft, high-pitched voice called him. Struggling through layers of dreaming he wondered if he hadn't begun a fresh nightmare. Moonbeams struck level through shadow to pick out a figure, cloaked and cowled, beside his bunk. The garment was of a kind worn by females; there were a few aboard to serve and entertain Olaghi and his higher-ups. But this wench was so tall—

"Hist, laddie," she whispered. "Busk yoursel' and come!"

She? No. . . . The cloak dropped off to reveal Hector on the shoulders of his petty officer acquaintance. The Hoka's left hand gripped his steed by the throat; his right hand held a knife under the Talyinan's jaw.

"What?" Charlie mumbled in his daze.

"Surely ye recall Flora Macdonald, laddie," said Hector, "the fair daughter o' Clan Ranald in the Hebrides, wha aided ye to evade the English guards on Benbecula whaur ye'd ta'en refuge after Culloden. What mon o' true heart can e'er fail tae hauld sacred the memory o' Flora, wha saved her Bonnie Prince Charlie?"

"Huh?"

"O' coorse, we've nae such aboord here, and I maun eemprovise," said Hector regretfully. "I snaffled a mantle frae ane o' the lassies and later tauld this loon tae meet me in a dark place whaur he wad hear what was to his advantage. I'd sounded him oot afore and knew him for greedy. So I swarmed up his coat,

seized his dirk, and stifled his yawp, the while I tauld
him the steel wad dirl in his gullet did he gie trouble.
Covered o'er, we walked past the sentries, who're
sleepy at this hour and anyhoo could scarcely see
mair in the gloom than a female on some errand.
They've nobbut contempt for females and didna think
tae question her, yon barbarians, wha ken naught o'
Flora Macdonald."

His fist smote the base of the Talyinan's skull. The
officer crumpled, not seriously hurt—his breath
rattled where he lay—but switched off for a goodly
time. Hector hopped clear, stuck the confiscated
knife in his belt, and urged, "Noo, Prince, quick, ere
they grow suspeecious."

Charlie kicked off his blanket. Bewilderment
rocked his mind. Chill sidled around his bare legs.
Against it, he wore a nightshirt Olaghi had given him.

"Ah, guid," Hector approved, "ye're clad as a
Prince should be when escaping, namely, like Flora's
maidsairvant, Betsy Burke. But let's awa'!" He swept
the other up across one shoulder.

Charlie writhed, to no avail. Hector held him
easily while opening the door and bounded on into
the hall. No guard stood outside; a watch in the entry
and one on the poop deck were deemed sufficient.

Meteoric, the Hoka traversed the companionway.
Charlie glimpsed wheelhouse, waters a-sheen beneath
a sinking moon, stars still bright though the east was
paling. Light glimmered off the helmet and pike of
an armed lookout. That male never had a chance.
Before he knew anybody had arrived, Hector leaped,
with a karate kick to the belly. Air whoofed from the
Talyinan. He folded over. The Hoka continued on
course.

"But—but wait—" Charlie stammered. Wholly
awake at last, he realized in horror that he was being

rescued. The ship dwindled below him as Hector shot up the rope rungs between the parallel cables which anchored the observation balloon.

The person in its basket saw what was making it bob. He bellowed an alarm. Charlie heard shouts respond from below.

A warrior on balloon duty saved weight by leaving behind armor and weapons which could be of no use, or so it had been supposed until Hector arrived. "Yo-heave-ho?" chortled the Hoka, and threw the Talyinan overside.

"Stop!" Charlie wailed. "You don't understand—"

He was too late. Hector had already cast loose the tethers. With a jerk and a sway, the balloon floated northward.

"Harroo!" exulted the Hoka. "We're on our wa', lad. Fair stands the wind for Belogh."

10
Wind, Sand,
and Stars

"You fool!" Charlie yelled. "What've you done?"

In the pale light, he saw the Hoka's puzzlement. "Wha hae I done?" Hector replied. "Why, wha but spring ye frae the grip o' your grim and treacherous enemy, tae bring ye again amang them wha love ye and wad win for ye' your richtful crown?"

"But they can't! I mean, I, I— It isn't my crown, none of this is any of our business, here we were finally safe and, and guaranteed a ride back where we belong, and you had to come spoil it—b-b-because it didn't fit that dream world of yours—you interfering idiot!"

"Is it really so, laddie?" whispered the Hoka.

Charlie turned his back on him.

Through mumble of wind and creak of rigging, he heard a thin, heartbroken voice choke forth: "Aweel, then, syne I hae been o' such dissairvice to my Prince, best I lay me doon and dee. God send ye better followers, but He canna find any wha'll care more for ye than did your puir auld thickheaded Hector MacGregor."

Charlie spun around, barely in time to see his companion leap out of the basket.

"Stop!" he screamed, but he was too late. "Hector. . . . Bertram . . . Hector, I never meant—I— oh, if only—Hector, I'd never say anything against you, I'd be anything you wanted—"

At which point he saw a hand clasp the wicker-work, and another, and he noticed how the carrier was tilted in that direction. The Hoka chinned himself till he could climb inboard. Full of good cheer, he said, "I thocht ye might change your mind, laddie—that 'twas nobbut weariness wha spake, and never Bonnie Charlie. So I clung to a sandbag hanging there for ballast, till ye came back to your senses." He laid a finger beside his black nose and winked. "Ah, rough I be, and nane too bricht, but we Scots are by defineetion unco canny."

Charlie, still in a state of shock, gave the kilted figure a very sharp look. No matter how thoroughly he acted out a part, the Hoka never seemed to let go of a certain basic shrewdness.

A few minutes later they examined their surroundings, by the light of moon, stars, and oncoming dawn. Secured at the middle of the basket was a sheet-iron stove, vented to the mouth of the bag so that the heat of a fire would expand the air inside and give lift. A supply of charcoal seemed alarmingly low. Charlie shoveled in more and peered across the glimmering waters. The desert isle lay behind him, but as yet he could not make out Vletska, the land on which Belogh stood. The wind wasn't moving at all fast. If they ran out of fuel far from shore, he and Hector might well drown.

Thus he had trouble hiding his relief from his companion soon after sunrise. Out of the north were bound six flying objects, crimson cigar shapes. They had to be Olaghi's blimps, in pursuit. Wonderful! They'd overhaul this motorless balloon, bring the prisoners back—And Charlie realized the king would doubtless order the Hoka's execution.

He *had* to prevent that. No matter the early-morning chill, sweat prickled him. How could he threaten or bribe or wheedle Olaghi into granting a pardon? No believable method came to mind. It didn't help his thinking that he grew ever more hungry and thirsty.

At last he forced himself to raise the subject. "And don't just say you'll go to your death with a stiff upper lip," he finished.

"Never," Hector agreed. "I'm nae bluidy Englishman. A firm lower jaw is for me."

"I don't want you dead, not any old way!" Charlie saw how to put it. "If I should be recaptured, I'd need you alive to help me get free again."

"Aye, there's that, and I dinna mind confessing the preenciple gies me a wee sense of relief." Hector pondered. "If we can make shore or swimming distance of it, we can descend till I can go doon by a rope. They'll na bother wi' me, when ye're the true prize." He pointed to a smudge on the southern horizon. "Yonder's Vletska. Mony a weary mile to gang."

Through a crude telescope, Charlie studied the nearest of his pursuers. Beneath a long hot-air container, a wicker gondola accommodated nine males.

Four of them rode bicyclelike devices which turned propellers; two adjusted control surfaces for direction; three stood by what must be weapons of some sort.

Only slowly were those awkward, underpowered machines closing the gap. From their bearing, Charlie deduced that a shift in airflow had forced them to maneuver crosswind, which was difficult for them. That gave him an idea. He knew wind direction often varies with altitude. Vletska Island was a big target, and he needn't care where he hit it.

Experimenting, he found he could sink by opening a valve in the fabric and dampening the fire. To rise, he could stoke up, or better, in view of the fuel shortage, he could discard sandbags. Gleeful, he caught a differently aimed breeze and watched the blimps fall behind. They fought their way to favorable conditions and once more approached him. But that took time, during which the hills of Vletska grew clearer to the sight.

He let the Olaghists draw so nigh that he heard warriors swear when he repeated his evasion. With their greater volume, the blimps could not match the speed of the balloon where it came to vertical movement.

But winds were dying down as the sun climbed and the warmth of day equalized temperatures. Charlie recalled the flat calms frequent around noon. His heart sank. His stomach, less loyal, growled.

A shout startled him. "Look, laddie, look! Deleeverance!"

Charlie's gaze swept past the Hoka's forefinger. Toylike at its distance, a ship which was a smaller version of the king's was bound from the island. Behind followed half a dozen more conventional craft. And off that flight deck rose one cigar shape after the next.

Hector danced for joy. Rigging complained and the basket wobbled dangerously. "'Tis the fleet o' the Vletska laird!" he caroled. "What else could it be? They've gane o'er to the side o' truth and reason . . . and noo, having spied what they surely ken is the royal air force, they're headed oot tae see what's afoot. . . . Och, lad, we're safe!"

"Not yet." Charlie moistened his lips. The baron's fliers numbered three; Olaghi's six were a lot closer.

In the near-breathless hush that had fallen, the blimps moved more readily than before. The balloon could dodge them only by bobbing up and down like an elevator. Charlie could not bring himself to protest when Hector dumped still-burning contents of the stove overboard, then refilled it soon afterward. They had expended their ballast. And it was a sinister sight, a gondola full of warriors gliding within meters, warriors who shook their fists and howled curses.

The time was actually about half an hour, but felt like a piece of eternity, while the balloonists labored to stay free. It ended abruptly. The baronial blimps arrived, and Charlie and Hector found themselves in the middle of a dogfight.

Furiously, crewmen pedaled and backpedaled, hauled on ropes which led to control surfaces, manned their armaments. Even in a calm, their vehicles were so clumsy that the difference in numbers between the two sides didn't much matter. A pair of opponents might lumber around for minutes to get within range of each other, and then the least lazy breeze pushed them apart again.

Arrows and crossbow quarrels flew between them. But the minor leaks these made in gas bags were not too dangerous, when amply fueled stoves supplied abundant heat to keep the fabric inflated. Telescoping lances and shears didn't work, in spite of valiant efforts, nor did water pumps, intended to douse an enemy's fire. An equal failure was every attempt to ram or to lay alongside, grapple fast, and board.

The typical encounter consisted of two blimps gradually working inward, passing near at last while crews struggled to inflict damage and captains exchanged abuse through megaphones, before they drifted elsewhere. The vessels would then try to come about for a fresh attempt. This went more and more slowly; the pedalers were growing exhausted.

Charlie stared as if hypnotized—until he became aware that the combat was now above him. Or rather, he saw with a gasp, he was below it. His supply of charcoal was gone. As the balloon cooled, contracted, and made shuddering noises, it sank.

"What can we do?" he cried.

"Swim," said Hector doughtily. He prepared a bundle of kilt, stockings, and shoes, to tie on his head. "Let me hae your sark, Hieness," he requested. "They'll be glad when I donate it to the Edinburgh Museum."

They might have gained time by jettisoning the stove. But it was still too hot to touch. When the basket struck, a cloud of steam hissed up. The bag followed, spread across a wide area. The passengers had to dive and go for some distance below the surface not to be dragged along as the whole apparatus sank.

The sea was cool. It tasted less salty than a terrestrial ocean. Sunlight skipped across waves. Charlie and Hector trod water while the ship bore down on them.

A glance aloft showed the battle finished. Olaghi's

aeronauts knew they had no chance to complete their mission and returned while they were able. The Vletskans trailed them at a cautious distance, to see where the foe had come from.

Their carrier lowered a lifeboat, which hauled in the escapers. Naked, chilled, starved, worn out, Charlie was just barely able to climb a ladder let down the ship's side. Warriors crowded the flight deck. Led by Mishka, they cheered him till his head rang.

Dzenko was also on hand. His robes billowed with his haste to greet the arrivals. "Congratulations, Charles," he said, low-voiced beneath the shouts. "We must confer at once. I managed to keep your disappearance quiet after we found your abandoned wagon—yes, even after we saw those aircraft from afar and I guessed what the case must be—but now let's plan how to get maximum propaganda value out of the episode. This can double your prestige, you know."

"Uh-huh," said Charlie, and fainted.

The last thing he saw before the darkness took him was Dzenko's face. It bore an expression of scorn.

11
The Social Contract

From his spies, as well as what had lately happened, Olaghi had to know that the augmented revolutionaries outnumbered his support. Blimpmen reported to Dzenko and his council that the king's flotilla had been quick to hoist sail and beat northeastward. Given such a head start, it couldn't be run down, and nobody tried.

"But won't he collect a huge force and come back?" Charlie worried.

"He will gather what he can," Dzenko replied. coolly. "I look for at least as much to rally to us at Lyovka."

They were bound there. Earthling and baron stood on the quarterdeck below the flagship's poop. It was beautiful weather. Whitecaps marched before a fresh breeze which sang in tackle, filled out sails, and drove the fleet swiftly in the direction of sunrise. Everywhere Charlie looked, he saw vessels. Warcraft were far fewer than tubby merchantmen or humble fishing smacks. Truly the common people of Talyina seemed eager to follow the Prince.

Recovered from his weakness of day before yesterday, Charlie should have rejoiced. But several things spoiled the time for him. Minor among them was the racket from the bows, where Hector was playing his pipes. They had been recovered with everything else in the wagon, which the kidnappers hadn't stopped to loot. Talyinans quickly acquired a taste for Highland music. A large group of off-duty enthusiasts crowded around the Hoka.

Worse matters plagued Charlie. He was back in the dangerous role of folk hero. The more he thought about a civil war, the more he hated the prospect, because of the suffering it must cause. And suppose his side did win, which looked nowhere near as certain as Dzenko claimed—suppose that, what afterward? He couldn't settle down to reign over this crazy kingdom! Yet could he in good conscience walk out on it? What chaos might not follow?

He cleared his throat. "Uh, Dzenko," he said. "Lyovka. Isn't that where the . . . the Riddling Priests live?"

"Yes. Don't fret about them."

"But I'm scheduled to— Well, how have you rigged things there?"

"I haven't. Remember, I have only a few men who are both cunning and trusty. And we must act fast. They could make detailed preparations for us in the first two instances. But every other place was too far off. Better to use them to spread the word about you as widely as possible, persuade the chieftains and rouse the rabble."

Charlie gulped. "So what about those Priests?"

"Don't fret," Dzenko repeated. "Actually, they're like the Brothers of Belogh: meant something once, but not anymore. The riddles were part of the ceremony when New Lemurian sacrifices were made to the god—mm, what's his name? —Klashk, I think. Nothing like that has happened for centuries. True, the cult still exists, in a fashion. But nobody seeks its temples, unless a scattering of beggars and grannies. The Three Priests would have to find honest work, or starve, did they not receive a pittance from public funds, inasmuch as this is reckoned a branch of the Lyovkan state church."

"Oh," said Charlie, somehow less relieved than might have been expected. "Then all I have to do is visit them and go through the motions."

Dzenko frowned. "No. You will stay well clear of them."

"What? Why?"

"Because you could fail their test. The riddles are secret. A man of mine sought to bribe the Priests to reveal them, but the pious witlings refused. Quite indignant, they were." Dzenko gave Charlie a meaningful glance. "If you attempt it, they might well fire up the old furnace."

"How do we handle the matter?"

Dzenko shrugged. "It's of petty consequence. See you, I judge I have crossed a threshold. We needed the inspiration of the Prince in the beginning. But the way recruits are now flocking to our standard, the sheer growth of our power will by itself attract more. Success breeds success. The wish to overthrow Olaghi, the hope of a share in plunder or other advancement, the simple stampede to join any popular cause—motivations such as these will suffice."

"Still, we can't ignore the original promise, can

we?" In a sudden wild hope: "Or can we? Could you smuggle me straight back to the compound?"

Dzenko shook his head. "No. That would be a disaster, as our enemies knew when they seized you. You must remain in our vanguard till victory. But as for the Riddling Priests, set your mind at ease. You are not required to seek them out at any particular moment. Upon arrival we'll explain that the time is not ripe for it. In due course we'll announce that it has taken place and naturally you triumphed. Given general tumult, nobody will pause to question our communiqué."

"The Priests will!"

"Belike. And perhaps a few others. Have no fears, Charles. My men will scout most carefully beforehand. They will know exactly what throats to slit, and when and where, and what 'explanation' we should offer for the disappearances—"

"No!" yelled Charlie, aghast.

Dzenko rolled a sardonic green eye in his direction. "Ah, yes. I had forgotten what odd prejudices you humans have."

Charlie smote his fist on the rail. "I won't let you I, I—if those murders happen, I'll . . . tell everybody the truth." He glared at the New Lemurian. Between his anger and the fact that they both stood in plain view of scores of warriors who adored him, he felt no fear, though he trembled with emotion.

"Well, well," said Dzenko soothingly. "Be calm. If you insist, I'll work something else out. Preventive detention, for example, until we've firm control of the kingdom. It'll not be as easy as assassination and for any problem, I prefer the most elegant solution. But an alternative can no doubt be arranged."

Fiery-faced, Charlie plowed ahead:

"What you wanted to do, that's, well, typical of

what's wrong in this country. There's no law except strength which offers little to the powerless. If a baron treats his commoners well, that's just because he happens to be halfway decent, or he knows that's how he can get more work and taxes out of them. They have no protection against the next baron being a monster—or the next king, like Olaghi."

Dzenko's whiskers bristled. "Full well do I know what Pomfrey and those liberals wish to happen in Talyina," he clipped. "Have you never thought, you infant, a . . . republic, do they call it? . . . a republic would deprive us nobles of our own rights? We have well earned them: aforetime when our ancestors took the lead against sea rovers and savages; in this day, when we keep the peace in unruly provinces, and manage estates large enough to be properly productive, and try cases, and conduct olden usage and ceremony which hold society together, and support learning and religion, and deal with foreigners—oh, everything needful to maintain what order and progress the realm enjoys. It's damnably hard work, I tell you. You have no idea how the other half lives."

"Well, maybe your class was necessary at first," Charlie argued. "But Talyina isn't a wild frontier any longer. It hasn't got any further use for warlords, including the biggest one who calls himself the king. You're overdue for something better."

Seeing the thunderclouds gather on Dzenko's brow, he added hastily, "Look, I'm not being hostile to you. I mean, of course we won't throw you nobles off your lands, or strip you of your titles, or any such thing. That'd be way too long a step. And actually, your class can, well, it can still supply a lot of leaders. It's just that we're ready for the common people to have a chance at leadership, too, and freedom in their private lives, and a better break all around."

"What do you mean, 'we,' Earthman?" Dzenko growled, clasping the hilt of his sword.

Charlie braced himself. "What's the point of this whole project if it doesn't lead to a real improvement?" he demanded. "Otherwise we'd only trade one despot for another. Oh, sure, I—you—whoever it was, he'd prob'ly be a, uh, benevolent despot. He'd do some worthwhile things. But what about those after him? And the people would still be tied down. Listen, I am the Prince of the Prophecy, and if we win, I'll want to see a lot of reforms made!"

For an instant, fear tinged him. Dzenko seemed angry enough to attack. But piece by piece, the baron mastered himself. His countenance turned into a smiling mask.

"Now, now, we can hardly afford squabbles among our ranks," he said. "You may in your youth be overhasty. Yet I'll not deny, I could be overslow. See you, from my experience of statecraft, I can foretell endless practical difficulties in carrying out what you propose. Nonetheless, you have at your beck knowledge of a longer history than Talyina's. And if naught else, certain changes might bring the League to loosen restrictions on what off-world traders may sell us." He paused. "You will agree, responsible leaders cannot enact far-reaching measures without long and prayerful consideration. Let us retire to mull over what has been said. Later we will hold many conferences, you and I and what wise advisers we can find. Does that sound reasonable?"

"Y-yes," Charlie whispered.

Dzenko bowed and departed. Charlie stayed.

He felt briefly dizzy, as if he were about to faint again, and then exhausted, wrung out. Had he really stood up to that Machiavellian veteran? It didn't seem like anything which shy Charles Edward Stuart would ever dream of doing. . . . Well, yes, he would dream of it. But here he had done it. And he'd even made his point—won as good a compromise as could be hoped for at this stage—incredible!

Charlie breathed the salt air. Strength flowed back into his heart.

A heavy tread, and a long shadow across him, brought his attention back from the sea. Mishka had come to his side. As head of guards to the chief noble in the Prince's retinue, he rated access to the quarterdeck.

"Why, hello," said Charlie.

"Greeting. I saw you by yourself and wondered if you'd like some company." Diffidence sounded peculiar in a rumbling basso, out of so towering a body. Mishka wore nothing today except a loincloth; beneath his golden skin, the muscles rippled.

"I would!"

"You seemed to be having quite an argument with my lord of Roshchak." Charlie nodded, and Mishka continued: "Watch out for him, Prince. Most nobles can't think. They never felt any need to learn how. Fighting, feasting, hunting, ordering the lowborn around, that's nigh all they know. During my wander-foot days, I watched many a one drowse off where he sat to try a lawsuit or preside over a folkmoot. Often as not, 'tis a hireling clerk who runs the real business of the province, and commoners live out their lives in their villages, seldom seeing more than the tax collector. Dzenko's different."

Charlie nodded thoughtfully. He had a similar impression. In that respect, he had overstated his case. Doubtless more aristocrats could be accused of laxity than tyranny. That didn't have to be an altogether bad thing. On the contrary, it caused people to get experience in self-government. The fact remained, though, the people were always too limited in what decisions they could make. A seed of democracy appeared to exist in Talyina, but it would never flower without roots.

"You're too solemn for a youth, Charlie," Mishka said.

"Well, I'm supposed to be the Prince." He forced a smile.

"Supposed to be? You are." In spite of his words, the giant spoke warmly, even familiarly. Like most of his kind, he accepted the supernatural as part of daily life. Charlie had a destiny, yes, but that didn't mean the two of them couldn't be friends.

"And you need more ease than has of late been granted you," Mishka went on. "D'you happen to remember, I'm from Lyovka myself? I plan to go visit my kin as soon as may be after we've landed. Would you care to come along? We can sneak off, the two of us. No fear of abduction this time. Nor fear of a great fuss being made over you; I'll see to that. Naught but a pleasant day's outing, and home cooking, and a chance to meet a few very ordinary folk."

"Thanks," Charlie said. "I'd enjoy it a lot."

Mad though his mission was, he could no longer feel sincerely regretful that he had been dragooned back into it.

12
The Return of
the Native

Glats, principal town on Lyovka, was the largest
Charlie had seen thus far. It enjoyed a spectacular
setting on a great semicircular bay, whose waters
could shelter hundreds of ships at once. The land
rose steeply behind, first the famous Seven Hills of
Glats—among them the one on which most temples
were located—and then higher and higher until the
horizon was walled off by low green mountains, and
distantly beyond them snow peaks seemed to float
in heaven.

Word had run ahead of him in a speedy sloop.
The news, not only of his latest Feat, but of his
capture and escape, confirmed citizens' belief that
he was their true Prince. He suspected certain

leaders privately doubted it but were willing to pretend. After he had landed on a jam-packed wharf and ridden in a parade walled by cheering throngs, he was received in the palace with overwhelming pomp and circumstance.

It got on his nerves. Besides his dislike for living a lie, his single steady companion was Hector, and he grew lonesome. Worse, he grew bored. Flattery and kowtowing were no substitute for fellowship. Every waking moment he must be on view, watch his behavior, wear clothes which, however gorgeous, were hot, heavy, and hampering. Every meal was a state occasion. He had to meet a seeming infinity of people and either remember their names or fake it. Still more than in Belogh, he must listen politely to hours-long pitches for persons and causes of no interest to him. Twice the local nobles escorted him off the grounds. The first time was to review troops and give a speech. The second time was to dedicate a new aqueduct and give a speech.

He might have been absorbed by the confidential councils of Dzenko and other Talyinan magnates who had come here. But the baron always gave some reason why Charlie hadn't been notified of the most recent such meeting. He considered insisting on his right to attend, then decided not to. If they really didn't want him present, they'd put on a dull charade and hold their important conferences elsewhere in secrecy.

At least the harbor was filling up at an encouraging rate. Every day vessels arrived, until no berths remained and ships anchored in the bay. That brought good business for ferrymen and, ashore, for innkeepers. Hector went out nightly to roister in streets turbulent with warriors, fishers, farmers, woodcutters, sailors, hunters, traders, artisans, tinkers, laborers

come to fight for the Prince. The next morning
Charlie would listen wistfully to the Hoka's account
of the fun he had had.

Thus, after a week, his heart jumped when Mishka
got him aside and they plotted their excursion.

Charlie announced that he wished to spend a day
or two alone in his rooms, to meditate. Nobody
objected; Dzenko seemed awed. As the head of the
Prince's guards Mishka had chosen males whom he
knew he could trust, to stand watch in the hours
before dawn. Hector must stay behind; he was too
conspicuous, and besides, somebody had to make
sure no one snooped. But wrapped in a cloak and
cowl, trailing along like a servant behind Mishka's
hugeness, Charlie left the area unnoticed. In an
isolated starlit alley waited two yachis.

By sunrise they were far into the countryside. A
thinly trafficked dirt road followed a scenic coast.
When the travelers stopped for breakfast, in an
enormous dewy quietness, the plain bread and cheese
seemed like the best food Charlie had ever eaten.

After three hours' journey, he came to Mishka's
home. This was his first look at a rural community,
such as the immense majority of Talyinans spent their
lives in. He was astonished at the contrast with the
towns. A small population could and did cope with
problems, like cleanliness, which were too much
when thousands of people crowded together under
primitive conditions.

This place reminded him of ancient Japanese
pictures. Perhaps twenty houses and buildings like
sheds or a smithy reached back from a pier where
nets on poles dried in the sun. Roofs curved high
above low wooden walls, their beam ends delicately
carved. At every corner hung a pot for catching
rainwater; the colorful fired clay made Charlie think

of Christmas trees. Through open doors and broad unglazed windows whose shutters had been thrown back, he glimpsed interiors which were sparsely furnished but airy, sunny, and immaculate. The whole village had a scrubbed appearance; the dock had no smell of fish, only tar. Some wives were sweeping the streets outside their dwellings. Others were spinning, weaving, sewing, cooking, or preserving. Each was done with a care that betokened love and created beauty. Most carried babies on their backs. Infants who could walk were in the charge of children just a little bigger than themselves.

The rest of the youngsters were hard at work, according to age and ability. Charlie spied a number of them out herding fowl or animals on a common pasture or hoeing in grainfields behind the settlement. Those fields were terraced; they rose gradually up the hillsides toward the forested mountains, intensely green, a lovely sight; but Charlie winced to think how much patient, backbreaking toil had gone into them, and still did.

Cries of excitement lifted when the riders bounded into sight, and of welcome when Mishka was recognized. Yet nobody ran to crowd around, as townsfolk did. Charlie asked why.

"It is the custom," said Mishka. "All know that first my kindred and I wish to be alone with our joy, before we share it."

He drew rein and sprang off. Two males waited outside a house. They expected this visit since Mishka had sent word in advance. So they wore their best robes, faded, darned, freshly washed. One was powerful, middle-aged, his features scored and darkened and his crest bleached by a lifetime of weathers. The other was big too, but full of years, bald, toothless, and blind. Besides the usual knife he bore a sword.

Mishka took his hands first, and bowed deeply "Foremost among my honored," the guardsman said, "your grandson asks for your blessing."

Gnarled fingers felt across his arms, shoulders, face, and came to rest cradling his cheeks. "This is indeed you," the old male whispered. "And whole and hale; I feel strength shine from you. Whatever god has been your friend, be he thanked. As for my blessing, that have you always borne."

He released Mishka, who turned to the other, likewise clasped hands and bowed, and said, "Father, your son has come home and asks for your blessing."

Wordless, but his lips not altogether steady, his parent touched him on breast, mouth, and brow. Then they hugged each other.

Charlie had dismounted and thrown back his cowl. His red hair blazed in the sun. Mishka bowed next to him. "Prince," said the Talyinan, "behold my grandfather, Vorka, and my father, Ruzan." To them: "Sires, behold the Prince of the Prophecy and my dear comrade, Charles Edward Stuart."

Ruzan went on his knees, palms together, but Vorka drew his sword hissing from the sheath and brought its deadly brightness aloft in a soldier's salute.

"I—I'm glad to meet you," Charlie fumbled. Mishka had told him to expect ceremoniousness but to be at ease because no one awaited similar actions from a foreign guest. Nonetheless, this dignity made the Earthling feel dwindled and awkward.

Ruzan rose. "We thank you for the honor you bring us," he said.

"And for our freedom!" Vorka's tone rang. Sightless, he scabbarded his blade in a single snap.

Mishka went inside. Charlie started to follow. "I pray you, Prince," Ruzan said, "We give him a short while to greet his mother. It is the custom."

"Oh . . . yes." The human shifted from foot to
foot. "Uh, he's told me a lot about you, sir. You're
a fisherman, you and your younger sons?"

"No more them," Ruzan said quietly. "Kyraz
drowned last year when a storm capsized our boat."
Now Charlie recalled Mishka's stoical mention of that
and flushed. "Arko has gone to Glats to enlist under
your banner, Prince. I would too, but someone must
troll our living from the sea."

Charlie tried to express sympathy. Vorka gripped
Ruzan's shoulder and said, "A proud blood flows in
my son, Prince. He has not chosen the easiest way."

"Your blood," Ruzan said low. To Charlie he
explained: "My father was the guardian of our village
aforetime. That was when the succession to the barony
of Lyovka fell into dispute, and for years fighting went
up and down this island. There were no patrols, and
folk grown desperate after their steadings had been
looted would often join the bandits that began to
swarm. The village then chose Vorka, who had served
in the troops and knew swordplay, to guard it. No
more than a single such man could the village support. But throughout the evil years he watched, and
fought, and slew, himself more than once wounded,
seldom given a full night's rest, and the village lived,
unplundered, unburned, its sons safe from death and
its daughters from shame, until peace came back upon
the land."

Charlie had heard the tale before. He would
sooner have cut his tongue out than interrupt Ruzan's
recital of it.

Presently Mishka emerged, to bid them enter. His
mother, his married sister, and the children of the
latter knelt on the reed mats in homage to their
Prince. His brother-in-law had joined the fighting
force.

Seated on low stools, Charlie and the family partook of tea. Mishka told the boy it was customary to refrain from eating at the reunion of kinfolk until ancestral rites had been performed at the temple.

Villagers hailed the party in soft voices as it proceeded to the halidom. This was little more than a roof over a shrine, inside a wooden fence where many-colored flowery vines climbed. The shrine held an altar, a granite block. On top of this was a blackened bowl-shaped hole. Its sides were chiseled with symbols of sun, moon, stars, sea, land, wind, and life. Otherwise the area was raked white gravel, carefully spaced and tended shrubs, and knee-high stone slabs which stood well apart, a different sign carved into every one.

The priest waited in sky-blue robes. He was also the community's master carpenter. His workscarred right hand held a blossom with great, flaring petals, his left a smoldering stick whose smoke perfumed the salty air. The visitors bowed to him, and he to them.

Mishka whispered in Charlie's ear, "A family keeps its own stone—" Then they were at his.

Again they bowed. Charlie found himself doing it. Vorka spoke: "Ancestors and beloved, you who are departed, rejoice with us this day, that a son of the house has come home. And beside him goes the Prince of the Prophecy, who shall deliver us from wrong and harm. Oh, but he builds on the work of your lives, which you left for us when you went down in darkness. Return now! May the Flower Flame call you back; may your spirits share our gladness."

Mishka went to the priest and received the bloom. He laid it in the altar bowl. With the incense stick he set it alight. A clear brilliance consumed it, and meanwhile the family knelt and said their prayers. Charlie knelt, too.

Afterward, shyly, the priest said, "Prince, my abode is but a few steps hence. If you could spare some pulsebeats, you may be interested—"

What he showed Charlie was a collection of books, preserved in fragrant wooden boxes. Their bindings were ivory, intricately carved. Parchment sheets bore illuminated texts. To create such a thing must have taken man-years, somehow stolen from toil for survival in the course of generations.

"There is much wisdom stored here," said the priest. "Very much wisdom for a small village like ours. Counsels from the gods; deeds of our forebears; poetry; music; and, yes, the workaday truths by which men endure, seasons, tides, the ways of water and of soil, what simples may help in what sicknesses— Well, my Prince knows. Now I will begin a new page for the latest of our chronicles, to tell how you came and knelt before Mishka's ancestors and how you guested at this house and held these books."

"Yes. . . ." Charlie felt utterly inadequate. An idea occurred to him. Though he wore plain Talyinan traveling clothes, he had at his belt a purse of money. From this he drew a fistful of gold and silver, a fortune by commoner standards. "Will you, uh, will you accept a donation?"

"I thank you, Lord, no." Gently, the priest closed Charlie's fingers back over the precious metal. "It is for our honor that we give what little we may, to the Prince who gives us our freedom."

"True," rumbled Ruzan. "Come, we must go make ready." To the priest, "We begin when the sun stands at noon."

"I wait in happiness," replied he.

The way back from here led within sight of the

beach. There lay an overturned hull on which several males used tools. Seeing Mishka, whose bulk hid Charlie from them, they waved and shouted.

"Why, yonder's Dolgo," the warrior said. "And Avan and—" He moved to go join his former shipmates.

His father stopped him. "No, son. You'll meet them at the feast. Disturb them not before then."

"Right, sire." Mishka rejoined his relatives.

"Why shouldn't he?" Charlie asked.

"It would delay them in their work," Ruzan answered. "You see what a big boat that is. We can ill do without it, for though every crew markets its own catch, it gives a tithe of what it gets to our treasury, for the care of the poor and to keep us all alive in years of bad weather. So we offered thanks when this boat drifted ashore after a hurricane not long ago, however much we mourned the ten men who did not return with it. Most of our fishers are out to sea. These must go back too, as soon as they can." He sighed. "I feel almost guilty myself that I stayed behind today."

Mishka squeezed his hand.

The revel was a communal affair. Every villager brought food or drink to a tree-shaded green. Lanterns, wind bells, and flags had been strung around to make the place festive.

For no matter how important the occasion, it was not solemn. In fact, Charlie had never been at a jollier party. The table was loaded, the shmiriz flowed unstinted, drums and wooden flutes rollicked to set feet a-bouncing, jokes crackled, and nobody talked politics. Charlie wasn't put on a pedestal; he was invited to join the songs and dances. Young and in top condition, he soon found the females could whirl him breathless.

And there Mishka capered with a New Lemurian girl who Charlie suddenly saw was quite pretty; and there the priest and his wife leaped by; and old blind Vorka joined the chanters as they roared forth the measure:

Swing your lady swiftly.
Sweep her in your arms, lad.
Do a dosey-do now,
Then double back and circle. . . .

Somewhere amid the noise and laughter, a part of Charlie wondered how many folk on Earth knew how to have this good a time.

When the foe might appear at any moment, unbeknownst before an aircraft or picket boat saw his masts on the horizon and beat home to report it, no leave could be for more than a day. Late in the afternoon, the celebration ended. Charlie stayed outside, making what conversation he was able, while Mishka bade his family a private farewell.

Thereafter the two of them saddled their yachis and headed back to town.

Mishka was about one and a half sheets in the wind. Jaws bandaged to save his teeth and tongue while he rode, he couldn't bawl out songs, but he hummed them as loudly as possible. No fears touched him. Maybe he would never see his kin again. But maybe he would. The coming of the Prince made that the more likely, in his eyes. And regardless of what some hostile god might do, he *had* seen them. He savored the memory.

Charlie, who had stuck to plain fruit juice, felt otherwise. He'd enjoyed his excursion, mostly, but that same fact got him brooding.

At a rest stop, he said, "They're so . . . so real, your people."

"Hoy?" Mishka responded. "Of course they're real."

"I mean, well, compared to the Olaghis and, yes, the Dzenkos and—" Charlie stared across a sea turned golden by evening. "And me."

Mishka blinked. "What are you talking about, Prince?"

That I'm *not real!* Charlie wanted to shout. *That I'm a liar, a puppet, a*—but he must keep silence.

"You seem gloomy," Mishka said. "Are you troubled by the morrow? Never be that. You are the morrow." He sat quiet for a while, before he asked almost casually, "By the way, when do you plan to take on the Riddling Priests? And is there any chance I could watch?"

It was as if someone else used Charlie's throat: "Why not tonight?"

13
Fahrenheit 451

That Klashk the Omniscient had been a great god early in the history of this island was evident from the site of his temple, near the top of Holy Hill. But these days the building was in ruinous condition. The roof leaked, the unpainted walls sagged, the fluting of the wooden colonnade was long lost to the knives of idlers, and most of the rooms were thick with dust and choked with junk that nobody had got around to throwing out. Charlie and Mishka did get a superb view from the porch, downward across the town and outward across the bay, which glowed beneath a lustrous sunset. But they were too intent on their purpose to give it much heed.

Charlie didn't think he was being reckless, anyhow, no more reckless than he had to be for the sake of his own self-respect. He couldn't force himself to tell Mishka's kind of person, later on, that at some point he had confronted the Riddling Priests, when in fact he had not. If Dzenko knew his purpose beforehand, the baron would find a way to stop him, quite likely murderous. Therefore he came unannounced.

But he thought he could hold his own in a battle of wits. At school on Earth he had always been the best of his class where it came to riddles. If he should be stumped here, he'd pull the trick of giving an answer that didn't make sense and then claiming the riddle he had been asked was only part of a larger one, which he should be clever enough to make up on the spot. Come what may, he didn't suppose the clergy of so impoverished a parish would really dare harm the Prince of the Prophecy.

Passersby stared when a giant warrior and a slight figure muffled in cloak and cowl tethered their yachis and strode through the temple door. Several trailed after them.

They entered a dark vestibule. As they approached an inner archway, an elderly male stepped from it. He was wrinkled and squinting, his green robe ragged and soiled, but a golden chain hung around his neck, carrying a pendant like an X superimposed on an O.

"Hai!" he shrilled. "What impiety is this? Weapons stay out here. That includes knives, younkers."

"Are you one of the Riddling Priests?" Charlie asked.

"Yes, yes," was the irritable reply. "What'd you think I was? The Hierophant of Druguz?" The New Lemurian thrust his bald pate forward. "Something funny about you, the short fellow. Not built right, you aren't."

Charlie threw back his hood. "I am not of your

race . . . uh . . . your reverence," he said. Louder: "I am the Prince of the Prophecy, come to join issue with you!"

The curiosity seekers, homebound laborers from the look of them, gasped. It disturbed Charlie that the Priest didn't seem much impressed.

"Well," he only said. "About time. Needed awhile to get up your nerve, did you? Very well, very well. When had you in mind?"

"Now."

"Hai? What? See here, I don't care who you claim to be, I'll have no levity in the House of Klashk."

This wasn't going the way Charlie had expected. He braced his feet, close to Mishka's comforting bulk, and declared as stoutly as he was able, "Sir, I do not joke. I insist. At once. This hour."

"But that's ridiculous!" sputtered the Priest. "First Riddling in . . . in . . . three hundred and fifty-seven years, is that right? Yes, three hundred and fifty-seven years. Milestone occasion. Needs days of advance arrangement. Temple swept and garnished. Magnates invited. Choirboys recruited. Vestments cleaned. Ceremonies planned and rehearsed. Yes, a six-day at least. Better a twelve-day."

"We will do it immediately," Charlie retorted, "or not at all. Remember what an impetuous young hero the Prophecy says I am." He added a flick of malice: "Or are you nervous about the outcome?"

"Certainly not," snapped the oldster. "It's a mere question of due respect, and—well, come on in and we'll talk about it." He raised his fist. "Leave your weapons here, I told you!"

Charlie and Mishka obeyed and followed him into the main chamber. It was pathetically bare. A few cheap rushlights flickered far apart along the walk, leaving the room full of murk. The stone floor was naked save for dirt and litter. A handful of worshipers (more accurately, perhaps, contemplators) squatted before an altar at the far end. They typified the tiny congregation Dzenko had described: decrepit females, males younger but still seedier. Behind the altar was a huge double door.

While Charlie and Mishka took this in and the slum dwellers gaped at them, the Priest tottered off to locate his colleagues. They lived on the premises and arrived in a couple of minutes with him. They too were getting along in years, attired in worn-out robes but splendid pectorals. It was obvious that they had donned these canonicals rather hastily, for one was still wiping sleep from his eyes and the other grease from his mouth.

The first Priest beckoned to the newcomers. "Over here," he ordered them. "Stop that babble of yours, and let's agree on a date that makes sense."

His associates were quick to become alert. "Yes," another said, "if you are indeed the Prince of the Prophecy—"

Low noises rose from the onlookers. Charlie had felt the amazement and tension grow in them as they stared. Now their guess was confirmed. He glimpsed two or three leaving, no doubt to fetch their friends. . . . Wait! Possibly someone would go to the palace and tell the nobles, in hopes of reward. He did have to keep things moving.

The Priest who had spoken last was still doing so. "—an extraordinary event." He leaned near and whispered, "Think of the converts, the donations, the glory of Klashk, and the honor of his servants."

Charlie wished he could inform them that delay might cost them their lives. Instead, he could merely say, "Tonight or never. I do have other business, you know, and it won't wait."

The first Priest gave him a stare of pure hatred. "As you will, then." Raising his voice till echoes flew spookily through the gloom: "Who volunteers to stoke the sacred furnace?"

Charlie was astounded and Mishka growled, when half a dozen males sprang forward. The boy turned to the Priests. "After all," he said, "it's just a matter of form. You know I'm going to win."

"We know nothing of the sort," answered the third of them.

"What?" roared Mishka. "The Prophecy says—"

"The Prophecy," interrupted the Priest, "is supposed to have been inspired by the god Bullak. It is no work of great Klashk, who indeed, once when they disputed in heaven, called Bullak a deceiver. Therefore the Prophecy is heretical, and we are the chosen instruments of Klashk to prove its falsity."

Charlie met his eyes and knew in a sudden chill that he had encountered three fanatics.

They bustled about, supervising the workers and making preparations themselves. Charlie and Mishka stood aside, nearly ignored. "This doesn't look too good, my friend," the guardsman muttered.

"No, m-maybe not." Charlie's glance followed the eager paupers. More were beginning to pour in. He thought of a discreet departure, but saw the exit so crowded that there'd be no chance.

The chamber brightened after the rear doors were swung wide. They gave on a walled courtyard where a sandstone idol loomed, eroded well-nigh to shapelessness. Before it lay a great rusty iron caldron with a lid. That must be the furnace, Charlie decided. Under a Priest's guidance, the people fetched wood from a shed in the corner and stacked it high.

"But why," Charlie whispered in despair, "why will

they help . . . against the Prince who's supposed to
set them free?"

"They are the very poor," Mishka said, "outcasts,
beggars, starvelings. They come to old Klashk
because every other god has forsaken them. What
difference would freedom make in their lives?
Whereas, if Klashk consumes you—well, King Olaghi
might be happy enough about it to scatter some gold
pieces around."

Then Charlie knew there is more to politics than
a simple opposition of good and evil. A democratic
government ought in time to help these folk, but how
could he make them believe this, when they snarled
and spat in his direction as they went by?

He gulped and husked, "I guess I'd better win."

"If you don't . . . hmm," Mishka murmured calmly.
His trained gaze searched about. "One of those
scrawny bodies, swung by the ankles, should clear
a pretty wide circle. First I'll boost you out this
window here. You go after help. I expect I can stand
the mob off, meanwhile. If not—" He shrugged.
"That's the risk my grandfather took."

Charlie swallowed tears. Mishka must not be torn
apart or roasted alive if they bore him down! Yet his
rescue, or his avenging, would involve the massacre
by armored soldiers of these miserable ignoramuses.

He prayed for word soon to reach Dzenko. The
baron would undoubtedly hasten here, a platoon at
his heels, and break this affair up before it went
beyond control.

Flames caught in kindling. Above the idol, the sky
turned deep violet, and the evening star winked
forth. The Priests got the people settled down on
their haunches in the nave. A hundred pairs of eyes
glimmered out of shadow. Solemnly, the Riddling
Three bowed, chanted, lifted hands, and genuflected.

Everything had taken time. If Dzenko or anyone in authority were coming from the palace, he would have arrived already. Sweat ran down Charlie's ribs. His knees felt like rubber, his lips like sandpaper, his tongue like a block of wood.

"You who would win to wisdom, tread forward!" intoned the Priests.

Mishka nudged Charlie. "That's you, lad," he whispered. "Get in there and fight. Remember, if it comes to a real scrap, keep hold of my belt so they can't drag you from me, and I'll slug our way to the window."

He followed Charlie as the Earthling went to stand before the altar. Behind it, the three Priests were faceless in the dark against the fire which leaped and crackled around their furnace. An absolute hush had fallen upon the watchers.

"Know, seeker of wisdom," the Priests declared, "Klashk the Omniscient bestows it freely, but on none save those who prove themselves worthy. The rest he—"

"Gives lodging," said one of them. "Takes unto himself," said a second. "No, 'gives lodging,' that's right," said the third.

They glared at each other. "'Gives lodging.' . . . 'Takes unto himself.' . . . Wait a pulse-beat, I seem to recall something like 'transfigures'—" The mumbled conference trailed off.

"Confound you, boy," cried a voice, "I *told* you we needed time to rehearse! But no, you wouldn't listen. You knew better."

A grim laugh escaped from Mishka. That sound was a draft of courage to Charlie. "No matter," he said, and was faintly surprised to hear how steady his voice, how clear and lightning-quick his mind had become. "The Prince of the Prophecy doesn't stand on ceremony. Ask me the first of the Riddles."

The Priests went into a huddle. Charlie waited.

It occurred to him that probably in former times the prospective sacrifices were quizzed in secret, lest the next victims be forewarned. That the present-day ministers had let this contest become public was a measure of their own confusion. Well, forget about culture shock and the rest. Some ethnic folkways deserved wiping out.

A Priest laid fingertips on altar. "Prepare your soul," he said. "The first of the Riddles: 'Why does an eggfowl cross the highroad?'"

"Huh?" choked the human. "That old chestnut?" Before he could stop to think what subtleties might be here, impulse had spoken. "To get to the other side."

A buzz of wonder arose at his back. The three dim shapes before him staggered. After a moment they went into a fresh huddle.

"The proper answer—" said the questioner at length.

Mishka growled and bristled his whiskers. He was very big.

"The full and proper answer," said the Priest, "is 'To get whither she would go upon the farther side.'" A stir and an undertone went through the audience. They weren't interested in hairsplitting technicalities. He must have foreseen this, because he continued: "Yet since your response holds the essence of truth, and Klashk is the most generous of gods, we rule you are correct."

It sighed through the high, dark nave.

"Besides," said the second Priest, "there is the next of the Riddles." He paused for dramatic effect. "How long ought the legs of a man to be?" Strictly speaking, an English translation would have to be "New Lemurian." But the natives naturally thought of themselves as the norm of creation.

Charlie kept mute while suspense mounted. He wasn't trying to develop his reply or even put on a good show. He was busy clarifying matters to himself.

As humanlike as these beings were, it was no surprise that they would invent essentially the same brain teasers. But on Earth those were schoolboy jokes. Here they were mortally serious. Why?

Well, when communications were slow, limited, and often disrupted, a new idea might never travel far. And if it happened to acquire a sacred character—yes, maybe riddles were a ritual in Talyina, not an everyday amusement—he must ask Mishka about that—

"I await your response, youth," said the second of the Priests, "or else your calefaction."

"Huh? Oh." Charlie shook himself. "Sorry. My mind wandered. How long ought the legs of a man to be? Why, 'Long enough to reach the ground.'"

This time a roar arose. Here and there he caught shouts like "He really is the Prince! The Prophecy really is true!" Meanwhile, the Priests conferred again.

On a sound of triumph, the third of them stepped forth to say, "Hearken well. For this is the Riddle that none has solved since first the world began, a dewdrop out of the Mists of Dream. 'What fares without legs in the dawn, on two legs by day, and on eight after nightfall?' Answer, or enter the furnace."

Blackness was fast gathering above the courtyard. The flames whirled higher. The paupers who fed them were tatterdemalion troll shapes. The caldron would soon glow red.

Charlie's heart stuttered. What was this?

It had started like the classic Earthly enigma, that the sphinx of myth had posed: "What goes on four legs in the morning, two at noon, and three at evening?" The response, of course, was: "Man. He crawls on all fours in the morning of his life, walks upright on his two legs in the noon of his manhood, and in evening must needs use a cane, making three legs together."

But this—

Silence descended, and grew and grew, save for the noise of the fire.

It burst upon Charlie. At least, what had he to lose? He said aloud, "Man."

The third Priest fainted.

The assembly screamed, sprang about, groveled on the floor before the Prince of the Prophecy.

An hour later, when things had quieted down and the temple been cleared, Charlie and Mishka sat with the three old males in the room which they shared. Their repentance had been so contrite that he couldn't bring himself to refuse their offer of a cup of tea.

Candles were too expensive for them. A wick floated in oil which a stone lamp held. The flame stank. Its dullness hardly mattered; there was little more to see than three straw pallets and three wooden stools. The visitors had two of these, while the Priests took the floor.

"Lord, how did you read the Final Secret?" asked the third of them meekly.

"Simple." Charlie felt he had earned the right to boast a bit. "As a baby, a man is carried around by his mother. Grown, he uses his two feet. Dead, he is borne to his grave by four pallbearers."

They covered their faces.

Charlie couldn't but feel sorry for them. They'd been ready to burn him, yes, but all their lives they had been told that this was proper and, indeed, the god made the victims welcome in heaven. Reflecting on past Earth history, he dared not be self-righteous. And here he had come and knocked their faith out from under them, the only comfort their lives had ever known.

He ought to do something. "Uh, look," he said. "You were mistaken about the Prophecy, but that doesn't mean you were about everything. As a matter of fact, I happen to know that the will of Klashk has gotten much misunderstood over the centuries. It would please him no end if you set matters straight. That's why I'm here, to help right wrongs—including wrong theology."

Three haggard visages lifted toward his.

He improvised fast: "It's simply not true that Klashk and . . . and the other god you mentioned earlier are at loggerheads. That's just a lie put out by an evil immortal named Satan, who wants to stir up trouble. Actually, Klashk himself made some excellent suggestions while the Prophecy was being composed."

The Priests shuddered and moaned with hope.

"However," Charlie said sternly, wagging a forefinger, "this business of live sacrifices has got to stop. It may have been all right for your primitive ancestors, but people know better today. Why do you think the worship of Klashk has nearly died out? Because his ministers weren't keeping up with the times, that's why. Get rid of that furnace tomorrow morning. In return, I'll issue a bulletin thanking Klashk for his hospitality and urging people to come pay him their respects. And I'll see about having your stipend increased."

It was heady to command such power.

Two of the Priests blubbered their gratitude. He who had first met Charlie kept a certain independence of spirit. "Lord," he said, "this shall be as you wish. Yet the service of Klashk has ever required the testing of wits. Is it not written, 'He shall require of them knowledge, that he may return unto them wisdom'? The Riddles were at the core of the faith. Now any street-bred fool can say them."

Charlie frowned. "I told you, those sacrifices—"

"No, no, Lord! We agree. Effective immediately, Klashk wants no more than flowers. He wasn't getting more anyway, these past three hundred fifty-seven years. Still, the duty of a Priest is to know at least one arcane conundrum. It needn't be used, except as a part of elevating novices to full rank. But, Lord, I pray you, in your understanding and mercy, give us a new Riddle."

"Well," Charlie said, "well, if you put it that way."

He pondered. Breathless, they leaned forward to catch every syllable he might utter.

"Okay," Charlie said. "You may or may not know this already, but let's see." He spoke the question weightily: "What is purple and dangerous?"

The Priests stared at him, and at each other, and back again. They whispered together. Mishka ran fingers through his crest, as puzzled as they.

"Lord," said the boldest of the three at length, "we yield. What is purple and dangerous?" Charlie rose. "A bellfruit with a crossbow," he told them, and he and Mishka left them to their marvel and delight.

Hubbub reigned in the palace. Lanterns bobbed around the grounds; inside, candles glowed from every holder; courtiers, military officers, servants scurried through rooms and along corridors, yelling.

Charlie's first concern was to return to his suite, unnoticed. In the chaos, that wasn't hard. Hector sat there, honing what he called his claymore.

"Weel, laddie," greeted the Hoka, "hae ye had a guid day amang the puir crofters?"

"Wow," said Charlie faintly. He had begun to feel how tired he was. "Let me tell you—"

"'Twas a wise idea to gang oot, mingle wi' the plain folk, and eat the halesome parritch, chief of Scotia's food. Ye grand ones need aye tae be reminded that a man's a man for a' that."

Noise from the hall reminded Charlie of something else: the strange fact that nobody had come to fetch him at the temple, though the news of his latest exploit must have spread through town like a gale. "Where are the nobles?" he asked. "What's going on?"

Hector's black button eyes widened. "Hae ye no heard, laddie? They're off tae whup their respective units into some kind o' readiness. Nae easy task on such short notice." He perceived Charlie's bewilderment. "Aye, not long before sunset the word came. Olaghi's fleet has been sighted, bearing doon on this isle, far sooner and larger than awaited. Nae doot his unmanly radios hae let his forces gather thus swiftly. Tomorrow we fight, Prince, we fight."

14

Beat to Quarters

Paradoxically, at first Charlie's latest success hampered the preparations of his side. By morning most able-bodied males in town and environs had heard about it and hastened to join the navy. From the quarterdeck of their flagship, he and Dzenko watched turmoil cover the docks.

"I . . . didn't expect this," he said, abashed.

"No." The baron's cold reply was barely audible above the shouts, foot thuds, and metal clangor. "It would not occur to you to consult me before setting our whole enterprise at hazard."

"Hold on, there, master," said Mishka, who stood behind. "You know as well as I do, we've gained, not lost. We've ample time to square things away; the tide won't let us pull out for hours yet. And those're some good fighters yonder—amateurs, but so are the king's pressed crews, and ours are here of their own wish."

Dzenko glared at him and snapped, "Speak to your liege lord with more respect."

The sergeant answered in a level tone, "I will, when he speaks thus to my Prince."

Dzenko stalked off. Charlie's uneasiness was soon lost in the excitement of watching the preparations. It was true that the commoners showed poorly at first glance, compared to the armored and well-drilled professionals among them. Not only did they mill about, but they looked as if they had outfitted themselves at a junkyard. But that mightn't make too great a difference. Judging by remarks and reminiscences Mishka had voiced during the journey, a medieval style of battle had little to do with close maneuvers under tight leadership. It was more like an armed brawl.

To be sure, a sea engagement required control, up to the moment when ships grappled together and crews fought hand to hand. Mishka gave Charlie a running commentary as they watched arrangements being made. The core of the fleet was the warships, and whatever civilian craft carried naval officers aboard. The rest—that wildly assorted, ragtag majority of freighters, smacks, luggers, lighters, jollyboats, practically anything which would float—were to steer wide of this cadre, on either side. The hope was that they could execute a pincer movement, get in among Olaghi's ships, and if nothing else, harass the foe.

"From what the scouts tell," Mishka said, "the enemy outnumbers us in regular vessels, which means he owns more firepower. But we've more keels and men in total. The way for us, therefore, is to close in as fast as may be and try to carry the day with boarding parties. I can see Dzenko and his

fellow nobles—but mainly him, I'd guess—are doing
a fine job of busking us for that strategy."

"He's very able, isn't he?" Charlie asked.

Mishka nodded. "Yes. Mayhap a shade too wily.
But no. I'll not speak ill of my lord. Although," he
added, "he's only my lord under you."

"Now, I—Mishka, please—"

Before noon the force was ready, and the tide had
begun to ebb. Tartan standards went to mastheads;
trumpets rang above chanteys; sails unfurled, oars
came forth; and the ships stood out to sea. Females,
children, aged kinfolk crowded the docks, shouting,
waving, sometimes weeping, till the last hull was gone
from sight.

About midafternoon Olaghi's armada hove in view.
There was no very strong breeze; wavelets glittered
blue and green. Some kilometers off, a small island
known as Stalgesh displayed a village, grainfields that
had started to turn amber, timber lots where leaves
blew silvery. The air was fresh and cool, tinged by
a clean hint of pitch. It was hard to believe that this
would be the theater of war.

But strakes and spars crowded the northern horizon. Rising from them were dozens of aircraft. And
between familiar bulwarks went a roar as males
fetched their gear and sought their battle stations.

On the quarterdeck, Mishka helped Charlie armor
himself in mail crafted to his measure. Himself an
iron tower, the chief guardsman said, "Let's just go
over our doctrine again, shall we, Prince? Frankly,
I wish your royalty didn't require you be in the
strife." So did Charlie, though he managed to con-
ceal his nervousness. "But at least we'll have no
useless heroics, agreed? You've had no real training.
You'd not last three breaths in a clash, and your fall

could doom our cause." Mishka gestured at a score
of troopers who stood nearby. "We'll hold a shield
wall around you. Never stick a finger outside it." To
Hector, who stood leaning on his basket-hilted sword
with kilt flapping from beneath byrnie: "You too, my
friend. Stay beside him if you insist, but keep out
of our way."

"Aye," said the Hoka cheerily. "Ever was it my
proud preevilege to guard his royal back."

Meanwhile, Hasprot, the minstrel, smote his horpil
and chanted:

Fearlessly faring and frightful to foes,
The Prophecy's Prince will prong them
            on bladepoint.
Happily goes he to hack them to hash.
No sweep of his sword but will slay at
            least five. . . .

With agonizing slowness, the fleets worked toward
each other.

Hostilities commenced in the sky. Olaghi must
have assembled his entire air force. It could virtu-
ally ignore the few blimps the barons were able to
muster. Awkward but ominous, it hovered above ships
to drop things on them.

Unfortunately for it, fickle breezes kept shoving
the fliers around. Thus almost all their missiles fell
in the water. Those which landed did small harm.
Alert soldiers and sailors shielded their eyes against
splinters from glass globes and suffered only minor
cuts. More to be feared were the fire bombs. One
set a fishing craft ablaze, but the crew launched
lifeboats and arrived on other decks. (Crews down-
wind did complain bitterly about the smoke from a
hull which year after year had been packed full of

fish.) As for the rest of the incendiaries, their fuses either went out as they fell or burned too slowly and could be plucked away before they ignited the spilled oil.

In a second attempt, the bombers descended to mast height. That brought them in easy range of catapults throwing giant quarrels. Bag after bag hissed itself limp and left its aeronauts splashing in the waves till boat hooks hauled them up to captivity.

If anything, the onslaught was a pleasant diversion, which took the minds of Charlie's followers off the serious business to come and greatly boosted morale. "I have heard," said Mishka, as he watched the survivors limp away, "that Olaghi has a slogan: 'Victory through air power.'"

Time wore on. Charlie, a mere spectator, saw Dzenko in bare glimpses. The lord of Roshchak was in overall command, which kept him moving. His regular and auxiliary units had only a crude system of signal flags to send him information and receive his word; his irregulars had nothing. Both winds and enemy dispositions kept changing; Olaghi must be making full use of his radios. Yet the baronial fleet responded well to every shift and always kept good order. Its professional center kept excellent order.

In spite of his growing distrust of Dzenko, Charlie had to admire the noble. Calm and self-possessed, he went about his work as if it were routine, not a clash which would decide the fate of the kingdom and his own life or death.

From historical shows he had seen and books he had read, Charlie unconsciously expected firing to begin long before it did. But the effective range of catapults, mangonels, bows, or air cannon was only a few hundred meters.

Thus combat erupted quite suddenly. Closer the nearest hostile vessel drew, and closer, and closer, until he could count the fangs in its figurehead and hear the shouts of its officers, yes, the creak of its tackle. The first strike was with quarrels and arrows, from archers perched high in the rigging. Shafts whistled in flocks, thunked into wood, and quivered.

Troopers crouched, made wary use of shields, but never flinched. Half-naked sailors took their chances and did their tasks. Charlie thought what courage that spelled: when the best that a surgeon could do for a wound was a rough stitching or an amputation, without anesthetics, and the sole guard against infection was a red-hot iron applied to the flesh, if this was not too likely to kill the man.

Man? Yes, he thought. If a man, or a woman, was a being intelligent, sensitive, brave, basically decent, then, regardless of biology, the New Lemurians were men and women as much as any Earthling. And that gave them the same rights, the same ultimate claim upon him, as his own kind had.

Artillery opened up. Staring across the waters, he saw most shots miss, and it flashed across him how ridiculously wasteful war is. But occasional ones went home. Barb-headed catapult bolts flew low, unstoppable, across decks, hunting prey or nailing down bundles of burning tow which set whole vessels afire. Stones from mangonels smashed yards and masts or punched through a bottom and sank a craft. It came to him how gruesomely wasteful war is.

Before the wheelhouse, in helmet and mail, Dzenko kept the poop deck. His voice drifted down to Charlie in snatches, through the clamor. He addressed the captain, who gave due orders to the steersman and, via stentorian boatswains, to sailors manning capstans, lines, and sails: ". . . We don't

want to close, not with these. It's Olaghi we're after.
Can you wear ship to get us between them? . . ."

They passed so narrowly through that gap that
Charlie saw the faces of his adversaries. Arrows sang.
Mishka's squad made him a roof of their shields. An
enemy cast a grapnel, which chunked its hooks into
a bulwark. At once, regardless of what sleeted around
them, men with axes were there to cut the thing loose.

The flagship sailed on. For a while smoke from
a burning galley blinded Charlie. When he could see
again, through reddened and weeping eyes, he found
that the lines of both fleets had splintered into
scattered individual combats. Dzenko had counted
on that. In close coordination with two other vessels, he had broken straight through.

And dead ahead, Charlie saw in a strange blend
of fear and fierceness, dead ahead was Olaghi's.

The great aircraft carrier loomed over the three
craft which neared it. And they must tack, while its
propeller should make it independent of the wind.
Yet they beat onward.

"I see what my lord has in mind," Mishka said.
"We'll grapple on either side and board."

"Board?" Charlie gulped. "How?" The flanks of
the carrier extended three sheer-meters above the
topmost deck of its opponents.

"Not easy," Mishka admitted. "However, in this
case we've the firepower over them. We'll keep their
heads down."

Charlie recalled how intensively he and, especially,
Hector had been quizzed about what they saw while
they were prisoners. He had described the gunports
which once again bristled menacingly before him.
Hadn't Dzenko believed?

Dzenko had, and rejoiced. The facts he learned
became the heart of his entire battle plan.

Olaghi's air cannon got busy. Dzenko's made no response. Instead, his crew stood to catapults, mangonels, crossbows, longbows . . . and sent forth a storm. The royal ship carried similar weapons, of course. But they were few in proportion to its deck area, and they were undersupplied with ammunition. Too many lockers were full of what the cannon delivered, feebly and at a much, lower rate of fire.

Moreover, a large number of its crewmen who might have been in direct action were below, exhausting themselves on the treadmill which worked the propeller. Windjammers were no such energy eaters. Though the carrier had sails of its own, it was not designed to get maximum work out of them. Thus it wallowed, unable to bring to bear its useful armament.

Mishka waved sword aloft. "Ho, ho!" he roared. "And earlier were those silly fliers! Olaghi's gotten too flinkin' modern to operate!"

Charlie thought of resources tied up in sophisticated technology that might better have been spent straight to the purpose. Had Earth nations ever made the same mistake, back in the days when they fought wars? Surely not. At least, surely the most advanced countries, those most familiar with engineering, had known better. . . .

The sun was getting low. Its light lay golden across waters on which here and there bobbed wreckage or a slick of blood.

The ships came together.

But however much he had overdone progress in some respects, Olaghi was no fool.

He had an efficient fire-fighting corps, equipped with hand pumps. It doused conflagrations. And when grapnels sank into his planks, he unlimbered a secret weapon.

Abruptly his cannon wheeled back from the gunports. Instead, those ports opened to man size, and gangplanks extended out of them like tongues. Spikes at the ends bit fast. Down them, to either side where his foemen lay, his shock troops thundered.

"They're boarding *us*!" Charlie wailed.

Mishka spoke harshly through the din. "There's no such thing as a certain fight."

Battle clattered below the quarterdeck. Swiftly outnumbered, Dzenko's crew reeled back. "Why stand we idle?" Hector cried.

"Go if you must," Mishka answered. "Here we ward our Prince."

"Ye hae richt," the Hoka agreed. "Yet och, the bluid o' my clan does seethe in me like whisky."

With a crash, one of Olaghi's assault planes struck centimeters from Charlie.

It hit Mishka and another guardsman a glancing blow, and pinned down the trooper between them. All at once, the wall around the Prince was broken. Through the gap, iron aflame in the evening glow, came the king's men.

Hector bounded to meet them. "Ah," he exulted, "the bra' music o' steel upon steel!"

In a shattering clang, his "claymore" smote a shield. The Talyinan behind it flew halfway across the deck fetched up against a rail, and lay quietly twitching. Hector cocked his head. "Aye," he decided, "E flat."

A huge royalist stalked toward Charlie. In both his hands he whirled an ax which looked huger still. The Hoka saw. "I come, lad, I come!" he shouted. "Ever wull Hector MacGregor ward the back o' his Bonnie Prince!"

"Not my back, you dolt!" Charlie screamed. "My front!"

Hector skidded on a heel, whirled his body through an arc, and caught the descending shaft on his sword blade. The ax tore out of its owner's grasp. The blade snapped across. Hector gave it a regretful look before he gripped the soldier's belt, raised the struggling shape over his head, and, after taking a proper sight, dropped him on top of another Olaghist on the main deck.

Battle ramped. Hasprot prudently stayed below the ladder to the poop and declaimed, not very loud:

How grossly ungrateful. No glory goes ever
To us who do also face anger-swung edges,
That tales of the deeds may be talked of in towns,
We careful recorders, we war correspondents. . . .

Mishka, briefly stunned, recovered. He lent his great strength to that of the Hoka and to the lesser but valiant efforts of his troopers. From above hastened Dzenko and his own guards. In red minutes, the quarterdeck was cleared.

Yet elsewhere ruin drew nigh. Better armed, better drilled, and in greater numbers, Olaghi's warriors drove back the baronial company. At masts, deckhouse, bulwarks, aloft in the shrouds and along the yards, clusters of crewmen fought with desperate courage. But the iron tide moved in on them.

Dzenko's voice came bleak: "It appears we are done for, after all. Well, we strove. Our names will endure."

"Our folk have lost their leaders," Mishka groaned. "If only—"

A volcano burst in Charles Stuart. "I am their leader!" he cried.

"What?" Mishka lifted a shaky hand. "No. You'd be cut straight down."

"Won't we be if we do nothing? Look, I don't mean to fight myself. But if they see me—I'm supposed to be the Prince who can't lose—"

"Whirlwinds and seaquakes!" Mishka bellowed. "Right you are! Oh, but there's heart in you, my King!"

He swept Charlie onto his shoulders. The Earthling unbuckled his helmet and cast it off. When the coif and cap beneath had followed, the level sunbeams flamed in his hair.

"Behold your Prince!" Mishka bugled, till it rang from end to end of the beleaguered ship. *"Now strike for your freedom!"*

He went down the ladder. Behind him came Hector, Dzenko, and the guards.

Swords belled. Axes banged. Arrows whistled. Men shouted. And they danced together to a terrible music. Across the deck did Mishka's band advance, hewing, hewing. Banner-high above them flared the russet head of Charlie—the red mane of the Prophecy.

The word flew among screaming seafowl: "He has come, he has come, he is here, and he leads us." Spirits rose anew in the men who would be free. Mightily they smote, carved a way to each other, then walked forward shield by shield. Soldiers sworn to Olaghi resisted them stoutly. But impressed commoners tossed their weapons aside and lifted hands in surrender—or, more and more, turned those weapons against their oppressors.

The ship was regained.

The usurper's men streamed over their gangplanks and cast these loose. Relentless, the Prince's men raised ladders and swarmed in pursuit. When aboard the carrier, they engaged its crew so fully that warriors off their companion ships became able to join them.

Charlie's memories were partly clear about the end of the battle. At first, Mishka, whom he rode, had been at the forefront. But when it grew plain to see that the revolutionaries would overcome, the sergeant hung back, not from fear but because of the very precious burden he carried. No longer in a maelstrom of violence, the rider could again look through sober eyes and understand what he saw.

The carrier was all but captured. Olaghi's standard was gone from its staff and masthead, where tartan flags blew in the sunset light. Elsewhere across the waters, royalist crews noticed, and despaired, and struck their colors. On many vessels the sailors mutinied in order to yield.

Still one forlorn combat raged. Olaghi himself and a few men held the bows. Against them came a band which Dzenko led. King and baron crossed blades, and Charlie never knew which of the twain showed more skill or courage. It was the baron who won. He forced his rival out from the rest of the defenders. Men of his fell upon Olaghi, pressed him between their shields, held him trapped. Then the last of the king's following lowered their steel, and peace descended with dusk.

In later years, Hasprot would chant of how the victors cheered until the western clouds were shivered apart and fell as a rain of gold. At the time, however, those remaining were too weary, too wounded. They croaked forth some dutiful noises while they wondered when they could go bathe their hurts, swallow a goblet of shmiriz, and sleep.

Wrists bound behind him, spears at his back,

Olaghi went to meet Charlie, where the Prince sat on a bollard under stars and a lantern. The prisoner's eyes were hawk-proud. Dzenko, in the best of moods, didn't mind consulting the human. "What about this wight?" the baron asked. "We can hang him in the main market square of Bolgorka. That would be a useful demonstration. On the other hand, since you're tender-livered, maybe you'd rather give him an honorable beheading at once. I leave the choice to you."

Charlie met the noble's gaze, and the fallen king's, and answered quite steadily, "Set him free."

Dzenko stiffened as if a lance had gone up along his backbone.

"We've had too much killing," Charlie went on. "Any killing is too much. I've thought about it while I waited here. . . . Amnesty. We start fresh, Talyinans together."

"*Him?*" somebody cried in the darkness.

"I think in his way, he tried to do his best for the country. And I think it's wrong to destroy people just because you don't like their politics." Charlie smiled. "What are you afraid of? What possible harm can Olaghi do? He's completely discredited. If he wants to save his life, he'll get out of this kingdom in a hurry and stay out forever."

The captive flushed angrily but did not speak.

"We'll give him a sailboat and supplies enough to reach the mainland," Charlie continued. "I'm told the dwellers there are savages. Maybe Olaghi can teach them something. That'd make the rest of his life useful."

"No!" Dzenko cried. "This is nonsense! I won't have it!"

Charlie gave him a cool stare. "Oh, but you will,"

he commanded. "I am the Prince. And doesn't the Prophecy say 'In terror, the tyrant who caused all the trouble, the false king, goes fleeing, unfollowed, in shame'? We have to see the Prophecy fulfilled, don't we?"

15
The Prince

Reaction set in. He was no hardened warrior. What he had witnessed shocked him more deeply than it would have a native civilian used to horrors long banished from Earth. Nor had he simply watched. He had run a high risk of being killed or maimed. He had pitted his will repeatedly against that of strong and ruthless veterans.

For a week, he spent his time in a dull daze or choking awake out of nightmares. Dzenko opined that it would be unwise, as well as bad for the patient, did the Prince arrive at the capital city in this condition. Yet it was important to ride the crest of success, take possession of the throne, reorganize the royal household, get started on a restoration of order and commerce throughout the realm. The baron proposed to lead the regular navy off and see to that. Charlie would remain behind until he recovered for a triumphal entry.

No one objected. The fleet steered for Bolgorka. It included those ships, with officers and crews, which had been Olaghi's. Medieval types of aristocrats had elastic loyalties. None of them accompanied the fallen usurper into exile. On this account, too, it was vital to nail down the victory, before any warlord might grab power for himself.

Volunteers dispersed to their widely strewn homes. They bore the news: that the liberating Prince had come into his own at the Battle of Stalgesh and now remained awhile on that island in order to meditate how best he might improve life for his people.

Only Hector stayed with him. Dzenko had pointed out that he, the baron, would need every able-bodied man he could bring along, as much to prevent trouble from starting as to quell it should it arise. The injured should be carried straight back to Glats. But Charlie would need a less hectic atmosphere than that of the court. The villagers would provide as many guards and as much service as he could possibly require.

Indeed they did. Their hospitality was humble, but what they lacked in facilities they more than made up in devotion.

So during that week, Charlie got well. Sunshine, fresh air, plain food, ample rest; later swimming, boating, fishing, hiking; the company of people who loved him, at first anxiously tender, afterward cheerful, chatty, eager to swap songs and stories—these things healed him.

He did feel as though there had been some basic changes in him. No longer was he unduly shy, and he didn't think he would ever again prefer daydreams to real-world action. At the same time he had grown more thoughtful, more aware of the troubles which haunt the universe but less ready to find simple causes or instant cures for them.

It was in this mood that he wrote a long letter to his father, after he learned that the spaceship still waited on Shverkadi Island. A miniradio wouldn't reach that far. Besides, Dzenko hadn't left him any of those captured from Olaghi—an oversight, no doubt. Charlie resigned himself to sputtering along with a quill pen and fish-gland ink on sheets of flexible bark.

He told the tale of his adventures, pointing out that on the whole he had never got a chance to turn back from them. Yet now, he declared, he must act of his own free will. No longer was he in danger. The same local skipper who delivered this message would gladly have taken him and Hector in person. But he *must* go to Bolgorka. If the Prince did not make an appearance in the capital of Talyina, doubts were sure to spread; ambitious barons would conspire; a full-fledged civil war might well ensue, instead of a single decisive clash such as they had mercifully gotten by with. Dzenko was obviously right. Between them the two could work out a formula which would enable Charlie to go home without disrupting the kingdom.

He begged everybody's pardon for this. He knew it might not be legal, but he also knew it was moral. And . . . the presence of outsiders would be disastrous.

The Talyinans had always found it difficult to believe that the mighty Interbeing League really did not plan to conquer them. Their trust in its good intentions was often fragile. Did a band of spacemen accompany Charlie to Bolgorka, many natives would jump to the conclusion that the Prince was

a stalking-horse for human imperialism. The new
government would collapse in a storm of rebellions
and secessions. Whatever leaders arose afterward
would tend to shun the Plenipotentiary and reject
his advice.

"Please, please, Dad," Charlie wrote, "sit tight, and
get Mr. Pomfrey to do the same. I won't be gone
more than another month or so. Why don't you
continue your route? I can use royal funds when I'm
finished here, to buy passage to a planet where we
can meet. Meanwhile, I'm perfectly safe, I swear I
am."

He left for Bolgorka the day before his courier
raised sail for Shverkadi. He would not directly
disobey his father. Therefore, he wasn't about to
chance getting an order to come straight back.

After all, he knew wryly, from now on he expected
to enjoy himself.

Like Glats, the royal town stood at the end of a
bay which formed a superb natural harbor. It too was
built on hills. The island whose name it bore was
still more rugged than Lyovka. To the west and south
rolled a great river valley, intensively cultivated, but
mountains walled those horizons, haloed with snow
and jeweled with glaciers Northward, the highlands
thrust a tongue out to sea in the form of a long and
steeply ridged cape. Too rough for farming, it was
forested almost to the outer bastions of the city. A
good road did go across the neck of it.

Several boats escorted the one which bore
Charlie to his throne. Pennons and streamers
adorned their rigging. The swiftest vessel went
ahead to tell the people. Thus a mighty crowd
greeted the Prince. Troopers lined the streets,
holding back throngs whose cheers echoed off

heaven, or slammed their thousands of boots down on paving behind his horse-drawn carriage in the parade which conducted, him to the palace. Their mail and helmets shone like new-minted silver; plumes and cloaks blew about them, as colorful as the banners beneath which their pikes gleamed and rippled; drums boomed, horns winded, deep voices chanted aloud the Prophecy. He wore brilliant fabrics and rich furs; he carried in his hands, naked, the sword which had been the Founder's; his head stayed bare, that the red locks might blow free. Beside him stood Hector, bowing right and left, waving, beaming, blowing kisses. The Hoka had been given a sack of coins to toss to the populace but did not think that became a thrifty Scot.

In glory they reached the stark stone pile of the kingly dwelling. Almost at once, Dzenko got the Earthling off in private for a business discussion.

It was curiously like their first encounter. They were alone in a guarded tower room, so high that they saw through the narrow windows only sky and wings. The chill of masonry was not much relieved by woven tapestries and skin rugs. The furniture was massive and grotesquely carved. Dzenko sat cool-eyed. Charlie perched on the edge of his chair and, bit by bit, felt sweat prickle forth on his skin.

"Yes, I have matters in hand," the baron said. "We must see to it that they remain thus. It will take quick and precise action to get you back where you belong, uncrowned, without provoking upheavals. I'll need your unquestioning cooperation."

"Uncrowned?" replied Charlie. "Why that?"

Dzenko twitched his whiskers. "Have you forgotten? The fifth Feat is left for you to do. It happens to be impossible. It's equally impossible, politically, to hold your coronation until you have done the deed. And, since the Grotto of Kroshch is quite near town, you would perform before many witnesses. There is no way to, ah, make prior arrangements."

"Well, what do you have in mind then?"

"That you stay here for, hm, about a twelve-day. You will move around, inspect your capital and its hinterland, meet people, attend ceremonies—a more extensive and elaborate version of what you did in Glats. Hence no one will afterward be able to deny, that you were indeed present, victorious. Mostly you'll be seen in my company, and will show me, every mark of favor. I'll give you a schedule for the honors you heap on me.

"Meanwhile, we'll start a new story going. I have some reliable priests, minstrels, and the like, ready to help as soon as they get their instructions. Probably you can give me a few ideas, though I've already decided in a general way. Essentially, the tale will be that while the Prophecy is true, it is not complete. Before he can settle down to reign over Talyina, the Prince must still overcome certain other difficulties—abroad—especially among the starfarers in whose image he has been incarnated. He must go suppress warlords of theirs who plot to overrun us. This will take time, but at last he'll return successful. Then will be the proper moment for him to enter the Grotto, and come out alive, and assume his throne here.

"In his absence, he will naturally require a regent. Who but his well-beloved Dzenko? And should Dzenko not outlive the years during which the Prince is away striving for the people, why, the heirs of Dzenko will succeed him. After all, since the Prince is to reign forever, it's reasonable that he may need a few centuries yet to complete his labors."

The baron smiled and bridged his fingers "There," he finished. "A most excellent scheme.'"

Despite Bolgorka's being the largest and wealthiest city in Talyina, Charlie found many sections antiquated as he toured it. The Sword Way, up which he had been paraded, was broad and straight, but most streets were crooked and stinking lanes creeping between overhanging walls. One reason for this was that earlier kings had had much reconstructed in expensive stone or brick. Consequently, it had not suffered the fires which, every generation or two, made most towns start fresh. It was frozen into a primitive pattern. Well-to-do homes, warehouses, marts were like fortresses here and there in the middle of slums whose wretchedness appalled Charlie. He thought of doing something to help the poor—then remembered that he wouldn't be around and Dzenko was not especially interested in reform.

Nobody showed Charlie bad conditions on purpose, or tried to hide them. They were incidental, taken for granted. One simply had to shout or flick a whip to get the filthy commoners out of the way while one was guiding the Prince from historic monument to quaint shop to stately mansion, then back to the palace in time for a major speech, a formal banquet, and picturesque traditional entertainment. If from time to time he stopped and tried blunderingly to talk with some work-broken navvy, crippled beggar, or gaunt woman carrying an infant, why, that was just his whim. Let him pass out a few coins if he wished and get him moving again.

Besides Hector, a hundred crack guardsmen were always with him in public. He recognized none of them and learned they were mercenaries who had

formerly served Olaghi. "Where're my travel friends?"
he demanded of Dzenko. "Where's Mishka?"

"I have to send my most reliable men out to
handle special problems," the noble answered. "'For
instance, if a baron fell at Stalgesh, we must make
sure the right successor takes over his province.
Mustn't we?"

The sergeant of Charlie's troop was not very
communicative. He would reply to direct questions,
of course. Thus, while inspecting the fleet, the
human saw a number of sailors tied wrist and ankle
in the shrouds of ships, under, a scorching sun. He
asked why. The sergeant told him casually, "Oh,
mutineers being punished."

"Not mutineers, Highness," said the captain of the
vessel on which they stood. "Such we'd flog to death.
These conspired to petition for discharge. That only
rates spread-eagling for one full day."

"What?" Charlie exclaimed. "They can't even
petition?"

The captain was honestly surprised. "Highness,
how could we let impressed men do that? It'd imply
they had some kind of *right* to go home before it
suits the king's convenience."

"You're still keeping them, this long after the
battle?"

Charlie contained his anger. But that night, in
English, he told Hector he meant to take the matter up with Dzenko, force the baron to release his
quasi-slaves.

"Maybe ye can," the Hoka said doubtfully. "Yet
is it no a waste of effort, when soon ye'll gang awa'?
Dzenko wad simply haul them back after ye're gane
or catch himsel' ithers."

"Why does he need that big a force, anyway?"

"A vurra eenteresting question. What say ye I poke

aboot on my ain? I'm nobbut your funny wee companion; nae guardsmen wull clank alang behind me; and I've found the Talyinans wull talk wi' me richt freely, once they're used to the sight and pairhaps a drappie or twa hae wetted their craws."

"All right." Charlie sighed. "I'm not sure what good it'll do—and I'll miss you in that hustle—bustle and dull ritual I'm stuck with—and lordy, lordy, how glad I will be to get through here!"

Hector did join him on an excursion to the Grotto of Kroshch. For this was a famous local wonder, its general area a picnic site for the aristocracy and bourgeoisie of Bolgorka. Dzenko himself wanted Charlie to visit there. Such a trip would lend credibility to his eventual announcement that the Grotto could wait until the Prince had disposed of what serious threats remained to the well-being of Talyina.

The Hoka was unwontedly silent, even glum. Charlie wondered why but didn't press the issue. After six days of officialism, it was too delightful to be out in the country again.

His yachi bounded along a winding, climbing road whose dirt lay vivid red under fragrant green of woods on either side, blue of sky and flash of gold off wings overhead. He had got used to riding native style, and his muscles fitted themselves happily into its thudding rhythm. Ahead of him, a section of guards made a brave sight in their armor and cloaks.

Behind him came the rest, along with scores of curious civilians.

The trip across the cape took a pair of hours. From the crest Charlie saw a narrow fjord, mercury-bright against the darkling cliffs of its farther side. Toward this the road descended, until it reached a cleared spot above the very end of the inlet. There stood tables, benches, fireplaces, and other amenities. Cooks had gone ahead to prepare a barbecue for the Prince. By now he had made his tastes known. Their simplicity was widely admired. With only salt for a condiment, the meat which he got was delicious. His wellborn seatmates were affable, flattering, proud to dine in his company.

After lunch, the party climbed down a trail carved out of the precipices to the water. Their outing had been carefully timed. The tide was low. Waves lapped quietly on rocks which formed a strip of beach. At its end, a mouth gaped black in a sheer granite wall.

"The Grotto of Kroshch, Highness," said the foremost of the magnates present. "The end of your destiny. No, the beginning of it." Awe freighted his tones.

Charlie knew what awaited him. He approached boldly. Yet he too felt a certain inner dread. The dimness down here, hemmed between dizzying heights; the opening before him, darker still, from which chilliness billowed forth; the mark of the sea, meters above its top—

He stepped through. Beyond was a passage, twice a man's height. For a while, light seeped in from outside, and he stumbled along on water-slick loose cobbles. Thereafter the murk deepened until he had to wait for flint and steel to kindle the lanterns his attendants carried. Shadows and glimmers ran eerily over the stone which enclosed him. He breathed damp cold. Afar he heard the ocean growl, through his ears and footsoles and bones.

The passage suddenly gave on the Grotto itself.

This was a roughly hemispherical chamber, perhaps the remnant of a volcanic bubble, about twenty meters in width and up to the ceiling, seamed with crevices, ledges, and lesser holes. The lantern bearers climbed along these until their firefly-bobbing burdens gave wan illumination to the entire cavity. He stared toward the roof. Blacknesses betokened hollows in it. But none, he knew, reached as far aloft as did the high-water mark he had seen outside.

Dzenko had explained beforehand. This fjord formed what on Earth was called a roost. It forced incoming tides to abnormal rapidity and power. Twice a day a wall of sea roared through, smashed against the cliffs, and wholly drowned the Grotto.

"Had you gills, you might wait in there and come out alive, as the Prophecy says," the baron sneered. "But you haven't. Nor have you along such diving gear as I'm told your people possess. In any event, the witnesses would never accept your going in with a load of equipment. If I remember aright, you're allowed a horpil, nothing else. No, I fear this is one test where I cannot help you. Luckily, you don't want the crown of Talyina."

As he stood in the sounding gloom, fingers plucked his sleeve and a nervous voice said, "Best we go, Highness. The tide will soon turn. Hear you not an awakened hunger in the noise of the waves?"

Back on top, the party waited to view the tidal bore. Charlie and Hector wandered a little distance aside. They stood near a verge amid blowing grasses, and gazed across the sky and down to the now-uneasy waters. Wind whittered; seafowl shrilled.

"I've found what's become o' Mishka, laddie," the Hoka said in English. "I wadna hae heart tae tell ye, save that a rough, tough Hieland clansman doesna ken hoo tae keep a secret frae his chief."

Alarm knocked in Charlie. "What is it? Quick!"

"He's a slave in the inland quarries. They say such canna hope tae live lang."

"What? But—but—why—"

"I learned this last nicht, in a low dockside dive whaur I've won the confidence o' the innkeeper. Ye see, I've sought tae make clear that everything done in your name isna necessarily done wi' your knowledge. But I canna say this tae the nobles or the well-off or even the small burghers, for then word might well get back to Dzenko. I've therefore gane amang the vurra puir, who hae naught to lose nor aught to gain by blabbering to him. For they're no a' slum-bred, lad; mony and mony o' them waur freeholders or boat owners, till Olaghi's greed uprooted them. They nourish a hope the Prince'll mak' it richt for them again, and they ken me for your friend.

"Yon landlord's hiding Kartaz in his cellar. Ye'll reca' Kartaz, o' Mishka's men, he who fought bonnily at Stalgesh. He waur wi' those who stood behind Mishka when the sergeant went before Dzenko tae protest, no alane the continued impressment o' seamen, but the new taxes."

"New taxes?" Charlie said. "I didn't know— whatever for?"

"Och, ye'll no hae heard, syne they're levied on little folk, crofters and foresters wha' dwell far frae towns. 'Tis clear, though, I think, that if Dzenko ha' a'ready begun wi' them, ithers may look for the same or fiercer erelang. Anyhoo, he dootless expected this deputation, for he had it meet him alane and unarmed. But then his new guards burst in at the ring o' a bell and arrested Mishka and the rest at crossbow point. The preesoners waur hustled off to the quarries that selfsame nicht. Next day their comrades waur fed a cock-and-bull story like the ane ye got, laddie, aboot special assignments in the ootlands, and syne, they're scattered far and wide on errands which hae no purpose save to scatter them. This I hae established frae ither reliable soorces.

"Kartaz got a chance tae escape and tuk it. His last sight o' Mishka was of our auld fere in chains, breaking rock, wi' a lash to hurry him alang. So Kartaz tauld me, and I've aye found him truthful."

Sickened, Charlie stared down into the gorge. The rising waters snarled at him.

"I'll collar Dzenko tonight," he whispered. "I won't have this. I won't. I'll denounce him in public—"

For now he knew what the baron intended: the identical thing Olaghi had tried to build, "an up-to-date absolute monarchy." That was why the navy must be maintained at full strength. Talyina had exchanged one dictator for another. And indeed it was worse off, because Dzenko was more intelligent, more efficient. And he ruled through Charles Edward Stuart, the Prince of the Prophecy!

Hector gripped the human's elbow. "Nay, laddie," said the Hoka. "Ye'd nobbut fling your ain life awa'. Surely yon scoundrel ha' made proveesion again' such an emairgency. Belike he'd stab ye the moment ye spake, then denoonce ye for an impostor and hope to ride oot the storm what wad follow. He might well succeed, too. Dinna forget, ye still lack the final proof o' wha ye are. Besides, when ye waur supposed to rule Talyina forever, your slaying wad in itself discredit ye.

"Nay, laddie," he repeated sadly, and shook his round head. "Ye canna but deepen the woes o' the realm, an' alienate Dzenko frae the League, which otherwise might pairhaps meetigate his harshness a wee bit, and yoursel' perish, when yonder lies a univairse for your exploring. Come hame wi' me! Hoo could I e'er face your parents or mysel', did I no bring ye back?"

"But how can I ever face myself again," Charlie shouted, "if—"

The sea drowned his words. Rising and rising, the tide crashed into the fjord, violence which trembled in the rocks beneath him. It marched like destiny, against which nothing may stand.

Nothing?

Charlie came out of dazzlement to see the many eyes upon him, made fearful by the trouble they saw in him. He dared not stop to think further, for he knew that then he would grow afraid. High above the noise of the bore, he yelled, "Hear me! Tomorrow I go into the Grotto as the Prophecy tells! And I'll come forth again—alive—*to claim my crown!*"

16

The Deep Range

Once more the sea was low, but drawn by a moon which hung day-pale above the cliff of the cavern, it was starting to rise. Sunlight flickered off wavelets whose chuckles took on an ever more guttural note. Chill and salt, a breeze piped farewell.

The dignitaries who had accompanied the Prince down to the beach lost their solemnity as they sweated and panted their way in single file, across the switchbacks of the trail toward the brink where a crowd of witnesses already stood. Hector wrung Charlie's hand. "We maun be off the noo," he said thickly. "Unless—lad, wull ye no reconseeder this madness? 'Tis ane thing tae hae read summat in a pheesics textbook; 'tis anither tae set your life at hazard."

"I've got to, Hector," Charlie said. He pointed at

the watchers, forestlike on the steeps. "For them. They trust me. And I can help them, if—" He clasped the Hoka to him. "I *will* come back to you. I promise."

Hector gave Dzenko an ominous glance. "If ye dinna return, there's more than me wull regret it," he muttered in Talyinan. Again in English: "Goodbye, Bonnie Prince Charlie, until we meet anew and ye enter upon your heritage."

The Hoka waded to a lifeboat in the shallows. Its ten rowers were not guardsmen; they were ordinary fishers and sailors, but each was armed, and each likewise looked grimly at Dzenko. They paused no longer, for already it would be difficult to escape from the fjord. No craft could live there while the tidal bore raged. The plan was for them to wait outside and come in after Charlie as soon as possible, in case he wasn't able to leave by himself.

Their coxswain struck up a chant. With Hector in the bows, oars bit water and the hull departed. Charlie and Dzenko stood alone. They were in sight of everybody but in earshot of none.

Except for a scarlet cloak, the baron was also dressed simply, in light tunic, trousers, and shoes. Both wore the usual knife, but his was long and heavy, a weapon rather than a tool. Charlie clutched to his breast the horpil he carried and met the stare of his rival with more resoluteness than he felt.

"Well, at last you grant me a private talk," Dzenko snapped. From the mask of his face, fury sparked.

"I wasn't going to give you a chance to pull some trick or . . . or assassination," Charlie retorted. "I made sure the whole town knew I'd do my final Feat today, and I stayed in public view till my bedtime, and Hector got those boatmen to watch over my suite, and you were the reason why!"

It was strange, he thought, how well he had slept. But as his moment drew near, every nerve was tightening.

Dzenko stroked his whiskers. "You are not overly courteous to your mentor, youth."

"I'm nicer to you than you've been to my people."

"*Your* people, eh? Your people? Well, well. A few of us might have something to say about that.

"Not after I've been in the Grotto."

"Ah, yes," Dzenko said with a sour smile. "You've gnawed your way to the secret of the Grotto, have you? I did myself, weeks ago. You might bear in mind, however, the Feat is dangerous just the same. For example, suppose the waves throw you against a wall and spatter your brains."

"Suppose they don't," the Earthling replied. "Somebody must've survived high tide in there once, to get the tradition started.

"Belike you're right. Yet I am anxious for you. Really, your suspiciousness hurts me; yes, it cuts me to the liver. I mean to wait low on the trail and myself be the first who goes in after you. This I will announce to the watchers." Dzenko bowed. "Therefore, fortune attend you, my Prince, until we meet anew."

He turned and strode off. A gust of wind swirled his cloak aside, revealing the pouch which bulged and banged at his hip opposite the knife. Charlie gulped. Chill went through him. What did Dzenko mean by that last remark?

Sarcasm, probably. He didn't expect his rival would live. But if that proved wrong—well, Dzenko would have to mend his own fences. It was understandable that he would make a point of hailing the new king before anybody else did.

Ripples lapped cold across Charlie's feet. The time was upon him.

He too was loaded down with a weighted pouch, which annoyed him by its drag and bump as he crossed slippery, toe-bruising rocks. Wasn't he supposed to be a legendary hero, above such discomforts and inconveniences? Instead, he stumbled alone through bleak, blustering hugeness.

He stopped at the mouth of the cavity. Far off, the boat which bore Hector was a white fleck under the cliffs. Closer, but still remote, patches of color along the trail marked the nobles. The commoners gathered at the top were a blur. Charlie wondered if they could even see him.

Yes, no doubt every available telescope was pointed this way. He must go through the motions. He plucked a few forlorn twangs and shook a few weak rattles out of his horpil. His lack of skill didn't matter. Nobody else heard him.

Quickly, before he lost courage, he entered the tunnel.

When well inside, he slung the horpil on his back and opened his pouch. It bore a glow lantern. This was a Talyinan invention, a glass globe inside a protective wire frame, filled with water which contained phosphorescent microorganisms. The dim blue light it gave was of some use to divers.

Nobody minded the Prince's bringing such a commonsense piece of equipment. He and Hector had kept quiet about the item which next he drew from the pouch. He didn't feel he was dishonest in taking it. But why give his enemies a chance to make snide remarks? The whole future of Talyina depended on his prestige.

The object was the bag from the Hoka's pipes. He blew it up and closed it with a twist of copper wire. He might have to stay afloat for well over an hour.

This would let him do so. Otherwise, if nothing else, cold would sap his strength and he'd drown.

It boomed in the gloom. He hurried onward.

When he entered the Grotto itself, the floor was already submerged a few centimeters. He splashed about, searching. Except at very short range, the glimmer from the lantern hung about his neck was less help than his memory of how his guides yesterday had scrambled around the irregularities of the walls.

Yes . . . this ledge slanted upward to a fissure, along which it was possible to creep farther to reach a knob, and from there— He took off his shoes and climbed. The rock was slick. It wouldn't do to fall, no matter how loudly the water beneath had begun to squelp and whoosh.

After what seemed like a long time, he got as high as he could go, onto a shelf which jutted from the wall and barely gave space for him to sit. He clenched fingers on every roughness he could find, and waited.

Here came the bore.

The tide noise grew to a monstrous bellow, rang through his skull, shook him as a dog shakes a rat. Spray sheeted over him. With one arm he squeezed the bag to his ribs. It was the last thing he had left.

Onward plunged the sea. Yet that vast mass could not quickly pour through a narrow shaft. Its vanguard struck the inner side of the Grotto and recoiled on what came after. Waves dashed back and forth, whirlpools seethed.

Through that brutal racket, Charlie felt a sharper pain lance his ears. He worked throat and jaws, trying to equalize pressures inside and outside his head. Amid all the chaos, his heart broke into a dance. The pain was a benediction.

It proved his idea was right.

When the tunnel filled with water, air was bound to be trapped inside the cave. As the tide rose farther, that air would be compressed. At some point, it must counterbalance the weight of liquid. And thus, no matter that the water outside stood higher than the roof within, here would remain a bubble of breath.

Charlie had no way to determine in advance where equilibrium would occur. He could but cling to his ledge.

The tide mounted. As the hollowness grew glutted, waves damped out. The earlier crashing diminished to a sinister mumble. At last the water was almost calm.

When it reached his breast, he decided to seek the middle of the room. He hugged his life preserver to him with both arms. His feet paddled him along until he guessed he was about where he ought to be. There he halted, lay in the sea's embrace, and thought many long thoughts.

This was what it meant to be a king, a real king— not wealth and glory, not leadership into needless wars, but serving the people, and if necessary, dying for them.

Yet kingship was not enough. The people themselves might want a Landfather to lift from them the weight of decision. But if they did, the people were wrong. The highest service a king could give was to lead them toward their own freedom.

Charlie smiled at himself, alone in the dark. Wasn't he self-important! Did he imagine he could save the world?

No, of course he couldn't. But he might leave it a little bit better than he found it.

Again the water roughened. Remembering what

he had seen the day before, he drew a glad breath. The tide had turned. The Grotto was draining.

But that brought fresh dangers. The height of the tide would recede almost as rapidly as it had entered. Charlie recalled what Dzenko had said: A current might smash him fatally against the stone around him. Even after the tunnel was partly clear, he shouldn't try to go out. The swift and tricky stream could easily knock him down, snatch away his life preserver, and drown him in the hour of his victory.

No, he must wait inside for quite a while, until it was perfectly safe to walk forth. . . . Maybe not that long. Hector's crew would row in as soon as they were able. But at any rate, what he should do now was find a wall and fend himself off it as he sank.

He did. The effort was exhausting. He was over-joyed when by the wan light of the glow lantern he identified a broad shelf newly uncovered. He could sit here till the Grotto was emptied, if the boat didn't fetch him earlier. It would then be an easy scramble to the floor. In fact, already the tunnel must be only about half full. He thought the darkness had light-ened a trifle.

The rest of the ebb would take considerably more time than had the showy bore and the initial out-flow. Charlie tried to summon patience. Miserably chilled, too tired to warm up by vigorous exercises, he slapped arms across body.

Maybe he could divert himself with the horpil. Besides—he grinned—the Prophecy did say the Prince would make music while the waters retreated. He unslung his instrument. Soaked, its strings twanged dully and its rattle gurgled. Scratch one more piece of glamor.

Wait. What was that new noise? Charlie peered

around. A vague blueness flickered and bobbed; eddies gave back the least sheen of it.

Following the beacon of Charlie's own glow lantern, it neared. A tall form climbed onto the ledge. The glove beneath its neck picked out the face in a few highlights and many shadows.

"Dzenko!" Charlie exclaimed. He leaped to his feet.

The baron's teeth flashed. "Did I not promise I would be first to come after you, my Prince?" he said, low above the lapping and swirling of the tide. "All praised my faithfulness, when I doffed cloak and shoes and plunged into the fjord. Fain would many guardsmen have come along, but I claimed for myself alone the honor of leading you back to the day."

"Well," Charlie said uncertainly, "that's very kind of you. I do want us to be friends, and I do need your advice. It's only, well, we don't think a lot alike, do we?"

"No," Dzenko agreed. "In many ways we do not. I believe your notion of slipping the ancient anchor which holds the commoners in their place is madness. Yet in some ways we are kinsmen, Charles. We share bravery and determination. My sorrow will not be entirely feigned, Charles, when I tell the people that I found you dead."

"What?" Echoes rang fadingly back, *what, what, what.* . . .

"You drowned." Dzenko reached forth crook-fingered hands.

"No—wait—please—"

The baron trod forward. "I suggest you cooperate," he said. "If you keep still, I'll cut off your breath with a throat grip. You'll be unconscious in a matter of pulsebeats. You'll never feel it when I stick your head underwater. And I'll always honor your memory."

Charlie whipped forth his knife. Dzenko sighed. "I too am armed," he pointed out. "I have a better weapon, a longer reach, and years of experience. I would hate to mutilate your body with rocks until the wounds are disguised. But the future of Talyina and of my bloodline is more important than any squeamishness."

Charlie sheathed the knife. "Excellent," Dzenko purred, and sidled close. Charlie slammed the horpil down over his head.

The string jangled and broke. The frame went on to enclose Dzenko's arms. He yelled, staggered about, struggled to free himself. Charlie left him in a clean dive.

Cursing, Dzenko got loose and came after. Charlie unshipped his glow lantern and let it sink.

From the set of the currents, he could probably find his way to the tunnel. He'd have to take his chances with riptides and undertows. Dzenko was more dangerous.

Charlie was no longer afraid. He hadn't time for that. He swam.

A splashing resounded at his rear. It loudened. Dzenko was a stronger swimmer than he, and tracking him by the noise he made. Charlie stopped. He filled his lungs, floated on his back, paddled as softly as he was able.

The baron's call came harsh: "You think to hide in the dark? Then I'll await you at the door."

Charlie saw in a white flash that his enemy was right. Either he, the prey, swam actively, and thus betrayed himself to a keen pair of ears, or he stayed passive, in which case the flow would bring him to the exit where the hunter poised.

His single chance was to find another surface halfway level and broad, and dodge about. He was more agile than Dzenko, surely. He struck out across the ebb. Behind him he heard pursuit.

Light broke upon his eyes, the yellow gleam of an oil lantern. Hector held it aloft, where he stood in the bows of the lifeboat. "Ahoy, laddie!" he piped. "Laddie, are ye here?"

"Help," Charlie cried.

"Aha!" said Hector. His free hand reached forth to haul a kicking, cursing, but altogether overpowered Dzenko across the gunwale, helpless in the powerful grip of the Hoka. "What *is* this farce?" demanded Hector sternly.

17
Earthman's Burden

For three terrestrial months, the Honorable Athelstan Pomfrey, Plenipotentiary of the Interbeing League to the Kingdom of Talyina and (in theory) the planet of New Lemuria, had received no direct communication from the royal town.

At first King Charles had been eager to talk with him, as soon as a man in an aircar brought a radio transceiver powerful enough to bridge the distance between Bolgorka and Shverkadi. He related what happened, to the moment of his coronation: "—And I sent Dzenko after Olaghi, into exile. His family and a few old retainers went along. I think they'll actually be a good influence on the mainland. They'll need to make friends with the savages there, which means they'll teach them some things. I did this right away, before I was crowned—"

"You!" Pomfrey had interrupted, furious. "You the king? Of Talyina? How dare you, fellow? How dare you?"

"I hoped you wouldn't blame me, sir," a subdued voice replied from the set in the compound. "Haven't I explained how I sort of got swept along?"

"Up to a point, yes," Pomfrey conceded before he reddened afresh. "But accepting the lordship of a native country— Don't you know, Charles Stuart, I can charge you with imperialism?"

The voice strengthened. "I don't think you can, sir. I mean, well, the plan Hector and I've worked out— Oh, I guess you haven't met Hector Mac-Gregor, exactly. Anyhow, we figure it's the direct opposite of imperialism. But maybe I should ask a lawyer first. Look, is my dad around?"

"No," said Pomfrey. "After my courier assured him that you were, indeed, safe, but wouldn't come back for some time, he wanted to visit you, but I forbade that. So he continued his voyage." His jowls went from crimson to purple. "If you have, in addition, the sheer gall to demand I obtain legal assistance for you— No!"

"Then maybe we'd better not talk anymore," said Charlie.

No total curtain fell between kingdom and League. Messengers went back and forth. Charlie was a gracious host to whomever Pomfrey sent. By degrees, the Plenipotentiary cooled off. At last he decided it might be best for himself that he check with a competent attorney. What he heard, coupled with what information he got from Bolgorka and from Talyina as a whole, made him very thoughtful.

When word came that the king would pay him a state visit, and requested off-planet transportation be available, Pomfrey got onto his subspace communication set. The *Highland Lass* was still in this galactic neighborhood.

Thus Captain Stuart was on hand when his son returned.

A sizable fleet docked at Grushka. The next morning a procession started north for the compound. At a leisurely pace, with an overnight stop, it arrived toward evening of the following day.

The humans who waited at the gates of the compound gasped. Not even their airborne scouts had prepared them for what they now saw and heard.

Autumn lay cool on the land. Leaves flared in multitudinous colors. The sea danced in whitecaps beneath a merry wind. High overhead went southbound birds. And up the road came the King of Talyina and his household troopers.

He rode in the van, on a horse rather than a yachi. His slender form was plainly clad for travel, but the sword of the Founder hung at his waist, and on his red hair sat an iron crown. The two who flanked him were similarly mounted. On his right, in kilt and bonnet, was a Hoka. On his left, in gleaming mail, was one of the biggest New Lemurians that anybody had ever seen.

Behind them tramped the guards. Banners fluttered; pikes nodded; boots smote ground in heartshaking cadence. But something new was here. Below their armor these warriors wore kilts, in the same tartan as flew above their helmets. And at their head, setting the time of their march, went the wild music of a hundred bagpipers and as many drummers.

The giant drew rein and wheeled his mount around. "Com-pan-ee-halt!" he roared. The troop snapped to a standstill. "Salute!" A thousand swords flew free. "Sheath!" Blades entered scabbards with a hiss and crash, as the pipes droned away to silence and the last drumroll lost itself in surf noise.

Charlie leaped from his horse and sped to his father. "Dad!" he shouted.

They hugged each other. "Sorry I made you so much trouble," Charlie whispered.

"I'm not, not anymore," Captain Stuart answered, low in his throat. "By all that's holy, you've made me prouder of you than I ever dared hope for."

They straightened. Pomfrey, gorgeous in formal dress, advanced upon them. "Ah . . . welcome, your Majesty," the Plenipotentiary said. He cast a nervous glance toward the soldiers, where they stood at statuelike attention. "I hope we can, ah, provide hospitality."

"Shucks, don't worry about that, sir," Charlie replied. "We brought supplies and everything. They can camp in the field yonder, can't they? It's only overnight."

"Indeed? I assumed . . . a certain amount of ceremony—"

"No! I've had enough ceremony! We'll throw a farewell party on the campground and enjoy ourselves, and that'll be that!"

"Well." Pomfrey was not displeased. "As you wish. I can understand it if you wish to abdicate quietly."

"Huh?" Charlie stared at him. "Abdicate? What're you talking about? Didn't I make it clear to you?"

Pomfrey began to swell. "Young man—I mean, your Majesty, *I* thought that in obedience to the laws prohibiting imperialism, you would retire as soon as feasible. It was on this basis that legal counsel advised me to file no charges against you."

Captain Stuart bristled. The Hoka, who had joined their group, broke the tension. "Plenipotentiary," he said, "dinna ye ken that to renounce the power isna the same as to renounce the title?"

"That's it," Charlie said in haste. "I . . . well, I am supposed to—Well, the Prophecy says, 'Righteous, the red-haired one rules us forever!' A mortal can't do that. But a legend can. If not forever, then long enough."

Pomfrey calmed. He stroked his double chin. He was not actually stupid, in fact, rather intelligent. "I believe I see," he murmured. "The last few messages you sent were pretty garbled. No doubt you were too busy to pay attention to their exact wording. . . . Ah, yes. You propose to take, shall we say, an indefinite leave of absence?"

"Yes," Charlie answered. "I've told the people this is part of my mission. I couldn't quite explain to them why it is."

Nor would he ever tell how that had been his last, greatest ordeal—the decision he must make, wholly alone in the night.

He could stay on as king. If he avoided the treaty zone, League law could never touch him. Rather, the Plenipotentiary would have to cooperate, like it or not. He, King Charles the Great of Talyina, could rule justly, bring in the benefits of civilization, and cover himself with glory. Nor need he be lonesome for his own kind. By offering trade concessions and well-paid jobs, he could attract as many humans to his court as he desired.

And he wanted to stay. Here was his realm. Here were his tested friends. Here dwelled his people, whom he had come to love.

But he harked back to a certain darkness in the sea and remembered that the highest service of a king is to give the folk their freedom, whether they ask it or not. Their descendants will bless him.

He, Charles Edward Stuart, must return to being an ordinary student on Earth. He could never visit this planet again.

"I'd have come sooner," he told Pomfrey and his father, "but it took a while to establish a Parliament—House of Lords and House of Commons, you know, and Commons has the purse strings—get organized, lay down some ground rules, hold our first election—that kind of thing. I'm ready to leave now."

"I see." The Plenipotentiary nodded. "If you, as the king who's supposed to reign forever . . . are not on hand . . . then nobody can succeed you, and the people will have to learn how to run the country by themselves."

"'Tis like British history," said the Hoka. As he spoke, his burr shifted toward an Oxford accent. "Bad though the early Hanoverians waur, yet they'd one advantage. The wee, wee Gairman lairdie—that is, the initial two Georges—couldn't speak English worth mentioning. So they didn't preside over meetings of Parliament. From this grew the practice of having Cabinets, Prime Ministers—in short, the whole jolly old structure of democracy, don't y' know? We trust the Talyinan national folkmoot will follow a similar course of development. QED."

"In other words," Captain Stuart said to Pomfrey, and his tone clanged, "my son has accomplished what the League has only dreamed of doing since it found this whole world."

The spaceship departed soon after dawn. Charlie and Mishka waved to each other all the time the human went up the gangway.

When the last airlock had closed, the warrior turned to his men, "Ten-*shun*!" he shouted into the frosty mists. "Salute your king!"

Swords flashed free and clashed home. A drumroll thundered.

Engines hummed. On silent drive fields, the ship lifted.

Mishka, Prime Minister to his Majesty Charles, Eternal King of Talyina, drew sword of his own. It was his baton, to direct the pipes which began to skirl. From the ranks of the fighting men, deep voices rose in the tongue of the Highlands.

Will ye no come back again?
Will ye no come back again?
Better lo'ed ye canna be.
Will ye no come back again?

DOOMSDAY CAME
ABOUT EVERY FIVE YEARS ...

Someone Out There really hated humans. Twenty years have passed since Shiva I swept aside Earth's crude defenses and rained down destruction. Now Shiva V has entered the Solar System, more powerful than any of its predecessors.

The Shiva cannot be destroyed by fleets of ships: we tried, and it was the fleets that were destroyed. There is only way way to defeat a Shiva: get inside and kill it. Once again, in the personae of five champions, four billion of us are about to do just that, using the ...

EARTHWEB
Marc Stiegler

"A high-voltage adventure story—and an intruiging look at what the worldwide web may become."   **—Vernor Vinge**

"A brilliant vision of our future networked intelligence."
                —Max Moore, Ph.D, President of the Extropy
                Institute and the *Extropy Newsletter*

ISBN 57809-X ◆ $6.99 ☐

EXPLORE OUR WEB SITE